Close Call

Gillian Slovo

A *Virago* Book

Published by Virago Press 1996

Reprinted 1996

First published in Great Britain by Michael Joseph 1995

Copyright © Gillian Slovo 1995

The moral right of the authors has been asserted

A CIP catalogue record for this book
is available from the British Library

ISBN 1 85381 816 X

Printed in England by Clays Ltd, St Ives plc

Virago
A Division of
Little, Brown and Company (UK)
Brettenham House
Lancaster Place
London WC2E 7EN

Chapter
one

I tried to concentrate on what Chief Superintendent Rodney Ellis was saying. It was hard going, not because he was more boring than any of my other recent subjects, but because I'd had a bellyful of jobs like this.

'Miss Baeier?' He had caught my inattention. I pulled myself together. I was there to listen; I put on my listening face. Satisfied, he fulfilled his part of the bargain: he talked. 'We're in a cleft stick,' he said. 'The public has impossible expectations.'

It was the same monotonous refrain he'd dealt me yesterday. But I was in control. I didn't do anything rude like yawning. Instead, to keep myself awake, I made a note.

Having dispatched my question, Rodney Ellis lapsed into silence. No problem. I pitched him another, something about clear-up rates and customer satisfaction. As he answered, I set my hand to the automatic recording of what he said. Meanwhile, I let my thoughts go rambling free. Regret was their focus: regret that I had let Charles bamboozle me into this profile; that I'd opted for a six-month lease rather than for three; that I had not made myself a second gruyère and ham on rye for lunch; that I had inadvertently switched the TV on to see . . . No. I severed that connection.

Rodney Ellis's monologue had been concluded. I looked up.

His weak grey eyes were fixed on me. He grimaced and his thin lips stretched so far they almost disappeared. His hands, white and more nervous than a Chief Superintendent's should be, were drumming an urgent tattoo against the dark wood. I wondered whether the rage that I suspected lay somewhere beneath the surface was finally going to erupt.

His eyes were on the move. They flicked over and beyond my head. 'What is it?'

I turned to see a man, a stranger, standing in the open doorway. Tall, dark, handsome – I just had time to name the cliché and to catch his eye before he transferred his cool gaze to the Chief Superintendent.

'I thought you might want to know that I'm off.' He had a voice to match the gaze: clear and self-confident.

Ellis was on his feet, volunteering a smile. 'If you should require any further assistance . . .'

'Of course.' The other man was quick. The door closed.

Leaving me and Rodney Ellis alone. He seemed about as thrilled as I; he turned away, looking out of the window. I did the same, seeing the jagged tangle of grimy rooftops backlit by the burnished red of a polluted Hackney sunset. I thought about other sunsets, about places I would rather be. After five years reporting from the world's war zones, I had thought I needed a break. Now, after a mere five months of writing vacuous profiles, what I needed was a complete change of scene.

I heard a chair scraping against the floor. 'Shall we?' The Chief Superintendent was already in motion, striding to the door.

I got up.

Not fast enough. 'Come on, Ms Baeier,' he said impatiently. 'Our driver will be waiting.'

*

I was in the Rover's back seat, strapped down against the luxurious velveteen while the police car trawled slowly through the Hackney streets, its radio burbling in the middle distance. There were no urgent messages, nothing for us to do. The pubs were closed; the clubs only just beginning to get going. The streets were deserted: those few people braving the chill looked like hypnotized extras from an ancient sci-fi movie. I soon got bored with them and turned my attention to Rodney Ellis.

He was sitting beside me, ramrod straight, staring out into the night. Against the darkness of the car's interior his hair seemed almost silvery, a distinguished contrast to the pallor of his face. But when he turned, suddenly, and caught me looking, his right eye twitched. What I had felt before with Ellis came again: a feeling that he was wired to blow and that, if I wasn't careful, I would be his detonator.

Wrong again. He wanted to talk. 'You must understand,' he said.

Of course I must. I was a journalist; my job was understanding.

'You must understand,' he said again, 'that educated intuition is the backbone of effective policing. And intuition comes from knowing your patch. That's why I go out on the beat.' His meaning was clear – this trip had not been laid on for my benefit.

Clear to me, that is. He seemed to feel it needed emphasizing. 'I do this regularly,' he said, 'to keep in touch with what's happening.' He paused, waiting for me to take down this little gem. I didn't bother – I had enough Ellis banalities to pad three times the length of any article – and lack of interest appeared to exhaust him. When he said: 'It's important,' his words had lost so much impetus they sounded anything but important. Still, he was a trooper, he finished

3

the sentence: 'Important to understand first hand what my men experience.' His voice faded. He stilled his eye's spasm, turned his head and resumed his aimless staring.

Silence. I stared out at the passing night. I saw that we were heading deeper into Hackney. Beyond us the desolate wastes of an estate, high rise jutting out of inhospitably flat land. It wasn't on our beat. We veered away, weaving through a maze of narrow streets, past batches of decrepit terraced houses. I sat, lulled by the car's silence, safe in its encapsulated warmth. The previous night's sleeplessness was catching up on me. And why not? At that moment it felt as though nothing would ever come to disturb the calm. My head began to droop.

Two words, roughly spoken – 'A fire' – roused me. I looked up hurriedly. I was in time to catch a quick glimpse of our driver's alarm. Ellis said it again, angrily this time: 'A fire.'

'But ... sir ... nothing's been ...' I understood the driver's confusion: there was no fire.

'Have you no sense of smell?' Ellis said. 'Ahead, man. And step on it.'

Another flick of the driver's eyes. I wondered whether he dared refuse.

Of course not: Rodney Ellis was the boss. The car accelerated.

Momentum threw me back and I lay for a moment bathed in the blueness of a light reflected back from outside. The sound of our siren came with us, more distant than I'd expected.

'Hurry.'

I breathed in, checking again. The air was clear – no hint of smoke. I let my breath go.

'Left, dammit. Go left.'

4

When the car did a hard left turn, I was thrown against Ellis. I grabbed the side strap, pulling myself straight. I was alert now and fascinated. What I had been waiting for -- evidence that Rodney Ellis was unhinged -- had finally materialized.

'And left again.'

This time I was prepared. I didn't fall. And so I was in a perfect position to discover that far from being unhinged, Rodney Ellis was right.

'There,' he said. 'In the middle.'

Chapter

two

Opposite was a terrace of small houses which had started life as workmen's cottages. They were still trying to look respectable but flaking paint and holes in the masonry showed how much of an effort this was getting to be. Some had lost the battle altogether: detritus from unkempt front areas spilled over into gardens whose sickly shrubs tried unsuccessfully to erase an atmosphere of genteel poverty.

'There.'

Rodney Ellis's hand had targeted one of the most dilapidated houses in the line-up. Its front gate hung off its latch, weeds choked the pathway that led to its front door, cardboard had been used to supplement the broken glass on its ground-floor window. And there, in an upstairs window, pinpointed by Rodney Ellis, was a light, flickering.

I looked around. The street was empty, the police siren slicing through its tranquillity.

I was still trying to catch up. Not Rodney Ellis. He was on the move. He told his driver to radio through, flung a curt 'You stay here' at me, shoved the door open, got out and strode across the road.

He went up the path and to the front door. His hand reached for its knocker and slammed down hard. Three doors down a light snapped on. The house Ellis was trying to rouse was still.

I saw a neighbouring door open. As Ellis's driver rapped into his mike and Ellis backed off, I came to. I pulled my door handle. It didn't move – they'd kid-locked me in. No problem. I shuffled over and using Ellis's exit made it out.

I crossed the street as a woman in a candlewick dressing gown came out of one of the houses. Her head swivelled, watching Rodney Ellis running at the door. A dull thud. The door stayed put.

'Out of the way, love.' This from Ellis's driver hustling the woman to the pavement opposite. Me he left alone – I suppose my previous proximity to his Chief Superintendent had made me seem official.

Another thud – Ellis hurling himself, shoulder first, against the door. I wondered why he wasn't using his powerful legs. He went again. I saw the door shiver – it was held by a single lock embedded at about shoulder height.

My eyes moved upwards. The fire was gaining hold, the vague flickering now a licking flame. His driver was having trouble holding back a hysterical woman. Ellis moved back. So did I. I ran to him and moved in sync, making my shoulder a battering ram, launching it against the wood.

The door juddered but held tight. A nod from Ellis, a few steps back and we relaunched ourselves. This time I hit the wood square on. Pain tore at my shoulder blade, jolting its way down my arm. Another nod. Another smash. Still no movement.

Rodney Ellis's determination kept me in there. 'Again,' he said. We went again. That did it. The lock gave way.

I fell forwards. Blackness, a blast of heat, a gelatinous smog rolled over me. I gagged. I had one single thought, one obsessive aim – I wanted out. But I couldn't see. I felt

7

around me, trying to find my balance. I touched hard ground and, pressing against it, tried to lever myself up. I was leaning all my weight on my sore shoulder. I toppled over. My head flopped back, hitting something sharp. I must have lost consciousness, if only momentarily.

When my eyes reopened, I was transfixed by what I saw. Through the fog, the dim outlines of a stairwell. Beside it, a door. My gaze was fixed on the door, watching as the smoke swirled elegantly around its frame, making dreamy patterns. It was so enticing. I stopped worrying about the smoke clogging my breath, about the heat, ever more intense as I raised my head higher. I concentrated on the unfolding display. What had seemed uniform had become a mesmerizing mix of sepias and greys, of purples and blacks. It was a living thing, that smoke; it surged forwards and then swished back, sucking me into its lazy beauty. It looks so pretty, I thought. I smiled. I felt myself sinking down again, secure in the smoke's rolling embrace. My eyes closed.

An image flickered through the descending darkness, a man's familiar face, dominated by his hawk-like nose, an image which once had frightened me. Now I welcomed its caress. I even beckoned to it, inviting it closer.

It backed off, dissolving into black. I felt myself relax.

A stabbing pain jerked me into the present. Before I could work out what had done it, it came again. This time it did not abate, instead the hand that was causing it squeezed my sore shoulder harder. I yelled at him to stop.

His mouth was close to my ear. 'Move!' he shouted and then again, even louder: 'Move!' His fingers dug into bone. All I wanted to do was to rid myself of him, but: 'Move!' That word again, accompanied by an increase in pressure.

Anything to stop it. 'All right.' I pushed myself up; he

lifted his hand off. Self-preservation told me to get out. But something that I had not yet put a name to held me back.

Chief Superintendent Ellis was heading deeper down the hallway. I looked again. What I'd vaguely registered was still there, a body lying at the end of the narrow corridor. Dead, I thought. Of course it's dead. I didn't want to know more. I wanted to breathe fresh air, to walk away. I wanted out.

Ellis was moving away from me, inching his way along the hall. In a moment even his outline would no longer be visible. It wasn't right. I followed him, crawling along the hall.

The body was slumped at the hall's end, at the foot of the stairs. It wasn't a corpse – not yet. As we inched closer, it – she – groaned.

My eyes were stinging, my throat thick. I couldn't imagine how, only moments before, the smoke had seemed enticing. Now it stunk: a sickening concoction of burning chemicals whose effect was instant nausea. I heard myself retching. I swallowed hard. I pushed everything – my fear, my sense of smell, my body's impulses – away. But I didn't think I could last much longer.

We were upon her. I stretched out my arm. She was impersonal, an obstacle standing between me and escape. I grabbed hold of her, holding on tight until I felt a tap on my leg. Then I pulled. She moved, but not enough. Another tap. I hauled again. Again no response.

I couldn't understand it. She was conscious; why wasn't she helping? It was too dark to see anything. I felt my way up against the outline of her body. I found her arm. It was stretched out. I traced it. It was taut, gripping at the banisters, clinging on.

That did it. The fire was burning in me now. I wrenched

9

at her, pulling her fingers back; her hand went slack so that this time when Chief Superintendent Ellis pulled, she moved.

Space was elastic: there were no walls any more, no doors, no floors – only smoke. The front door was a million miles away. Each hard-won inch closer to it a torment. I heard somebody crying out, jangled words without coherence. They might even have been mine. I couldn't tell. I couldn't tell anything. All I knew was I had to keep on going, pushing the woman in front of me.

We fell, heaving, out into the open. The air stabbed my chest. My vision was blurred. I lay coughing, sprawled beside the woman. I saw the vague outlines of shadows moving towards us. I lifted my head and my eyes began to refocus. An ambulance, its blue light flashing, came speeding round the corner. Beyond it, in a frieze, a refugee encampment: inhabitants from neighbouring houses huddled together.

I heard that same voice calling out. It was hers, a cry of hopelessness endlessly repeated. It jangled in my head and, merging with the dying of the ambulance's siren, it made no sense.

Chief Superintendent Ellis was on his feet, leaning down, speaking loudly. 'Where?'

Where what? I thought.

She said the words again. This time I heard them clearly: 'My son.'

Now I understood her tenacious hand. I closed my eyes.

'Where?' I heard again. I reopened my eyes in time to see the woman's smoke-blackened hand pointing up. I felt sick. As a war correspondent, I'd got used to almost anything. But the death of a child, and the grief of a mother who couldn't save it . . . I didn't want to witness that, not again.

I didn't want to be part of the beginning of an emptiness which would for ever dog this woman's life.

I moved my head, meaning to turn away, but found myself transfixed by the sight of Chief Superintendent Ellis. In his eyes, a mix of fear and resignation.

Footsteps. The ambulance men coming closer. A voice: 'Where's the sodding brigade?' Rodney Ellis's face hardened. He turned.

I grabbed his leg. 'Don't.'

He whirled round. 'I have to. What if he were Steven?'

He pulled away from me. Uncomprehending, I let him go.

I pushed myself up and watched him heading for the burning building. At the void that had once been a door he stopped, briefly. I could see his chest expand. His arms lifted up, pulling his jacket up so that it shrouded his head. Then he was gone.

A brave man, and a foolish one: he must have known that what he was doing was hopeless. I sat there, thinking vaguely that despite the hours I had spent interviewing him, I had not really got to know him. My eyes misted.

I heard a sound. Cheering?

I looked up. It was cheering all right. Rodney Ellis was at the top-floor window, leaning out. In his arms, a bundle. I saw his thinning hair, lit up by a background of flames. A phalanx of black and yellow flashed past me, a ladder was raised. He didn't wait for it; he stretched his hand out and dropped the bundle.

Chapter

three

'Come on, love.' The taxi-driver's voice jolted me awake.

I came to. I was sprawled across the back seat, my mouth open wide. I shut it, closing in the acrid taste, and righted myself.

'Hurry up.' He was staring at me. 'I haven't got all night.'

I fumbled in my pockets and produced coins which I shoved in his direction. When the closing of his fist told me I'd paid enough, I got out of his cab.

I was still half asleep. As my memory came back on stream I thought about what had happened after Rodney Ellis had climbed down the ladder. They'd sent us to hospital two by two: first mother and baby and then Rodney Ellis and me. We'd had nothing to say to each other. We'd sat on opposite bunks in silence while he rationed the oxygen mask that they kept on offering him. I had watched him, thinking that although my respect for him had risen, my liking had not.

Oh well, no law says you must like your subject. And no law says either that you need to think of him twenty-four hours a day.

I looked around. Not much to see: a line of parked cars; a

skip overladen with the neighbourhood's unwanted junk; a drunk, his hand raised, tottering after the departing taxi. High neon lamps hissed out vague smudges of light. I squinted at my watch. Four-thirty, which meant I'd spent more than five hours waiting for a doctor to tell me that my shoulder was 'merely bruised'. I flexed it experimentally. It hurt like hell. Wincing, I started across the street.

There was a long black saloon car, the kind that ageing rock stars and South American dictators covet, parked by my front door. As I came closer I wondered vaguely who its owner was. Some accountant, probably, I thought, and dismissed it from my mind.

I was alongside the car when its headlights clicked on. I froze. But then: no, I thought, it can't be. I talked myself into relaxation as I waited for the car to move on out.

It remained stationary, lights on, engine quiescent. I heard a dull whirring. I turned my head, watching as the smoked glass window was slowly lowered. I knew who must be inside: the man whose face I'd seen when I was inside the burning house, the man who'd been on the lunchtime TV news shaking the hand of a junior minister. My father.

The window was halfway down. I was wrong. It wasn't my father. It was someone almost as familiar. I swallowed, and said his name: 'Zetu.'

It was more than ten years since we'd met but when he smiled I saw his face softening just like it always had. His voice was mellow. 'It's good to see you, Kate,' he said in Portuguese.

I stood there, tongue tied.

Glancing at his chauffeur's peaked cap, Zetu switched to English. 'You are out late.'

It was the kind of opening gambit he used to use. But

that was years ago and I was now too old to play. I exaggerated my frown. 'Why did he send you?'

'Kate,' Zetu said without missing a beat. 'Do you think that I did not want to see you?'

I turned my wrist, showing him my watch face.

He nodded. 'It is true that if this were strictly pleasure, I would have chosen a more orthodox hour,' he said. 'But it is also true' – his hand appeared, reaching for mine – 'that I have missed you.'

I stared at his generous, strong hand and saw liver spots that hadn't been there before. I felt myself wavering. I'd clasped that hand when I was a toddler; it had been lifted in defence of me when I was a child; it had stopped me from falling when I was a teenager. Could I reject it now?

'I've followed your career closely,' he said. 'You've done well.'

Clever. It had been Zetu who had encouraged me to write and got me my first rookie's job.

But then he said, 'The General thinks so too.'

And it came back to me what I had been in danger of forgetting, that no matter how much I loved Zetu or how much he loved me, his soul belonged to my father. I backed away. 'I'm not interested.' My voice was hard.

He knew he'd blundered. 'At least send him a message.'

A message? I looked across at him. Age had bleached the brown from his eyes, moisture made them doleful. 'Tell him to keep away.' I started walking off.

'Kate.' His voice pursued me, pleading.

I kept my pace as even as I could.

'You are not really hard like this,' he said.

I didn't hesitate. I walked straight up to my front door and went in.

★

The terraced house had been divided into four separate flats. Mine was on the third floor. I climbed the stairs to the anonymous grey door, opened up, walked through the square hallway and went into the sitting room. I didn't bother switching on the lights. I went over to the window and pulled up the blinds.

Despite the years we'd lost, Zetu could still predict what I was going to do. When I looked down, I saw him looking up. His eyes caught hold of mine. In the yellowing of the streetlight, he seemed frail. He'd always been a friend to me; I felt myself relent. I almost gave in. I almost went downstairs.

But then I thought about the gangster car and its silent chauffeur. Neither were Zetu's style. Which meant that he was here entirely on my father's, the General's, orders. It had always been this way. While the General lay tucked up in bed, his employees did his bidding. And no matter what he'd once been to me, Zetu was one of my father's employees. He could not be trusted.

I yanked at the cord. I heard the engine kicking in, the car driving off. I left the window. I went to the bathroom and stared at myself in the mirror. My face was streaked with grime, my cheeks scratched, my hair wild. I wondered why Zetu hadn't commented.

I shook my head. I wasn't going to wonder. I took off my clothes and got into the shower. I stood motionless as the water washed away the stench of the fire, the news that the baby Rodney Ellis had rescued might not survive, and the memory of the hurt in my godfather's eyes. I stood until all of it was gone.

The water was cold by the time I got out. Wrapping towels around me, I went to the kitchen. I didn't have enough milk for hot chocolate and I was too far gone for coffee. I made myself a cup of tea, managed two sips, and threw the rest down the sink.

Back to the living room. I switched on the light. I stood in the doorway looking round. It was clean, tidy and adequately furnished, this rental in the heart of Camden Town. It was also utterly anonymous – that's why I had chosen it – and would never be home.

The only thing of mine in the room was the answerphone. I saw its red light blinking. I pressed 'play'.

'Kate.' The voice sounded out against a background of hard static.

I didn't move.

She said it again: 'Kate. It's Carmen.'

I knew that already. What I didn't know was what she wanted.

But of course, it being Carmen, all she said was: 'Ring me.'

Her message was punctuated by the answerphone's electronic whine. I pushed down on buttons, silencing it. Ring her! If I hadn't been so tired I would have laughed. I wasn't going to ring her, not then, nor any time. We'd once been close – she'd been my assistant in my detecting business – but we'd had our last meeting and our last argument. Nothing would change that. Ever.

I'd had it with the living room. I took myself to bed.

I couldn't get to sleep. I was too angry – not with Carmen, nor Zetu, but with myself.

I should have known better, that's what I kept thinking. I should have kept away. When my lover Sam had been killed, I'd junked my failing detective business and left England. I'd gone back to journalism, earning my living as a war correspondent. It had been an effective strategy – by the end of five years touring the world's trouble spots, my grief no longer kept me awake at night.

16

That's when I messed up. That's when I came back to London.

My visit was supposed to have been fleeting, but it didn't turn out that way. Within days I was embroiled in an investigation of Sam's death. I couldn't help that, and I suppose the past had needed burying. But what did I do when it was over? Did I follow the intuition that had served me so well before? Did I get the hell out? No, I did not. I succumbed to pointless nostalgia, took out a short-term lease, and lined up some freelance work.

It had been a disastrous decision. After the preceding year's constant adrenaline rushes, writing profiles of the likes of Rodney Ellis kept me less than half awake. And one month in London was enough to blow a hole in the delusion that I could rebuild my life here. I couldn't believe that I'd been so naïve. It didn't matter who I knew or who I didn't, I no longer fitted in.

I should have known. After all, leaving England had not been my first major relocation. That I'd done when, as an eighteen-year-old, I had fled my father's home in Portugal and ended up in London. I'd been younger then but wiser, I'd known that there is no going back.

My eyes focused on the blankness of a coffee-coloured wall. London was full of ghosts and of people I didn't want to see. Like Carmen, which was bad enough. And now my father.

I turned restlessly, pulling the duvet closer, and the solution came to me. It was so simple. I'd had enough. I didn't care, not any longer. Blow the lease, that's what I'd do. I'd finish the Ellis article and that would be it. I was out of there.

That decided, I closed my eyes, welcoming the onset of sweet unconsciousness.

Chapter
four

I dreamt about my father. I dreamt about his powerful patrician's head, his scowling lips, his gaunt cheeks, the coldness in his fierce brown eyes. In the dream, his domination was total. As his granite face came closer, his image, twenty years younger than he had since become, gripped me tight.

'You don't scare me,' I told him, my voice too fragile to cross the space between us.

He smiled. And spoke. '*Nunca perdoe.*'

Never forgive. I'd heard those words before, many years ago. It's the same old thing, I told my dreaming self, don't panic.

But it wasn't the same. Last time he'd turned and walked away. Now all he did was open his mouth.

It widened unnaturally. I backed off, struggling against the pull of the dark chasm that threatened to engulf me. I tried to move. My legs were fused. I felt so heavy I couldn't raise my arms. I was being sucked into darkness, swamped by a vast black void closing in on me. I struggled against it. 'Don't,' I shouted, trying to counter his fury. I heard his sound, a rumbling. My protests were drowned out by his roar and by the blood pounding my ear drums. 'Don't.' I jerked my arms out, fighting against the tangle of suffocation.

The tangle of sheets. I was awake, half in bed, half out, and the telephone was ringing. I stretched out, wrenching my shoulder, knocking off the clock. I grabbed the receiver and croaked a barely audible hello.

Charles was brimming over with his own special brand of bonhomie. 'I'm paying you to write the news,' he said. 'Not to get into it.'

I picked up the clock. Eight a.m. I groaned.

'Nice to speak to you too,' he said.

I forced out words. 'Hello, Charles.' My tongue was thick.

'That's right, sweetie, Charles. The man who bankrolls your lavish lifestyle.'

What this meant was that he tossed me the occasional freelance piece, including the profile of Rodney Ellis. There was a glass of water by the bed. I didn't care that it was musty, I gulped it down.

'In case you're interested,' Charles said. 'The prognosis on the baby is good. Rodney Ellis is a hero, his photograph's front-page news. Your mug shot even made it into one.'

I pushed myself up, enduring the spasm of pain that the movement provoked. I never could take Charles lying down.

'Quite a transformation,' Charles said. 'Him, not you. From dreary chief super to saint. And we have the in-depth interview. Which reminds me, when exactly will I get to see the copy?'

I shrugged. 'He's polishing his halo at a charity do tonight. I'll deliver tomorrow.'

'Splendid. Can't wait.' His voice, which had gone distant in preparation for severance, was suddenly revived. 'By the way, you did have a bit of a flutter with Mrs Chief Superintendent, didn't you?'

'Charles.' My head was beginning to hurt almost as much as my arm.

'You know who I mean. Did you speak to her? Mrs Rodney Ellis. What's her name? Flavia? Fiona?'

'Frances.'

'Of course. Frances. Give her a whirl, will you? Get the little woman's angle. You know the kind of thing: the thrills and spills of being hitched to a hero. Take another thousand words.' His voice dropped. 'And another day if you have to.'

'Same rates?'

He groaned as if he were the one in pain. 'Of course,' he said and, without another word, hung up.

I followed his example. But instead of going to my desk, I threw painkillers down my throat and sank back into sleep.

The function room was a monstrous space. Its floors and ceilings were polished wood, its walls lined with red brocade. A criss-cross of chandeliers shimmered over tables laid formally in white starch, burnished silver and translucent crystal. I stood in the doorway watching as overdressed contributors to the Children's Aid and Welfare Fund pecked at each other's cheeks. As the crowd swelled, I was shoved from my vantage point until I ended up pinned to the wall. Not that it mattered. I was a real party-pooper. All around me was laughter, the clinking of glasses, the wobbling of chins – everything a decent function needs. None of it made me feel any better.

Nursing a glass of dry white, I kept a vague eye on Rodney Ellis. He was in full policeman's regalia and surrounded by an armoury of well-wishers. Sharp elbow action would soon have cleared a path, but there was no point. I'd already spoken to him on the phone and got his reluctant consent to interview his wife. And I'd already heard more than enough of his clichés. The only reason that I was there was because once, when I'd been a cub reporter, my failure to turn up to a function just like this had meant I missed a scoop.

A man resplendent in maroon tailcoat hit a miniature silver triangle. 'Ladies, gentlemen. Dinner will soon be served. If you would all locate your tables . . .'

With food in mind, the casual groupings formed flying wedges. I didn't have the energy to compete. I waited until the first wave had parked themselves down and then, having located my name tag, did likewise.

Journalistically speaking, the function was a dud. Since the cuisine and cellar were not much better, I seized the first break in the proceedings to leave. Once outside, however, I stopped congratulating myself for the smoothness of my exit. I had other things to preoccupy my mind: namely that my slinky, low-backed dress would not survive the rainstorm. I stood at the edges of the hotel canopy, searching for a taxi. But, of course, this was London, and it was raining: there would be no taxi.

I inched forwards. A gust of wind spat water at me. I started cursing slowly under my breath. I'd never liked the rain, but since Sam had died – on a night just like this – my dislike had bordered on the phobic.

'Hello? Excuse me?'

Shivering, I looked up and saw an old Saab convertible stopped at the canopy's end. The dark outline of its driver was smiling.

'Would you like a lift?'

I'm too old for casual pick-ups. I turned round, expecting to see the object of his desire. No one there.

The man was beckoning at me. Of course I knew who he

was – an employee of my father paid to track me down. I didn't know whether to be impressed that the quality of the help had so improved or scared that I was worth the bother. I did know that there was no way I was going any nearer.

He leaned across and opened the car door. I heard a blast of Archie Shepp. That was out of character: my father thought of jazz as devil's music and, amongst his devotees, what my father thought was gospel.

I looked again, this time more closely, and recognized the man – he was the one who'd made a brief appearance in Rodney Ellis's office. One mystery solved, another raised. What did he want from me?

To introduce himself apparently. 'Gavin Dowd,' he said.

I returned the favour: 'Kate Baeier.'

He smiled. 'Look, there's a bomb scare at Oxford Circus.'

So?

'You'll never get a taxi.' He looked at me.

My move. I chose to let the silence stretch.

He didn't seem the least bit disconcerted. After a decent interval he spoke again: 'I could take you to a rank outside the area.'

I shook my head.

When he smiled again, the blandness of his expression was undermined by the flashing of his grey-green eyes. A challenge. He was daring me.

I'd grown past the stage of needing to rise to challenges. 'Thanks but . . .'

'It's no bother,' he said.

I was beginning to feel exasperated. 'Look . . .' I began.

Except, before I could crank my indignation up, I was

the one who looked. He was still smiling and he no longer seemed dangerous. I saw myself through his eyes – wet, bedraggled and affronted by the offer of a lift. I couldn't keep it up. After all, he was a policeman and this was Britain. What would he possibly do to me?

A dollop of rain landed on my neck and started sliding down my back. 'Thanks,' I said, quickly, before I could change my mind.

His response was calm acceptance. Reassuring enough. He sat back, waiting for me to get in. I did, and clicked the safety belt into place as he pulled out, expertly, into the stream of traffic. 'Where to?' he asked.

'Any taxi rank will do.'

A quick glance in my direction and, 'Camden's on my way,' he said.

How could he possibly know where I lived? I reached for the door handle.

He read my mind. 'You can't keep anything secret,' he said. 'Not in a police station.'

Of course. I was being paranoid. Policemen are hypersensitive about the press: every casual word I had let drop in the Parchment Road nick would have spread like wildfire.

'You're a journalist,' he said.

I nodded. 'And you're a policeman.'

He returned the nod.

I guessed what age he was – early thirties? – and then his rank. 'Chief Inspector?'

'Chief Superintendent.'

Well, well. I almost whistled. I looked more closely, comparing him to my mental picture of Rodney Ellis. They were of entirely different genres – while Ellis fitted the stereotype of a stolid career policeman, Gavin Dowd was much more modern, with little of the predictable plod about him.

'Where in Camden Town?'

I told him and then sat in silence, enjoying the way Archie Shepp breezed through a saxophone solo and the way Gavin Dowd handled the car. The route was elegant as well but I stamped down on my admiration. Being a policeman he would naturally know his way around.

Around what? an inner voice inquired. I stamped on that as well.

He drew up alongside my house.

'Thanks,' I said. I held out my hand. 'Nice to meet you.' I felt the firmness of his grasp, the warmth of his touch. I was curiously reluctant to let go, but I slid my hand out, saying: 'Would you . . .' and hesitated, wondering if I was really going to go ahead.

A rap, brisk, against the window pane. I jumped and turned to see a face pressed hard against the glass, its features distorted. I saw dark hair slicked against puffy flesh and wild staring eyes. Oh Christ, I thought, the maniacs of Camden Town have finally pinned me down.

'Kate.'

I wound down the window.

The face took shape – not mad but terribly dishevelled. Well, that was no surprise, she was a woman who had long ago elevated self-neglect to the heights of political correctness. 'Valerie,' I said.

She never had gone for idle conversation. 'We have to talk.'

'Now?' I don't know why I bothered: with Valerie it was always now.

'It's urgent,' she said. It was always urgent, too.

I sighed and turned to Gavin Dowd. 'Thanks for the

lift,' I said, thinking that I liked the way he hadn't heavied himself into the conversation. In fact, I thought as he smiled, I like him. Full stop.

'Any time.' He leaned across and pushed the door wider.

I got out. 'Thanks again.'

He nodded.

Valerie cut in. 'Come on. It's a stinking night. Let's go upstairs.'

Chapter
five

As I climbed the stairs, Valerie stumped after me. I could hear her jaws going. Some things never change, I thought. Five years ago Valerie was also always masticating.

'Hope I didn't break up anything,' she said.

I was wrong. Things had changed. In the old days Valerie would not have admitted to the possibility of a heterosexual encounter, never mind think that there was anything wrong in breaking one up.

'It looked promising,' she said.

'It was only a lift,' I said.

We'd reached the third floor. I opened up and ushered Valerie into the living room.

'Nice place,' she said.

'It's rented.' Valerie always made me feel defensive, as if I was getting more than my fair share of life's goodies.

'Still. It's nice.' She plunked herself into the sofa. Her smile was friendly. I felt bad. Just because she was different from the rest of us – nun-like in her devotion to poverty – didn't mean she had set herself up as judge. 'It's lovely and warm as well,' she said. Where her body had touched the sofa's dark blue linen back, a stain was spreading. She wasn't merely wet, she was soaked through.

I wondered how long she'd been waiting and why she hadn't rung first. 'I'll fetch a towel,' I said.

'That's OK.' Valerie had always hated being mothered. 'I'm fine.'

But I wanted to be mother. I needed to be, if only to let me buy some time alone to make the transition from Gavin Dowd's racy Saab to Valerie's embattled cosmos.

Having handed her a towel, I went into the bedroom to change. It was a relief to roll my soggy dress off. If I had invited Gavin Dowd instead of Valerie up, I would never have done the same. I'd have sat there, damp and uncomfortable, anything rather than give the wrong signal to a man I didn't know.

'You been back long?' Valerie called.

'A few months.' I pulled on a pair of jeans, topped them with a sweater and went to join her.

She was on her feet – she never could sit still – and staring at the bookcase. She'd tied her straggly hair up in the towel. She smiled and she was beautiful. I looked at her moon face and saw how much her fat had protected her from ageing. 'It's been a long time since we last met,' she said.

'More than five years.' She hadn't changed much in other ways either. The jeans were what she'd always worn and, by the way her red sweatshirt hung, I guessed she was still boycotting bras.

Nor had she changed in her predilection for getting down to business. Intensity took the place of her smile. 'I need your help.'

I opted for delay. 'Coffee?'

She didn't even bother saying no. 'We want you to do something for us.'

'We?'

'The Hackney Rape Crisis and Battered Wives' Centre. We need you to find somebody for us.'

I held up my hand. 'No,' I said, loud enough to stop her. I meant it. Ever since I'd discovered that Sam had been killed because of me and my investigations, I had decided my finding days were over. And anyway, yesterday's decision still held fast: I was going to polish off my outstanding commitments and then I was getting out.

'But, Kate . . .'

'No,' I said again.

Valerie stood in silence, looking at me. Only after a long, long pause did she speak again. 'Carmen said you might react like this.'

Carmen – my one-time partner in detecting, my one-time friend – so that's who'd given Valerie my address. And that's why Carmen had rung me. I wondered what else she'd said.

'She said you're slow to forgive, that you're hard on everybody, but hardest on yourself.'

Trust Carmen, I thought, to bandy around not only my address but also my pain.

Valerie must have taken a recent course in interpersonal relationships. Instead of pressing the point, as she would previously have done, and getting me really angry, she threw me her most charming smile. 'I'll have that coffee.'

As I watched the water drip through the filter, I listened to her description of the difficulties of keeping the Rape Crisis Centre open, and of the women who passed through its doors. She spoke with animation and empathy. I found myself thinking that although she was a fanatic, without the dedication of people like her, we might all feel a lot less safe.

'It's a policewoman,' she said.

I looked up. 'What is?'

'The person we need you to find.'

I nodded. Non-committal.

'WPC Janet Morris.'

The name sounded vaguely familiar.

'You might have met her. That's why Carmen thought of you, because she heard you were doing a profile on Chief Superintendent Ellis. Janet Morris was based at his station.'

Of course. I remembered that I had met her. Only briefly, but long enough to absorb her name and to register a solid, muscled frame, short straight brown hair, a wary smile. I heard an echo of what Valerie had said. 'She *was* based at the station?'

'She's not there now. Or at least we don't think she is.'

'I see.' I didn't. But then I didn't want to.

'We've tried phoning. We even sent someone in. Undercover, of course.'

I sighed. Save me, I thought, from Valerie and her undercover.

'Which is why we've come to you. Carmen –'

'Leave Carmen out of it,' I snapped.

Valerie blinked. 'She said she couldn't do this. Only you.'

Great, I thought. When I had last seen Carmen she'd accused me of playing detectives. So what the hell was she doing setting Valerie on to me?

But I wasn't going to think about Carmen. 'Why do you want me to find Janet Morris?'

A long pause and then: 'I can't tell you.'

Suited me. I got up. 'In that case . . .'

She didn't hesitate. 'Janet Morris phoned the helpline about a week ago. She'd been raped.'

29

I grimaced.

'One of our volunteers counselled her on the phone. We offer routinely to accompany rape victims to the police station – it should be done sooner rather than later – but in her case, this didn't seem appropriate.'

'Because she's with the police?'

Valerie shook her head. 'Because her rapist is.'

'Oh.' Now I got it. 'From the same station?'

'We think so. We can't be sure. We arranged to meet her but she didn't turn up.'

I shrugged. 'Changed her mind.'

'Perhaps.' Valerie didn't even pretend that she believed it. 'We phoned. To see if she was all right. She wasn't there, not any of the times we phoned. In the end they told us she'd been transferred elsewhere. We sent someone in . . .'

'Undercover.'

She nodded. 'Carol said she was a friend who'd lost touch with Janet. Nobody would talk to her.'

'Has it occurred to you that she may not want to be found?'

'Of course.'

'But you're pressing on anyway?'

'We want to hear it from her own mouth,' Valerie said. 'If she tells us to leave her alone, then we will.'

I didn't say anything. I was too busy thinking that a rape inside a police station was Valerie's kind of case. What better way of making the point that no woman, not even a policewoman, is safe?

'We can pay you,' she said.

That was a surprise. In the old days, Valerie never paid. 'How much?'

'Forty pounds a day,' she said. 'Plus expenses.'

Forty pounds. It was a joke.

'It's all we can afford,' Valerie said.

But it was money, and money for which I didn't have to produce an article. That made it more attractive. I told myself that what I'd thought before was irrelevant – this was nothing like the case that had done Sam in. And how hard could it be to find a policewoman? It might, I thought, be a good way of passing the time as I arranged my departure.

I checked it out. 'You just want to find her?'

'Yes.'

'If I do, I won't tell you where she is. Not if she doesn't want me to.'

'Of course.'

I opened my mouth to throw in another proviso. I couldn't think of one.

Valerie's gaze was even.

'I'll see what I can do,' I said.

Chapter
six

I was almost out of the door when I heard the phone ringing. I rushed to answer it. 'Hello.'

'Kate Baeier? It's Gavin Dowd.'

My bag slid off my shoulder and on to the floor. 'Hi.' I didn't ask how he'd got my number.

He didn't say. Instead: 'Don Cherry's playing at the Royal Festival Hall.'

Great, I thought. A chief superintendent with the time to keep departing journalists up on the latest jazz news.

'I wondered whether you would like to go,' he said.

I was so surprised all I could manage was a perfunctory: 'When?'

'Tomorrow night.'

My eyebrows lifted.

'I realize it's short notice,' he said. 'I'm sure you must be busy.'

No, I wasn't busy. I was . . .

I was thinking that there wasn't any point. I had made up my mind: I was leaving. The last thing I needed was another connection to sever. So of course the answer was no.

Before the sensible, prudent me could frame a polite refusal, I spoke. 'I'd love to come.'

A moment's pause before: 'Oh.' He was as surprised as I, but had quick reflexes. 'Great. I'll pick you up. Seven o'clock?'

'No, I'll meet you there,' I said. 'Seven-twenty?'

If he was disappointed by that, he didn't show it. 'Sure. I'll see you at the bar.'

I had a little trouble putting the receiver back on base, but I didn't have time for nerves. I had to pick up the car and get over to the Ellises' house. Grabbing my jacket, I left the flat.

Downstairs was my father's limousine. No Zetu this time, only the chauffeur. When he got out of the car I saw he was short, with the squat build of an undernourished Algarvian. He opted for the Algarvian man's way of getting attention. When I tried to walk on by, he stood mid pavement, cutting me off. On his face was the kind of menacing sneer that all my father's heavies learn to perfect. He also had their same regard for language. His lips solidly zipped, he shoved an envelope at me.

I took it.

He was a veritable mime artist. He gestured that I should open the envelope and then his finger slashed across his neck, indicating what would happen if I didn't comply. His smile left me in no doubt that cutting necks was what made him love his job. So much for being the boss's daughter. I opened the envelope.

The note, on hotel stationery, was the first direct contact my father and I'd had in over a decade. Despite that, it was circumspect almost beyond belief. *Kate*, he'd written in his constipated, spider's hand, *I must speak with you. Room 504.*

He hadn't signed it. Which was no great surprise. When

33

I'd been young, when my father still had visions of turning me into a female version of himself, he'd endlessly repeated his first rule of business: never sign anything. In case you need to disclaim it later, you understand. Probably why I became a journalist who fights ferociously for the largest possible by-line.

I crumpled up the note. Mr Charm grunted. I gathered he was waiting for an answer. Well, no problem, I had one. 'The answer is no,' I said.

Although I had spoken in Portuguese, he blinked as if he hadn't understood. I knew exactly why: in the universe he inhabited, nobody said no to *O General*.

I went one step closer. 'Unless you have specific instructions to beat my brains out,' I said, 'I'd be grateful if you'd get out of my way.'

His mouth opened wide. I reached up and gently nudged his bottom jaw shut. Then I moved, fast. Before he could react.

It took me just over an hour to pick up my hire car and drive to Richmond. It was like journeying to another world. The place was bright and clean and optimistic – all those things that had long been bled out of Camden Town. Even the sun was out, wiping away the memory of last night's ferocious storm. I parked the car and walked under trees heavy with candy-floss blossom, past gardens whose stiff order was disrupted only by blousy camellias.

The Ellises' house was bay windowed, red brick and semi detached. A short stretch of crazy paving led up to their combination wood/glass door. The bell push, white and inlaid into an adjacent wall, produced a set of melodic chimes and – disconcertingly fast – an open door.

Frances Ellis was small, with dyed honey-blonde hair

and a face more wrinkled than her fifty or so years should warrant. Her smile was crooked with apprehension. My heart sank. I'd seen this kind of smile before; it told me she was going to be one of those hard-work interviewees, the kind who want to help but who are made terminally uptight by nerves.

'Miss Baeier,' she said, stepping aside. A long beat and then: 'Would you like to come in?'

I was already in.

She blushed. 'Let's go into the living room.' She moved on down the hall, leaving the front door open. I shut it before chasing after her.

I found her in a bay-fronted L-shaped room. She was gazing round as if ashamed by what was there. A cursory inspection showed me why. It was a good-sized room but badly furnished. In one corner a neglected-looking dark green three-piece suite stood near by a shining mahogany sideboard. That was all. The rest of the space looked as if it had long given up waiting for a someone to move in.

If Frances Ellis could have stretched her smile out any further, her lips would have snapped. 'It's . . .' she began. But she didn't say what it was. She smiled inanely in my direction.

I looked away.

I was immediately transfixed by a huge, landscaped garden which wound its way almost to the horizon, the stuff of stately homes rather than suburbia. A lush, smooth lawn swayed past borders so deeply layered they must have taken years to establish. In a far corner, I saw clusters of azaleas and rhododendrons in bloom, their zingy reds, pinks and oranges an exaggerated slash of colour against the brightness of the grass's green. To one side was a rock garden, its purple heather so densely planted that, even from this distance, it was visible. I kept on looking, taking in more of it, the clump of fruit trees at the back, the climbing roses massing against the background of a clematis-covered trellis. The sight was mesmerizing – a free, untethered Richmond where lace curtains and crazy paving and even bay windows were unnecessary distractions. Against the turquoise of the sky, it glistened, beckoning. I wanted to go out there; I wanted to touch and feel its beauty.

No wonder the living room was so neglected: the garden must have taken all her energy. I tore my eyes away. 'You're a gifted gardener.'

'Not me. Rodney.'

The thought of those restless white hands delving in the soil to create such loveliness seemed utterly implausible. My eyes widened.

'He likes to make things grow.' She said it plaintively and her smile was nervous. 'He works so hard.' Another smile, disparaging this time, the little woman behind the great man.

I thought about her husband and the edge of ferocity I'd suspected lay within and I thought her behaviour was perfectly matched. I could see it all: the chief superintendent at work, the tyrant at home. By the looks of it, any tender loving care he had was reserved for his garden. Which didn't endear me to Mrs Chief Super. In fact the opposite: it made me want to kick her.

'Tea?'

I was beginning to feel slightly queasy. I said yes.

After she had scuttled out, I pulled myself together. One thing I've learned, journalism can be interesting, even fulfilling, but no good ever comes from delivering the unexpected. If you're being paid to write character assassination then you can put diamond-encrusted spades on your expense sheet and the meanest editor will pay up without demur. But if you get an assignment to produce a profile on a chief superintendent for a middle of the road woman's magazine then a hatchet job on the superintendent's wife is likely to get you flung out on your ear. So the bottom line was, nobody cared if Frances Ellis was a doormat.

She was back with tray. While she set to pouring, I got out my notebook. She handed me a cup. I sat down with it and took a sip.

'I was a nurse, you know,' she said.

I didn't, but it was a start.

'We met in A. and E. I was a nurse.' Her face folded in on itself as if she were reliving the days when she'd worn white and he'd been a junior enough policeman to be in and out of Casualty.

I waited patiently for her to come out of her trance. The seconds dragged on; my writing finger began to itch. 'Did you stop working when you had your son?' I said eventually.

Her eyes focused. She stared at me with enough astonishment to suggest she might have forgotten I was there. 'My son?'

I flicked my eyes towards the sideboard, where a row of silver-framed photographs catalogued the transformation of a gap-toothed baby into a young man.

'Oh yes. Of course.' She was on her feet and at the photos. 'Isn't he handsome?' She was holding one of the photographs, turning it so I could see. 'On his twenty-first birthday.'

I agreed, yes, he was handsome. He was also looking straight at the camera, unsmiling, with something hard about his eyes.

'But then of course so is his father,' she said.

I was given photo number two, a wedding snap. In it stood the young Frances, serene in gauzy white, with Rodney, a proud arm circling her waist, looking strangely raffish. There was none of the stiffness which characterized the man I knew. I wondered whether it was the responsibility of family or the constraints of the job which had so permanently strained that cocky smile.

She took the photos from me and carefully put them back. Then, sitting down, she raised her cup to her lips.

My turn. I got down to business – Charles's kind of business. I asked the kind of 'little woman' questions I knew he thrived on. She was perfectly co-operative. She told me that her son was an accountant, that she kept house and worked voluntarily in an old people's home, that now Rodney had reached such a high position she no longer worried about his safety but that she felt for the younger wives who did not have this security, and that, contrary to my first impressions, she seemed to be a nice, balanced, boring woman who had too little in her life.

Like me, I thought, interviewing women about their husbands and sons. I wrote down what she said while all the time I was dying to get out of there. I was even beginning to feel grateful for my father's attempt to contact me, which had pushed me into leaving. I closed my notebook. 'Thanks,' I said.

'Is that all?' She sounded only mildly surprised but the look that crossed her face was one of immense relief.

She and me both. We got to our feet. She smiled, an ordinary woman who had provided me with an ordinary interview, the kind that Charles would relish.

'Thanks,' I said again and followed her to the door. She opened it and I stepped out.

'Drive carefully,' she said.

Chapter
seven

I drove fast and sure, heading into inner London. The more I put between myself and Frances Ellis, the more my mood lightened. By the time I reached my desk, I was positively euphoric. I rode the high, speeding through the Ellis profile before e-mailing it into Charles's computer.

It was evening by the time I pushed open the smoky glass door which lead to the Parchment Road police station enquiry desk. Two steps in and I saw a man standing by the counter, his silvery-grey beard trailing down to his stomach. He was in fancy dress, his overlapping shreds of long red, pink, purples and puce material arranged around him. I knew him from the old days – he was a fantasist in flowing robes who spent his days wafting along the Hackney pavements and his nights sleeping rough. I was glad he'd survived the years since I'd been gone.

There was no one at the other side of the counter. As I came up beside him, the fantasist's head darted sideways. I said hello.

His slit eyes latched on to mine. 'Forgiveness is a gift from God,' he said.

I did a double-take. I'd not heard him speak before.

'Unless you can find it in yourself to forgive,' he said, 'you will never be at home.' He looked at me so intently, I found I couldn't look away. He spoke again. 'I *know*.'

His bloodshot eyes showed how much the years had ravaged him. But I saw something else in them as well – a will to make me understand. I found myself wondering what he knew.

'No matter how far you travel,' he said. 'You will always be travelling with yourself.'

The ravings of a madman, but I was intrigued. He didn't go on, because at that moment an inner door opened and a policeman came through to the other side of the counter. The old man addressed himself to the new arrival. 'You have no right.' He had upped the volume and added outrage. 'It's mine. You should give it back. I have nothing. Only that. You should give it back.'

The policeman was young and patient. 'Come on now, Jim. It's . . .'

'I am not Jim.' The old man flung out his arms. 'I am James.' There was so much thunder in his voice, I took an involuntary step sideways.

The policeman wasn't so easily intimidated. He moved out of his antechamber, through two double glass doors, and into our area so fast that he had his hand on the mad James's arms before the old man realized he was there. 'James,' he said. 'Play fair. You've had your tea. Now come on mate, you don't like being locked up, do you?'

He had pitched his voice low and easy, infusing it with that perfect combination of jocularity and condescension they learn at policeman's school. And it worked. The fight went out of James. He started shuffling to the door.

Before he left he turned to me. I found myself hoping he'd continue on the forgiveness theme.

No such luck. 'Keep hold of your valuables,' is what he said.

I tried a half-smile. 'See you later.'

Our eyes connected, only for an instant, and then he was gone.

The policeman retraced his steps. 'I won't be a minute.' Behind the counter once again, he picked up the phone. 'James took off at last,' he said. 'But you better tell the lads to keep an eye on him. He's heading for one of his funny turns.' He put the phone down and came towards me. 'How can I help you?'

'My name's Kate Baeier,' I said.

His face lost some of its careful neutrality. 'Ah yes.' He started smiling. 'I'll call through to Mr Ellis.'

I stopped him with a hurried: 'Actually, I'm after somebody else.' A moment's pause while I worked out which was the best approach. I decided to go head on. 'I'm looking for a WPC, name of Janet Morris.'

His voice was casual. 'I'll see if she's in the station.' He went back to his desk, spoke quietly into the phone. I couldn't hear what he was saying.

Whoever was on the other side was into the short report. Within seconds the receiver was in its cradle and the policeman was addressing me. 'I'm sorry. Jan's not here right now.'

'Do you know where I could find her?'

He was perfectly impassive – 'She could be on the beat. Or on another shift' – drip-feeding me, in that policeman's way, with only the barest minimum.

I hung in there. 'Could you find out which it is?'

'Hold on.' Back to the desk. This time he was on the phone for longer. When eventually he hung up, he didn't look my way. He sat himself behind the desk instead, and pulled a file closer.

I stood and waited. When that got boring, I inspected the waiting room. There wasn't much to see: three steel chairs bolted to the floor; two wooden doors with lighted letters above, each saying 'IN USE'; two smoky glass doors – one leading to the street, the other into the station's depths – and two posters giving anti-theft advice. The only thing that didn't come in twos was the leaflet holder which was stuffed with anti-domestic-violence leaflets. I stretched out for one.

The phone rang. The policeman picked it up and listened. When the call was over, he looked at me. 'No joy. She must be on another shift.' His pleasant face had closed down on me. I've done my best, it plainly said, now give up.

I didn't feel like giving up. 'Could you tell me which shift?'

His expression was now full-blown policeman's impenetrability. 'It's not policy to give out such information.'

'Well, would anybody else be able to help me?'

He shook his head.

This was like drawing teeth. 'The station sergeant?' I tried. 'Or the inspector?'

At last some words. 'The sarge is busy in the custody suite,' he said, 'and the guv's out on a call.'

His phlegmatic impassivity was getting to me. I thought of upping the stakes, of asking for Ellis. But knowing Ellis, I wasn't sure how far that would get me. 'Think I'll have more luck if I try the next shift?'

He shrugged.

I wasn't going to get any more from him. I glanced at my watch. 'I'll come back,' I said.

His answering smile was pure formality. 'You do that.' He was already turning away.

The next shift came on stream at ten. Since I was going for a quick completion, I decided to come back then. Which left me with three hours to kill. I was hungry so I went in search of food. I found an Indian restaurant that served me a chicken with mango and green bananas which was more than palatable. Pity about the atmosphere though – it was the kind of low light and dense-packed tables that made a prolonged stay a recipe for depression. I left in search of entertainment.

What I found was certainly engrossing – a pub on the edges of Dalston packed by middle-aged white couples laughing uneasily at the mean gibes of a bitter comedian. Red faced from drink, he clobbered us with pitiless caricatures. At least he was even handed – nobody escaped his rancour. Halfway through, I realized the laughter was the audience's way of stopping him from aiming his venom at them. I couldn't work out why they didn't leave. I got up and did just that.

Out in the streets, Dalston's nightlife was getting going. A gang of rangy young men had coalesced around a video store. They were leaning against the glass, talking softly amongst themselves. They were taking up so much of the available pavement space that I was forced into the gutter. As I passed by, I saw a small package flit from one casual hand to another. I must have shown that I was watching. A jacket opened, allowing me a flash of the butt of a handgun. I got the message. I walked off fast, heading for the police station.

Chapter
eight

The policeman, a different one, barked a bullish, hard-cop 'Yes?' at me.

'I'm looking for a WPC,' I said. 'Name of Janet Morris.'

'Oh yes?' His smile was perilously close to a smirk.

I kept my voice even. 'Would you see if she's in?'

His eyes, deep set in a high forehead, were fixed on me. He didn't move; he didn't do anything. Just stared.

I heard the sound of the street door opening. I turned and watched two women, one young, one in her mid-sixties, entering together.

A knuckle rapped on the counter: the policeman calling me back. 'Name?'

I sighed. 'Janet Morris.'

'No. Your name.'

'Kate Baeier.'

He nodded. 'Take a seat.' And walked away.

I took a seat. The other punters – the women and two middle-aged men – stayed where they were in front of the counter. Their weary posture showed that they'd done all this before, their resignation that they expected to keep on doing it.

The station clock was marking time. I looked around trying to stop depression settling on me. There was nothing much to see. Both the wooden-doored interview rooms were still 'IN USE': the domestic-violence leaflets still waiting to be read. Beside them hung – I don't know how I'd missed it previously – a garish colour portrait of Rodney Ellis. I stared up at him; he grinned uneasily back, the picture of a law-enforcement nerd.

'Yes?' PC Charmer was back.

'I want to know what's happened to my husband,' the young woman said. 'Mr Johnson.'

The policeman nodded but didn't stir.

Another blast of chill night air as a man came in. There was nothing casual about him: his suit was grey but flecked with enough metallic thread to make it silver, his shirt was garish reds and oranges woven into the finest silk, his briefcase was dark leather, and his shoes looked as if they'd stepped off the back of a slinky crocodile. As he strode past me, I saw gold – lots of it – on fingers, wrist, neck and front teeth, glistening against his honey-brown skin.

He had reached the counter. Not for him the hushed submission of a plaintiff. 'I've got my brother's food.' He said it loud.

He got the stock response. A nod and: 'Take a seat.'

There were seven of us now and only two chairs. Nobody fought for the unoccupied one.

The policeman went through an inner door. Nobody spoke, nobody moved. The policeman came back. 'Your husband's being interviewed,' he told the woman, and then said to one of the middle-aged men: 'Your son's just being charged. You can see him after that.'

'Hey, man.'

The policeman moved along the counter until he was in front of the young man and gestured impatiently with his hand. 'Show me.'

The leather briefcase was opened and a straw lunch box extracted. The policeman's movements were sluggish, as if he were under water. I smelled rice and beans and dashin and something more pungent. My mouth watered. The policeman's gaze, directed at the food, was bleakly disparaging. His hand hovered, for a moment I thought he was going to poke a finger into the centre of one of the cartons. But he didn't go that far. He looked up. 'Your brother's Melville Adams?'

'Come on, man. You know he is.'

The policeman closed the cartons. 'I'll see he gets these.'

The young man's assertive voice stopped the policeman in mid-turn. 'I want to talk to him.'

'I'll speak to the custody sergeant.'

'It's my right,' the young man insisted.

Leaving the food on the counter, the policeman disappeared again.

Time passed. The young man closed the lunch-box lid. The street door opened and a woman's head inserted itself into the space. Her body didn't follow through. Her mouth was frozen Munch-like, locked in a scream without sound. Her jerky eyes leap-frogged from one to the other of us and then, abruptly, as if she had seen something she didn't like, she withdrew. The door swung shut. The man whose son was being charged pulled down a leaflet and read what to do when threatened by domestic violence. The young woman clicked her tongue impatiently. The young man rocked back and forth on his heels. Apart from that there was only the sounds of night: the distant traffic, a dog snarling, a passing and almost immediately curtailed burst of laughter.

The policeman came back. Seeing no one new he gave the counter a miss and settled himself down at the desk which lay some feet away.

46

'Hey, man.'

The policeman looked up.

'What about my brother?'

The policeman's movements were on the other side of measured, his voice was automaton dull. 'The custody sergeant is busy.'

The young man's voice rose. 'When can I see my brother then?'

The policeman shrugged and made another pass at sitting.

'Hey.'

The policeman stopped, half up, half down.

'I'm talking to you.'

The policeman was on his feet.

'When can I see my brother?'

The policeman's face was still as granite. 'I told you,' he said, 'the sergeant's busy.'

The young man reached into his jacket pocket. The policeman's eyes flared. I thought about what I had seen in the street and held my breath. But instead of a weapon the young man took out a small, leather-bound notebook. 'It is my right,' he said.

The policeman moved closer. 'Only if the custody sergeant has the time.'

The young man's fist closed on his book. He leaned forwards so that his face was near to the policeman. For a moment, as the silence turned crystalline, they eyeballed each other – two adversaries locked in an ancient combat.

'If I were you,' the policeman said quietly, 'I'd go home.' I couldn't miss the warning that underlay his words.

Neither could the young man. He did not back down. Slowly, slowly he began opening his address book and, at the same time, upped the stakes. 'You think I'm stupid?' he sneered. 'You think I don't know what you're up to?'

The policeman made a stab at chortling. But when he asked, 'And what is that?' there was no humour there.

'You and your spot searches. You think we don't know that you're trying to scare us?'

The policeman shrugged. He looked as if he were trying not to yawn.

The young man turned a page of his book. 'I've got your number,' he said, as if it were written there. 'I've had it for a long time now.' I could see the build-up of tension in his back. 'This isn't the way you usually work.'

The policeman opened his mouth.

'Not on the Richton estate, you don't,' the young man said.

The policeman's face was stilled, his yawn pulverized. His question: 'What does that mean?' was delivered on such an undercurrent of menace that the air seemed to shimmer.

I was sitting on the far edge of my chair. Looking round, I saw the others were similarly alert. We watched the young man as his expression went from purposeful through a moment's indetermination to resolution. It was obvious to all of us – he was going for broke.

My eyes moved back to the policeman. His finger was hovering over what could only be the panic button. The young man didn't care. The way he bent his legs showed that he was about to destroy his future by vaulting over the counter. I sat there, watching, thinking he was a fool but that there was nothing I could do to stop him. I saw the two other men, both shaking their heads in sorrow, both moving out of the way.

But one of us was prepared to act. The woman in her

sixties reached forward and touched him gently on his arm. 'Leave it,' she said.

He looked as though he was going to flick off her hand. The policeman's finger went lower.

The woman pulled the young man round, fixing him with the force of her own determination. 'He's not worth it.'

A beat: the young man glared at her.

'Save your strength, brother,' the woman said.

She'd got to him. 'You're right,' he muttered. He looked away. 'Fucking idiot.'

That was it. Over. The policeman went back to his desk. The younger woman dipped her head, acknowledging her companion's feat. The two middle-aged men exchanged a smile of relief.

Behind the counter, the phone trilled. When the policeman had finished speaking he got up. He addressed himself first to the older woman, 'Your son's being charged now. You can see him afterwards,' and then: 'Mr Adams? The custody sergeant will see Melville gets his food.'

The young man moved the lunch box along the counter. The policeman stretched out for it. The young man backed off. The policeman lifted out the cartons and reinspected the food. When he looked across at the young man his eyes were narrowed. 'Anything else?'

The young man looked back. But not for long. As the policeman kept on staring, the young man dropped his eyes. Submission. The policeman made no attempt to erase the victoriousness of his smile. It didn't make me like him any better. Still, it was none of my business. I turned my attention to the pattern on the floor.

'Miss Baeier?'

I looked up to find a man with sergeant's stripes sewn on his jacket sleeves standing in front of me. 'I'm sorry to have kept you waiting,' he said.

I wondered who he was.

'The name's Harrison, Tom Harrison.' He was in his mid-fifties, big and broad, with a friendly face. He seemed vaguely familiar. I couldn't think why. Maybe it was because he looked like everybody's model father. 'This way.' He held one of the 'IN USE' doors open for me. I walked through and into a dingy room. 'Have a seat,' he said, closing the door.

There was a scratched wooden table and two wooden chairs. I sat in one of them. He took the other.

'You've been writing an article on Chief Superintendent Ellis.' His smile was wide and friendly. 'You've finished now?'

I nodded.

'And you're looking for WPC Morris?'

'Yes.'

'Well, Miss Baeier . . .'

I had the feeling that at last someone was going to give me the gen on Janet Morris. I breathed out, relieved.

Too soon. A fist rapped on the door but couldn't wait. A man, in plain clothes and a furious hurry, burst in. He nodded at my policeman. 'A word, Tom.' It was an order. Tom Harrison got up, grimaced apologetically, tossed a 'Won't be a minute,' my way and left.

He was longer than a minute – much longer. I sat, containing my irritation, doing a quick inventory of the room.

The table was scratched and wonky. I looked up. Several of the ceiling tiles that should have covered the space above were missing, exposing a mass of jumbled aluminium pipes and boxes. I dropped my gaze. The walls were painted a slate-grey which had long passed its sell-by date. Somebody had shown their distaste by throwing coffee at them; nobody had bothered to wipe the splashes off. That, apart from the mud–brown of the skirting and door architraves, was it. I threw my head back, looking up again. A long strip light looked down.

I leaned my chair back against the wall and set myself to wait. I kept looking at my watch. After about ten minutes, I made myself stop.

After about twenty minutes, I'd had enough. 'This is ridiculous,' I said. Out loud. Checking out the acoustics.

They weren't worth staying for. 'I'm going,' I said, and so I was. But something – perhaps the time I'd wasted to wrest mundane information out of the police – had made me wild. I felt like making an impact. So, instead of going out through the door that had admitted me, I tried the other one.

Chapter
nine

Whatever was taking Tom Harrison so long had made him careless. When I nudged the door, it opened easily. I went out into a corridor whose brick walls were painted a pale canary yellow. In front of me was a tall metal cabinet, both doors gaping wide. I saw grey blankets, a pile of white paper overalls, a basket of plastic gloves, a mish-mash of different-sized white trainers and someone's half-eaten cheese sandwich. When I'd been here before, the place had been obsessively neat – I wondered what kind of panic had led to this disorder.

There was nobody to ask; there was nobody in sight. The only evidence of life was distant voices, so distorted that I couldn't make out a single word.

I thought about going back. I even tried to. But I'd been more efficient than the sergeant, I'd closed the door behind me. It must have been on an automatic deadlock: no matter which way I twisted the handle, it wouldn't budge. Which meant I'd have to find somebody, anybody, to let me out.

Turning right would have taken me to the police side of the reception counter. I didn't feel like braving Action Man's smirk, so I turned left. As I walked slowly along the stone floor, the voices got louder. I still couldn't make out what was being said.

I reached the corridor's end at an unmarked door. I hesitated, looking back along the corridor. It was still yellow – although from this angle closer to regurgitated buttercup than to any living bird – and still empty. I knew that if I succeeded in opening the door, I would be in the bowels of the police station. Thinking that it surely couldn't be this simple to infiltrate a police station, I pressed down on the handle.

It was that simple. The door was heavy but when I leant on it it opened.

I was at the entrance to a custody suite which bore about the same relationship to a hotel suite as an English hamburger does to a sane cow. It was an uneasy claustrophobic space, its walls the same yellow as in the corridor but much higher. It was the stuff of disorientation – none of the angles or the proportions made sense. Since this was the first port of call for any new prisoner, you would be forgiven for thinking that the effect was deliberate.

When Ellis had shown me round the place before it had been a focus for uniformed hyperactivity. Now it just looked dead. By the door was a sealed time clock where policemen punched in prisoner movement. Opposite it were a sink, a fridge and enough coffee and tea equipment to satisfy a small battalion. There wasn't a single customer – not even the custody sergeant, who should have been parked behind his long desk.

Curiosity took irritation's place. Letting the voices guide me, I made my way down the narrow passage that led to the men's cells. I was still expecting somebody to spring out and demand what I was doing there. When it didn't happen, I kept on going.

The first cell was a psychologist's fancy, designed to house the most uptight of prisoners. A narrow space, its walls were painted a sickly pink. It was supposed to calm the agitated, but only for a limited period. After four hours, apparently, the incarcerated started seeing red again.

Its door was open. I looked in. I saw a policewoman sitting on the hard bunk. Perhaps her four hours were up: she was drooped so far down that all I could see of her head was one tight central plait. I stood for a moment, watching her. She was too involved in herself to notice me. I could have said something but I decided that her misery brooked no interruption. I turned and continued down the passage.

The next cell along was closed. I stopped, moved its metal shutter gently to the right and looked in. What I saw was the kind of thing you expect to find in a police station – three men locked up. One, white, in his mid-forties, dressed in a business suit, was ranting loudly – the source of most of the clamour I'd been tracking. As he marched from one end of the cell to the other, his mouth motored with him. There were vowels and syllables and even the occasional verb but all strung together so wildly that I still couldn't make out what he was saying. I guessed that nobody could. Certainly not his two companions. One, white again, was lying with his back to the door, curled up in a foetal position, his hands clamped tight against his ears. The other, a young black man, dressed homeboy style like – I guessed – his brother but much more casually, was sitting on the floor. By the way his hand kept swiping at the dripping from his nose, I reckoned it wasn't food he needed but something much stronger. He sniffed and wiped again; the madman glared at him.

They were in no position to help themselves, never mind a passing stranger. To keep things tidy, I closed the shutter. I moved on. There were only two cells left, both with their doors wide open. After that lay a dead end, the police station's external wall. I was driven. I went on, my only concession to sanity being that I went more slowly.

The nearer I got to the next cell in the line-up, the more words separated themselves from the general mêlée and started making sense. Two more steps and I was in a position to hear clear sentences.

'You checked on him when you made your rounds?' The question was delivered loud and unsympathetic and topped with a hectoring: 'Right?'

A mumbled reply: I couldn't make it out.

'When was that? Twelve-forty-five?'

Another murmur. I looked at my watch and saw that it was gone one o'clock.

'You wrote down when you phoned the MO.?'

More jumbled words that seemed to signal assent.

'Good.' The voice got louder still. 'Now you know what you do? You sit and you write down what happened. You all on your lonesome – not in the canteen, not with your mates holding your dick. You take a pen in your hand and I don't care if you end up with the worst case of repetitive cissie injury the MO has ever seen, you don't let go until you've got down every detail. You make this the model report of your whole sodding career. And when you think you've finished – that's when you begin again. You read it over and you think about whether you've left anything out – anything, I don't care how stupid it seems, anything that happened -- and you write that down as well. Understand?'

There was a moment's pause during which the recipient of this short course in report writing must have found the right thing to say, for his tormentor's voice went down a notch, changing from bullying to a paternal, 'Good man. Go on, get yourself a cup of tea.'

I should have waited for them to come out. I knew I

should. But even as I told myself that I was going to wait, I took off. I fled into the final, open cell, pulling the door partially closed. Peering through the space between door and wall, I watched a policeman in shirt sleeves and sergeant's stripes shoo his junior forward.

'Show me that report as soon as you've finished. Right?'

It didn't take them long to reach the end of the passage and disappear. About as long, in fact, as it took for me to come to my senses and realize that I'd walked myself, literally, into a brick wall.

I didn't panic. I took stock of my situation. I was alone, in a police cell – a man's cell – in Hackney. I wasn't going to waste time berating myself for having got into this stupid situation, I was going to get out of it. And I knew how. I had no alternative. I would have to follow the men down the passage and I would have to ask them the way out. Simple as that. Taking a preparatory breath in, I reached for the door.

I don't know why I saw it then rather than before. Too busy concentrating on the policemen, I suppose – or maybe the fit of pique that had led me here was tinged with more madness than I'd assumed.

Once I saw it, there was no denying what it was. A dead body. Stretched out on the bunk and covered with a sheet. It had to be a body: nothing else looks quite like that, nothing else has the form of a man, the outline of the head, the nose, the distended stomach, the feet pointing to the ceiling, nothing else can be all that and yet lie so still.

Dead, then.

Corpses no longer unhinged me. They were never the worst thing anyway, it was the people left alive who were so hard to face. So I didn't overreact. I stood and invited coherent thoughts in.

They came sporadically. I wondered which of the people in the waiting room would mourn this lonely figure. I wondered how he'd died. I wondered whether he was in fact a he. And I wondered all this so hard that I found myself going over and lifting up the sheet.

I knew his face immediately. I think I would have known it anyway, but I had seen him so very recently. It was James. James the bum, the wearer of exotic costumes and fabulous fabrics.

I thought about the contact we'd had that day. He hadn't looked well then but he was alive. More alive to me than I'd expected, because what he'd said had meant something.

And now he was dead.

I take back all I said about corpses. I never had got used to them, I had only pretended to myself I had. Now, faced with the waxen sheen of his skin, which took away his humanity, I felt melancholy. I laid the sheet down, covering him up. But I couldn't wipe out the memory of what I'd seen. It stayed with me – eyes bleached of colour, staring out, mouth slack and open, sallow skin turning yellow. I closed my eyes, felt myself swaying.

'What the hell are you doing here?'

It was a good question. It brought me back to consciousness.

'Who let you in?

I didn't have an answer.

He didn't need one. He had me in a disabling armlock before I'd even registered movement, and he was brutal. He yanked me hard. I yelled.

'Shut up and come with me.' He shoved me out of the cell, past two paramedics with stretcher in tow, and straight down the passage.

Chapter
ten

The air in the room was stale. So was my inter-rogator's breath. 'What were you doing there?' He leaned forwards.

I edged out of range. 'I told you. I left by the wrong door.'

His head was so close, I could see his tonsils. I wondered whether he knew they were infected. 'The wrong door!' He moved back, exposing a belly which, bulging out of crumpled brown trousers, put extra strain on already overloaded shirt buttons. 'Geographically challenged, are we?'

He had a point. But what was I supposed to say? That I'd been deliberately naughty out of pique? Somehow I couldn't see that as a winning line.

'Come on, Kate.' He had see-sawed again both physically and emotionally. He was sitting straight, trying to be nice. The tautness of his smile showed what an effort it was. 'You can tell me.'

I kept my mouth shut tight.

He guillotined his smile, shoved his chair away and stood up. I hoped he wasn't going to pace. The room was already suffocating – we could do without the extra loss of oxygen. And besides, the last time he'd gone walkabout, he'd ended up behind me, blasting rancid air down my neck. I turned to look up at him.

He was looking down. He definitely had the better view. While I was merely exhausted, his stomach was distended by too much bitter, his sallow face puffy from too many late nights, and his mouse-brown hair tousled during unending repetition of the same question. He tossed it out again. 'Why were you walking round the station?'

'Look,' I said. I was still trying to stay calm. 'We've been through this. I came to the station to get a simple answer to a simple question. When it looked like I was going to wait up half the night for it, I decided to leave. I was tired. I made a mistake. I went out the wrong way. There was nothing to stop me. The door closed and I couldn't get back. So I walked down the corridor, looking for somebody to let me out.'

'Why didn't you turn right? You knew there was an officer there.'

Because he's got a personality almost like yours, I nearly said. I didn't have to. I didn't have to say anything. He was on a repetitive roll. 'What were you looking for?'

It was once too often for me. I got up.

He swerved into hard-cop mode. 'I told you to sit down.'

I yawned. 'As a matter of fact,' I said, 'you *asked* me to take a seat and I co-operated. But now I've had enough. So if you're planning to charge me with walking unattended around a police station, do it – in which case I'd like my phone call. If not, well, it's been great but you know what they say – all good things must end.'

A good enough speech, delivered with some bravado. The only problem was my heart wasn't in it. Brown Suit was between me and the door and he wasn't going to let me pass. And even if I managed to side-step him,

59

outside lurked other policemen ready to have a go. I'd penetrated their inner sanctum and the glares they'd thrown me told me how little they appreciated the feat.

'Sit down, Miss Baeier.'

What choice did I have? I sat.

'Now tell me.' He had a limited repertoire and had gone back to his old leaning trick. 'Why were you in the cell?'

I didn't like the look of him, especially up close. I put my elbows on the table and dropped my head into my palms, covering my eyes. It felt great: dark and quiet and restful.

'Why go there?'

The tips of my fingers massaged the place where my forehead ended and my scalp began. I felt the tension circulate. If I continued long enough I might even drive it out.

'Hey.' He sounded really angry. 'You can't sleep here.'

Small circles were definitely the most effective. I decided to be methodical about it, working two fingers simultaneously from the centre out.

I felt a faint disturbance in the air. Him playing with the idea of getting physical? I kept my head down, wondering what I would do if he made contact.

I heard my name: 'Miss Baeier,' spoken by a different voice. I didn't feel like facing another one of them. I didn't feel like anything. My head was heavy. I let it lie.

It came again: 'Miss Baeier.' Of course, I knew that voice. Brown Suit's voice, telling the tape recorder that the Chief Superintendent had just entered, confirmed it. I looked up.

Rodney Ellis was standing just inside the door. He'd obviously got dressed in a hurry. His tie was askew, the top button of his starched shirt still undone. It was the first time I had seen him looking anything other than supremely in control. I suppose I shouldn't have been surprised – a death in a cell was the kind of nightmare that must throw even the most serene of chief superintendents off course.

His nervous fingers yanked his tie straight. 'I'm sorry to have kept you waiting,' he said.

I'd been there long enough to forget what it felt like to be on the receiving end of normal courtesy. I nodded gratefully.

'I gather you stumbled across Mr Shaw's body.'

'She says it was a mistake, guv.' This from a sneering Brown Suit.

Rodney Ellis's eyes flared and shifted to the other man's. The result was unexpected. Although he was the target of his station commander's glare, Brown Suit did not seem cowed. His gaze was lazy, languorous, almost insolent. Ellis amplified his expression so that he was pumping out enough stern disapproval to exhaust the most trenchant opposition. It worked eventually: Brown Suit dropped his gaze. I felt a moment's triumph, for that's exactly what I had wanted to make him do.

Ellis's eyes were still on Brown Suit. 'Do me a favour,' he began, although it was the mutual eye action which was transmitting information. Watching as messages were semaphored between the two, I came down to earth. I was tired but not that tired. Brown Suit wasn't really being insubordinate, this was just some kind of organized hard-cop/soft-cop routine featuring Rodney Ellis as Mr Nice Guy.

'Get us some coffee, would you?' He looked at me inquiringly.

'Or would you prefer tea, Miss Baeier?'

What I would have preferred was sleep, or in its absence, a single malt or five. 'Coffee would be good,' I said.

'Two coffees,' Ellis said. 'Please.'

Brown Suit stayed long enough to indulge in more eye talk, which this time had him going over to the tape deck, muttering into the machine and switching off. An electronic whine of closure punctuated his lumbering exit. I'd been trying to get rid of the man for well over an hour. I should have been pleased. All I felt was wary.

Rodney Ellis came to sit by me. 'Tell me what happened.'

I sighed.

His voice was gentle – 'I know you've gone through it over and over again' – and hypnotic as well – 'but tell me. Just this last time.'

What I half wanted to tell him was that I knew he'd used Brown Suit to soften me up. I decided not to bother. I was so tired I no longer cared.

I told him, and it took all of four minutes. When I had finished, he nodded and put a final full stop to his notes. His voice was as businesslike as his words. 'I'll get your statement typed up on a witness form,' he said.

On cue Brown Suit appeared with two mugs of instant coffee. Mine he placed in front of me. Rodney Ellis took his out. The coffee was undrinkable. I sat and drummed my fingers on the table. Brown Suit fixed his doleful eyes somewhere in the middle distance.

We didn't have to sit there long. Rodney Ellis returned with my statement all neatly typed. I read it through and signed. With a 'Thank you, Brian' Ellis handed it to Brown Suit who took it away.

Leaving us alone. Rodney Ellis started to rise. His expression told me I was supposed to follow suit.

I stayed put. 'How did he die?'

He looked at me, deciding, I suppose, whether I deserved an answer. He delivered a compromise: 'We'll only know for sure after the PM,' and then watched me, waiting for my response. Well, two could play the waiting game. I bit back words.

He let me win. 'At a first guess,' he said, 'we think a heart attack.'

I wasn't surprised. If you ruled out murder, a heart attack was probably the obvious deduction. Except . . . 'Inconvenient place to have it,' I said.

His gaze was so ferocious that I wondered whether his staring down of Brown Suit had really been an act. I felt my own impulse to look away, but I'd had enough of being bullied. 'Inconvenient for the smooth running of the station,' I said.

He repeated the word: 'Inconvenient,' as if trying it out for size. It didn't seem to fit. His face softened; so did his voice. 'I've known James Shaw for over thirty years,' he said, musingly, almost as if he were speaking to himself. 'A strange soul. He lost his wife and children and he never picked up the pieces. Used to walk the streets adrift in his own world. He was part of the community. I'm sorry that he'll no longer be there – he reminded me of the days when I walked the beat.'

I was fascinated. The Rodney Ellis that I had known before, the efficient functionary who, although he would always be fair, had also by-passed normal human emotions, had gone. In his place was someone other, someone who could talk with compassion and what sounded like regret. I held my breath.

He had caught the intensity of my concentration and he didn't like it. When he spoke again, he was back on robotic stream. 'Mr Shaw was phobic about doctors in general and hospitals in particular. When he felt ill, he would get drunk and make a nuisance of himself until the beat officer had no

63

choice but to take him in. They were waiting for the MO to arrive when he died.'

This time not an ounce of warmth was displayed. I wondered whether the compassion I thought I had heard before, had all been in my imagination. Oh well, I thought, easy come . . .

'If there's nothing else?' he said.

There was something else – time for me to cut the contact. I stood up. So did he. 'It's late,' he said. 'Go home and sleep. Sergeant Turner will show you out.'

Chapter
eleven

Sergeant Turner – Brown Suit – took me past the custody sergeant's desk, through the heavy doors, down the yellow corridor, into the witness interview rooms and out the other side. The reception area was deserted, although Action Man was still in situ on the other side of the counter, behind his desk, making jerky finger music on his typewriter. He was so caught up in the rigours of composition that he didn't even look up when I passed.

The sergeant was by the outside door, fidgeting with its metal handle. We exchanged a nod and then I went out into the grey dawn. I walked down a row of steps and on to the empty pavement. A newspaper lorry rolled into vision and then swished by. I thought about the fact that James Shaw would never walk these streets again. I looked back up at the police station. Sergeant Turner had gone. I continued walking, making for my car. So that I wouldn't waste any time, I got my keys out.

But I didn't use them. Not then. Obstinacy wrestled with my longing for sleep. It was an uneven contest, and sleep lost out. I knew I had to finish what I had started. I shoved my keys back in my jacket pocket, made my way along the pavement, up the stairs and into the police station again.

There were two of them behind the counter – Sergeant Turner and Action Man – both seated at the desk. As I approached, they exchanged a glance and then both looked down.

'Excuse me,' I said.

While his junior concentrated on a particularly fascinating section of the brick-red linoleum, Sergeant Turner lumbered to his feet and over to the counter. 'Miss Baeier,' he said. He was smiling. 'Come to wander through our back passages again?'

I guessed it was a joke. I didn't find it funny, but then stumbling upon corpses does tend to make me ditch my sense of humour. 'Janet,' I said.

'Janet?'

'Janet Morris,' I said. 'Remember? I came in looking for . . .'

'Janet Morris,' he said. 'Of course. I'm afraid she's not here. Been moved on to another station.' Fixing his eyes on me, he followed through with a deadpan: 'That's a policeman's life for you.'

I cut to the chase. 'Which one?'

'I beg your pardon?'

'Which police station?'

This time his smile was skewed, apologetic. 'I'm afraid I can't tell you that.' He shrugged his sloping shoulders. 'Policy.'

I didn't say anything.

'If you want to leave a message,' he continued, 'I'll make sure she gets it.'

'Thanks.' I didn't know why I was thanking him. I wanted to be bloody minded. I paused.

He had his pen and notepad out, waiting patiently for my dictation.

Fatigue welled. 'No message,' I said. I turned away.

His voice pursued me. 'Sorry for what happened.'

I couldn't work out now whether he was apologizing for his interrogation technique or for the fact that I had found James Shaw. Either way, it didn't matter, a nod delivered casually over my shoulder seemed adequate response.

He wasn't finished. 'If there's anything else you need,' he said, 'feel free to contact me.' He wouldn't let it rest: 'The name's Brian Turner. Don't forget.'

The way he said it, it sounded like a threat. I didn't rise to it. I turned and walked away.

The motion was effective: my annoyance drained. Except that, when I reached the door, I heard them both softly chuckling. My fury almost erupted once again. Once again I stamped on it.

I was out and walking along the pavement. There was no reason, I told myself, to think that they were laughing at me. And as for the rest – I got out my key – it wasn't their fault that I'd stumbled upon James's corpse – I slipped the key in the lock – and not their fault, either, that they couldn't tell me where Janet Morris was. Probably.

So why then, I asked myself as I got in the car, did I feel so suspicious?

As the engine kicked into life, the answer came. If I put aside the corpse, what was bothering me was simple. It was that none of them, neither the first station officer, nor the second, nor their sergeant, had asked the obvious questions, like why I was looking for Janet Morris and whether they could help instead. Which made me think that perhaps Valerie was right. Perhaps something nasty had happened to Janet Morris.

I'd taken Valerie's forty-pounds-a-day job as a way of

passing time. Now, with the memory of James Shaw's dead body fresh in mind, it felt like more than that.

When I got home, I went straight to the bedroom and threw myself down on the bed. The next thing I knew, sunlight was hitting at an unaccustomed angle. I stretched my arm out for the clock. It wasn't there. Hardly surprising since I was sprawled across the bed, with my head where my feet should have been. Would have helped if I'd taken off my shoes, I suppose.

I felt grimy and uncomfortable and as if I had inherited Sergeant Turner's breath. I got up, stripped off, threw clothes and sheets into the washing machine and myself into the bath. Precisely what I needed. I lay, luxuriating, so relaxed I almost went back to sleep. When the phone rang, I ducked under the water, re-emerging only after the answerphone had clicked on.

I heard her voice. 'Kate.' Angry. Righteous. 'It's Anna.'

Oh shit. It struck me what I had done. Or to be more accurate, what I hadn't done. I was out the bath and running.

'Where the hell were you?'

I reached the living room as her message roller-coastered on: 'If you'd warned me, I would have made another arrangement.'

I picked up the receiver. 'Anna.' I was breathing hard. 'I'm so sorry.'

'You're there!' Her voice went up a notch. 'Do you know what I had to go through this morning rearranging everything? Not to mention how disappointed the little one was.'

My stomach did a double dive. The little one was Anna's five-year-old daughter, my namesake, Kate. She'd been

born while I was travelling and her uncomplicated acceptance of me on my return had done something to heal the
hurt that Anna, my oldest friend, had felt when I'd walked
out of her life. But now I knew I'd messed up on both of
them. I was supposed to have gone over to waken, feed and
take Kate to school so that Anna, a television editor, could
leave early for a dub.

'I'm sorry.' It sounded weak. 'Did you find somebody
else?'

'Sure I did. Two somebodies. One to wake her and one
to take her to school, which is what she hates, which is why
you offered to do it.'

I said it again: 'I'm sorry.'

'Christ, Kate, stop apologizing.' She dropped her voice
to a semi-whisper: 'My bloody mixer's bad enough – he's
got the personality of a slug and the manners to match,' and
strengthened it again: 'Just tell me what happened.'

'I overslept,' I said and then, quickly, before she could
butt in, I told her why.

The story brought temporary silence. When she finally
said, 'Hmm,' she no longer sounded indignant. 'Some
excuse. Kate would love it – especially the gory bits. Why
not come round this evening and tell it to her?'

'No.' I hesitated, but felt I had to tell her. 'I've got a
date.'

'A date?' She seemed amused. 'You mean, like, with a
boy?'

'Something like that.'

'Not a girl, surely?' Her voice rose. 'Not this late in life?'

'No,' I said. I swallowed. 'A policeman.'

She was always fast, was Anna. She didn't miss a beat.
'One from last night?'

I told her no, and then I had to tell her how I'd met

69

Gavin Dowd. I expected disapproval at the streetside pick-up. What I got instead was an impressed: 'Well, well. Progress.'

I laughed. 'Because I'm going out with a strange man? This must be what they mean by post feminism!'

'No.' Her voice, deadly serious, rebuffed my laughter. 'Progress because it means you might finally be ready to trust someone again.'

It was a familiar theme, Anna's favourite, its gist being that Sam's death had turned me into an emotional cripple. She moved on to its chorus. 'Face it,' she said. 'It's been a long time. And you're not getting any younger.' I was going to tell her just how wrong she was, but she got in first: 'Hallelujah. Return of the lugubrious slug. Gotta go,' and hung up.

Leaving me with what I had wanted to say to her reverberating in my head. She was wrong. Completely wrong. I'd had relationships since Sam's death – quite a few in fact. And if none of them had stuck, well, that wasn't my fault. I mean, it's not easy when you're constantly on the move. Not when your average thirty-plus man is undergoing a kind of menopause which means that, at the same time as he's attracted to strong women, he's also terrified of them. And besides – I was warming to my theme – Anna had no right to come on heavy with me. Since her divorce, her dual commitment to daughter and work made dating an impossibility. Who was she to act as judge?

I was working up quite a head of steam when the phone rang. I grabbed it. 'Yes?'

My bark was loud enough to faze even her. 'Kate? Is that you?'

'Yes, Valerie. It is me.' I sighed. 'How can I help you?'

'Janet Morris,' she said.

I was fed up with that name. I kept my mouth shut.

'Have you found her yet?'

That got me talking. 'For God's sake, Valerie, I've only just started.'

'It might not seem long for you,' Valerie intoned, 'but for a rape victim it can be . . .'

'All right.' I was too cold to stand listening to one of Valerie's empathetic speeches. 'I'm working on it. I've got a lead to follow. I'll let you know. Don't ring –'

'Kate, wait a –'

'– me, I'll ring you.' I hung up. It wasn't right, I know, but it's what I felt like doing. And Valerie was quite capable of looking after herself. I didn't think she'd put up with what I'd done, not for a moment. I waited by the phone anticipating her call back.

It never came. Oh well, I thought, Valerie's one of those people who thrives on rejection. I discarded the guilt, went back to the bathroom, and towelled myself vigorously, more as a way of stimulating my circulation than of getting dry. As I got dressed I thought that at least Valerie's call had distracted me from Anna's barefoot psychoanalysis. I pulled a leather jacket on over my jeans and T-shirt. I wouldn't think of what Anna had said, not any longer. I had other things to do.

Chapter
twelve

At the local newsagent, I rooted through cards until I found the perfect combination of cherubs and saccharine kittens, the kind of kitsch that little Kate adored. I wrote a message on the card, apologizing for not pitching up and promising I'd come by soon to tell her all the bloody details of my night's adventure. Then I dropped it into the post box, walked back to my car and drove off.

The Neville Brothers were into the last chorus of 'Fearless' as I reached my destination. All the way there Anna's insinuations had kept twisting in my guts, leaving me feeling anything but fearless. I turned the music up high to drown the inner voice and only when the track was over did I switch off and get out of the car.

I was in one of those in-between areas that are London's speciality. Ahead was the forbidding tunnel that leads into the Barbican, to the left an interconnecting sprawl of low-rise housing estates and to the right what I'd been looking for – the police section house. I stood for a moment, taking in its measure. It was a housing block reserved exclusively for the police, an undistinguished slab with a student look about it, its short, wide windows each packaged by orange curtains. It had been constructed at a time when mosaic was in vogue and black and white swirls covered the walls, competing vainly with the only other decoration, some mottled cladding. The rest was concrete, with only a few puny rose bushes sitting dutifully in square holes to show that somebody had once cared.

I fed coins into the meter. It ate them but carried on telling me that my time had expired. I looked up and down the road: no traffic wardens, nor any other parking spots. I left a note on my windscreen telling anybody who was interested that I was technically legal and then I crossed the road.

I reached the entrance and walked up the short flight of stairs. Above the glass door a tiny Metropolitan Police emblem was stuck high up. I pushed the door. It didn't budge. There was an entry phone stuck below a notice warning visitors to report to the warden. I pressed the buzzer.

When a distorted voice asked me what I wanted, I spoke into the mike. 'Janet Morris.'

The voice got more distinct. 'Not here.'

'Can leave a message for her?'

This time the voice was crystal clear. 'I told you,' it said. 'There's no Janet Morris here.' I heard a disconnecting click.

It had always been a long shot, me acting on a memory of Rodney Ellis gesturing at a group of policewomen, telling me they lived in the section house. There was no reason to think that Janet Morris was amongst them. And yet, long shot or not, it was an in. I didn't feel like giving up.

Reactivating the intercom seemed like a waste of time; so did standing there. I turned. And heard a sound behind me. I looked back. Nobody there – either at the door or to left or right. Only the twitching of a curtain so slight that I probably imagined it. I shrugged and kept on going.

There was a traffic warden by my car.

'Hey.' I ran across the road.

She was speedwriting the final line, then she ripped the paper from her clipboard and stuck it on my windscreen – over my note.

'Hey.' I was upon her.

'Parking is not permitted when a meter is out of order.' She walked away.

Having counted silently to ten and down again, I retraced my steps. But this time I kept on going, doing a quick reconnaissance around the section house. It was the kind of institution that makes me want to bolt. It was also impregnable – bars blocked every ground-floor window, security lights lit all strategic places, and high gates activated by remote control guarded the fenced-in parking area.

I kept on going, doing first one circuit and then another, telling myself that if nothing developed by the third, I would attack the buzzer again.

Third time lucky. As I came round the corner, I saw a policewoman making for the door. She was holding some keys. I got mine out and, jiggling them ostentatiously, went closer.

She reached the door, opened it and, going through, held it for me. But I wasn't out of the woods. She looked at me and frowned.

I spoke rapidly. 'You been doing overtime?'

Her face relaxed. 'I made the mistake of bagging a D and D just before shift end. When will I ever learn?'

Nodding sympathetically, I walked past her.

Her frown had reappeared. 'You new here?'

I nodded. 'I'm a friend of Janet Morris.'

Her face relaxed. 'Oh. Janet. Yeah. Haven't seen her around for a bit. But then she spends all her time in the gym, doesn't she?' And with that, she walked away through a swing door and up some stairs.

Leaving me alone. There was a desk and a chair in the entrance hall, the warden's I assumed. There was nobody by them but I couldn't count on that; I'd have to hurry. There were postal holes on one wall – numbered only. There was no index anywhere to tell me which room was Janet Morris's. Luck had got me in the place, but if I started knocking blind on people's doors I reckoned that the same luck would soon desert me. So I went down instead, heading for what, from the outside, had looked like the communal spaces.

The glassed-in stairs led to the basement and to three doors, all closed. You didn't have to be a genius to guess what lay behind them, each had been neatly labelled: 'GYM', 'BAR', and 'TV LOUNGE'.

I tried the TV lounge first, opening the door and sticking my head in. The TV was on – a cartoon character screeching wildly. It had the room entirely to itself, the overflowing ashtrays testifying to a crowd that had long since deserted. I stepped back and let the door swing closed.

A burst of laughter as the bar door opened. I wasn't ready with a story. As footsteps sounded, I kept on going, fast, acting like I belonged, going into the gym.

As soon as its door shut, I stopped. I heard a sound, an eerie swishing accompanied by a rhythmic thud. I looked round. What I saw was a sizeable room, dimly lit. All I could make out initially were the outlines of machines, dull grey and unoccupied. The asthmatic thumping continued. I went forward. The floor was dark green lino, scratched and worn, the windows blanketed by off-white net and huge steel bars, the light source a couple of strips, only one

75

of which was working. The place had a bleak, joyless feel about it and I wondered what had driven Janet Morris here.

And not only her. Someone else, too. The sounds were human, I was almost sure of that. My eyes flitted from one empty machine to the next until, there in the corner, I found out what was making the noise. It was human. Of the male variety. A huge muscled man lying on a workbench doing push-ups. The swishing was his breath, the thud the sound of metal weights hitting base. I stood there, he carried on. He'd seen me, I was sure of it, but he didn't make a sign. He continued, while I stood watching, his forearms bulging, thick, angry-looking veins swelling out as the effort consumed him. His concentration was so complete, I gave up thought of questioning him. With that degree of self-absorption, I didn't think he would have noticed Janet Morris anyway. I shrugged. Tipping my hand to my head in a mock salute I turned away and walked out.

One more room to go – the bar. Its door had glass portholes. Looking through, I saw a group of uniformed police gathered around one of the low tables littering the room. They were at the extreme end of the room and I couldn't see their faces, only the whiteness of their starched shirts, dazzling against the black trimmings. It was quite a party they were having – discarded beer cans lay littered at their feet. As I watched, one of the men stood up and, raising his can high, said something I couldn't hear. His audience cracked up, several of them doubling over.

It seemed like as good a time as any. Pushing the swing doors open, I walked in.

The comedian wasn't finished. 'And then, he pushes

himself up on to his elbows, looks at me, says: '"If you're room service, this must be the hotel from hell," and falls back unconscious.'

I didn't get it – you obviously had to be there at the beginning to appreciate the humour – but his audience roared with laughter. Tears ran down the face of one of the participants, while another was reduced to clutching her side and groaning helplessly. None of the group noticed me. I moved closer.

They saw me then; at least, two of them did, their laughter abruptly stanched. Their reaction had a domino effect. Within seconds, they had all turned their faces my way.

The joker in the pack dropped his arm. His face was blank, expectant. I flicked my eyes round the circle, checking out the others. There was only one I recognized – the woman officer who'd been crying in the cell last night. I addressed myself to her.

'I'm looking for Janet,' I said. 'Janet Morris.'

She looked back. Her brown hair was still pulled hard back into a plait to reveal an oval face, brown eyes set against high cheekbones, a long, aristocratic nose and a generous mouth which showed no sign of speaking.

I came a step closer. 'You know her,' I said. And got no further.

'Miss Baeier.'

It was so unexpected, coming from behind – I hadn't heard the door – that I jumped and turned.

'Nervous, aren't you?' he said. He, Action Man, last night's station officer, was out of uniform, dressed in blue jeans and a white T-shirt which stretched across his hefty chest. His thin, mean mouth opened. 'And you're persistent,' he said. He was close. Too close. I could smell his breath, soured by beer. He smiled. 'But all journalists are nosy. Part of the job, I suppose.'

His smile stretched wider. I stood there, trying to remain calm, telling myself that there were witnesses behind me and, anyway, that he was smiling.

'I was looking for Janet,' I said.

He nodded. 'She's moved out,' he said. 'Found better digs. Lucky her.' His eyes flicked over and beyond me.

I turned and followed the direction of his gaze. His eyes, I'm sure, were fixed on his policewoman colleague. She didn't move. She stared back.

Action Man spoke again. 'Janet's gone, hasn't she, Gracie?'

Gracie dipped her head.

'And we can't of course give you her address.'

I nodded. Of course they couldn't.

'Why don't I show you out then?' he said.

Chapter
thirteen

He was perfectly polite. When we reached the entrance hall he pointed at the desk and said, 'Next time it would be better if you signed in,' almost as if he didn't mind if there was a next time. Then he opened the door. 'Take care,' he said.

'Oh, I will.' I fixed him with a hard stare and then I left.

A stream of traffic held me up. I stood, waiting for it to pass by, thinking that if Valerie had been tracking me, she would have said that I wasn't worth the money. And perhaps she would be proved right. Perhaps Janet Morris had gone voluntarily underground and was determined to stay that way. By the reaction of those I'd tried to talk to, I was no longer so sure.

I got into the car and drove away. Halfway home when I looked in the mirror, I saw a sleek black car so close it was almost nudging my bumper. I kept on driving. It never made contact but it followed me all the way to Camden Town.

I parked outside my house: he double-parked beside me. I got out: his darkened window opened smoothly. He was going for repetition. When his hand thrust out, it was holding a white envelope.

I took the envelope. It was blank. I turned it over. It was

sealed. I tore it into four pieces, which I dropped neatly through the open window. Then I walked off.

I watched out of my living-room window as the chauffeur talked into his mobile phone. The conversation over, he threw the receiver to one side, pushed a button which sent the window up and drove off. Knowing what my father thought of failure, I thought I understood the squealing tyres.

I shredded my vague stirrings of sympathy along with cheese and ham for a chef's salad. But while I ate, I couldn't stop fragments of memory from invading. I remembered sitting at the table with my father after my mother had died, and I remembered how we had had nothing to say to each other. It had gone on like that for years, our contact reduced to his ordering me to behave more like a daughter of a wealthy general, or my denouncing him for the atrocities that were committed in his name in Angola. Our final confrontation – the one where he had stopped me having the satisfaction of walking out for ever by evicting me – was branded on my brain. I remembered each word, each movement, the vengeance in his face and the way he had sworn he would never see me again.

And now?

Now he was sending me letters. It didn't make sense.

Not that I wanted it to. I cleared up and went to my desk, finishing odd bits of work until dusk and my impending date came closer.

I scoured my wardrobe then, trying to decide what to wear. I thought of going casual – I didn't want to give the wrong impression. But in the end, what the hell, it was a date: I chose a black suit with a skirt which hugged my hips and a three-quarter-length jacket which showed its pedigree by enlarging my shoulders and reducing my waist. I went all the way after that, using a scarlet chemise to provide a flash of colour.

I walked into the entrance hall. Gavin Dowd was already there, standing by the bar. I was nervous. I walked slowly in his direction, delaying the moment when he would spot me. He turned before I reached him, unsurprised to see me there. It crossed my mind that nothing much could surprise this man.

He'd solved the smart/casual dilemma by going for both. He was wearing a gleaming white T-shirt, lightning-blue brushed silk zipper jacket, a pair of black Levi's, and, on his feet, black leather penny loafers. He looked fantastic.

He started walking towards me. Although his face was making a bid at relaxation, I saw my own wariness reflected back. 'Can I get you a drink?'

I shook my head.

He stopped. 'Shall we?' He gestured at the auditorium.

I nodded – I had seemingly dispensed with language – and began going that way.

I could feel him close. Too close. 'I'm glad you could make it,' he said.

Given my general state of speechlessness, I wasn't sure that I was glad.

'Here we are.' He touched me, gently, on the elbow.

We found our seats and waited until the lights dimmed and Don Cherry drifted on to the stage. With his wide pantaloons and a brief waistcoat he was like a demonic grasshopper, skipping from piano to one or other of his strange reed instruments, weaving his eerie magic. From quiet beginnings the music intensified. I felt myself relax.

As the numbing constraints of everyday life receded, I stopped worrying about Gavin Dowd.

Afterwards, when the rest of the audience had already filed out, Gavin looked at me. I thought he was going to suggest a drink. Instead: 'A walk?'

An alarm bell went off: walking was what Sam and I used to do.

'Unless you're tired?'

No, I wasn't tired. And I couldn't let what Sam and I used to do stand in my way. 'I'm fine,' I said. 'I like to walk.' As we went together towards the door, I filled my embarrassment with words. 'You're not at Rodney Ellis's station, are you?'

'No.' A pause. 'I'm not based anywhere in particular. I deal with manpower allocation in the whole metropolitan area.' He opened the door.

I went through and out into a night which had turned surprisingly warm. When Gavin joined me we wandered to the edge of the embankment. The sky was cloudless, dark but tinged with midnight blue, giving the glistening cityscape on the opposite bank a special clarity.

Gavin turned to me. 'Baeier,' he said. He pronounced it perfectly. 'Unusual name.'

'Comes from a long line of Portuguese Jews with enough pretension to sneak in an extra "e",' I explained.

He smiled. 'I saw a Baeier on the news recently. A relation?'

'My father.' I hoped he'd only been half watching.

No such luck. His gaze was interested. 'Wouldn't have thought you were the type to have a general in the family.'

I didn't know where to look. So much for steering away from the personal. He was on track now, and with a vengeance.

'Your father fought in Angola?' It was only half a question.

He murdered in Angola, I thought. I kept my mouth shut.

'Must have worried your mother.'

I shrugged, wishing he'd leave it alone, wishing I hadn't agreed to go out with a policeman not only clued up enough to realize that mothers worried but also eager to talk about it.

And persistent as well. 'Your father's involved in some kind of talks with the government, isn't he?'

I nodded to show that I also watched that news.

'And your mother? Is she in London?'

'She's dead.'

That usually generated some variation on embarrassed silence or polite condolence. Not in this case, however. Gavin looked expectant: he was waiting for more.

I gave it to him. 'She dived into a bottle,' I said, 'and forgot to come up for air.'

'Whisky?'

Whisky? 'As a matter of fact, only the finest of Oporto's port wines ever passed my mother's lips. She pickled her liver in sugar.'

A pause. I was sure he was going to back off. But no, he upped the stakes. 'My father was a cheap drunk.'

Oh Christ, I thought, surely this isn't what attracted us to each other? Alcoholic backgrounds? It was too corny.

'He had no problem downing anything as long as it was alcoholic.'

Although Gavin had spoken lightly, there was no mistaking the pain that underlined his words. I felt an impulse to reach out, to touch him, to tell him that I knew how he felt. But I didn't. I couldn't. It felt too intimate a gesture to make to a stranger, especially to this stranger. I blinked and looked across the greyness of the Thames, thinking that Anna was right, that I was scared.

I felt Gavin Dowd stirring beside me, so I did what I am good at. I turned, looked him straight in the eyes, and changed the subject. 'Could you do me a favour?' I asked.

He looked back.

Which didn't scare me. 'A man – name of James Shaw – died in the Parchment Road police station last night,' I said. 'Could you find out the cause of death?'

His face was so impassive, I thought he was hiding something. But why should he be? 'Why do you want to know?' he asked.

The lie came easily. 'Because I used to see him walking the streets,' I said. 'I'm curious. And sad to hear he's gone. Seems wrong not to find out why.'

Gavin kept on looking.

'If it's a problem,' I said, 'I'm sure some of my journalist friends could find out for me . . .'

He shook his head. 'No problem.'

'Thank you.'

His return smile was brief and businesslike. He knew as well as I did that the feeling between us had been lost. He looked first at his watch and then at me. 'Can I give you a lift anywhere?'

I shook my head. 'I've got my car.'

We smiled uncomfortably.

'I'll walk you there.'

'No,' I said. 'I'm fine. Thanks.'

I could have gone with him on to Waterloo Bridge and taken the long way to my car. I decided not to. I held out my hand. I was fine. In fact, I was great. I'd done what my friends kept urging me to do, I'd had a date, and I'd enjoyed it, and I was pleased that it had come to nothing. I shook his hand, both of us businesslike again, shaking on a deal that hadn't quite worked out. 'Thanks for a nice evening,' I said and, turning, walked away.

Chapter
fourteen

It was very quiet on the walkway. I quickened my pace. I knew there was a flight of stairs somewhere, which would take me down to street level. All I had to do was find it.

The ramp forked. Was this the turn or was I walking myself into one of those dead ends which are a speciality of the South Bank? In the distance, I could see what looked like a concrete tube. That must be the stairwell. I turned.

I reached the stairs and started going down. My feet tiptapped past wall lights set in the bare concrete walls. They were all dead, the architect's brutalist style perfectly realized. At least I wasn't alone. I could hear other feet slapping against the steps above me.

I looked up, but the bends were too steep: I couldn't see anything. I waited a moment to find out if the sound came again. It didn't. I started walking.

It was dark at the bottom of the stairs. I was sure the road was to the left. I went left, rounding the smoothed stained concrete corner. And found that I wasn't alone. Something had moved.

I glanced to the left trying to work out what it was. As I did so a dazzlingly bright light snapped on. I was blinded.

I had no time. Literally. No time.

Something fanned the air beside me. Something long and hard and straight. Because the light had wavered I saw its outline. It was a wooden club, heaved from shoulder height, aimed at my head. I jinked to one side. Although the light tracked with me, the club missed.

My back was pressed against the wall. I had nowhere to go but forward. I would have to go forward, aiming myself at the figure behind the light. The club was raised high into the darkness. I took a deep breath.

'Kate.' A voice echoed down the stairwell. Before I could call back, it came again. 'Kate.'

I glanced back and up in time to see Gavin running down. His feet drummed against the stairs.

I turned to my assailant as his club strobed down.

I dived. My chin grazed the concrete. I shielded my head with my arms, waiting for the blow. It never came. Nothing did. I looked up to find that my attacker had switched off the beam. I could just make out the outline of a tall thick-set man stepping back into the darkness.

'Hey.' I raised myself up.

He started running, easily, like a man accustomed to working out. I knew that I would never catch him.

Gavin was almost at ground level. All I could think was that I didn't want him to find me prone. I got up. By the time he reached me, I was wiping dust off my jacket.

I liked the fact that he didn't smother me with sympathy. Instead he threw a compliment – 'You stood your ground' – over the space he'd maintained between us.

My hands moved down to my skirt, straightening its creases. 'Years of facing bullets, I suppose,' I said. There, I was in one piece. I looked across at him. He wasn't even breathing hard.

Nor was I hurt. To prove it, I took a step forward.

My legs caved in on me so completely that the only reason I didn't fall was that Gavin had gripped my arm, steadying me. I didn't try and shrug him off. 'Just relocating my balance,' I told him.

He waited while I breathed in and out, in and out, closing a trap door on the piece of my mind which wondered whether the man only left me in one piece because Gavin had appeared. I knew who my attacker must be – my father's muscleman come to punish me for the snub against his boss.

Gavin's calm voice smoothed out my growing rage. 'Ready?'

I leaned on my right leg. It resisted the pull of gravity. I tried the left one out. No problem. I was ready. I began to walk.

Gavin came with me, his arm linked to mine, as we went slowly towards my car. I felt his hand, light but steady, holding on to me. It was a long time since I'd had a man this close. When we reached the car, he let go. I got out my key and slipped it in the lock. He waited until I had opened the door and then: 'I'll come with you,' he said.

I shook my head. 'Thanks for the offer.'

'It's no trouble.'

'I'll be fine,' I said.

Gavin hesitated, but didn't press it. Instead: 'Did you know that man?'

'No.' It was the truth. Three quick street-side meetings hardly qualified as knowing someone.

'Do you know why he came at you?'

I said it again, 'No.' Which was near enough the truth. After all, I didn't really know what my father wanted, did I?

The way Gavin looked, so sure and straight, told me that

he didn't believe me. I met his eyes head on; they were more green than grey, and they had a steely edge about them. He trapped my gaze and gripped it tight until I thought I was going to choke. Only after he looked away suddenly, releasing me, did I breathe out.

I didn't like the way he'd made me feel. I went on the offensive. 'You followed me.'

He shot me a half-apologetic smile. 'It's dark. I wanted to check that you got back to your car.'

My look was as sceptical as his had been.

He shrugged, caught but not embarrassed. 'The truth is I wanted to ask you something,' he said. 'I'd like to see you again,' adding quickly: 'if you're interested.'

That was the last thing I had expected. It threw me. I didn't know what I thought. I gave my emotions a quick sound check.

What I discovered came as a surprise. Upstairs, I couldn't get away quickly enough; now I didn't want him to go. Nothing like your father setting his goon on you, I suppose, to make the seductions of normal men attractive.

'What do you think?'

'I'd like that,' I said.

'Tomorrow?'

I laughed. 'You're not into hard to get, are you?'

His answering smile was open. 'Or the next day.' I didn't know how I could have seen those sparkling eyes as cold.

'Tomorrow's fine,' I said.

He leaned over and kissed me, quickly, on the mouth. 'See you at seven?'

I nodded.

He turned and began walking away, heading back to the bridge.

And me? I stood there watching. My lips were burning. I licked them once or twice. That didn't help.

After a while I felt stupid standing there. I got into my car, closed the door, started up the engine and drove off.

Chapter
fifteen

I slept long and soundly and woke up knowing what I had to do. I showered, dressed, drank two cups of strong coffee and dialled a number.

A telephonist's nasal voice told me I had reached my father's hotel. I told her I wanted to speak to the General; she asked me who I was. The name I invented had enough of an aristocratic ring about it to get me through to a second filtering system, but that's when my luck ran out. The General, I was told, was resting. If I wanted I could leave a message.

After last night's little adventure, I didn't want to risk being prosecuted for corruption of the airwaves, so I said no, no message. I hung up and then made my way out of the flat and back to my car, thinking that it was lucky he'd been unavailable. He was a master manipulator of words, especially on the phone. I needed to see him in the flesh. Only that way could I drive my message home.

His hotel in west London turned out to be a set of apartments serviced by a kitchen, a switchboard and a gang of security staff. Its foyer, fronted by glass and decorated by a Conran lookalike, said clearly that only the very wealthy could afford to stay there.

The place was guarded like a fort. Behind the reception desk sat a man who was about as broad as he was tall. He controlled the electronic gate that barred access to the lifts. If things got too much for him he had back-up in the form of two grey-suited heavies who lolled on plush sofas dividing their attention between their fingernails and the backsides of the smartly dressed women who swayed in and out of the building.

At the desk, I told the gorilla I wanted to see the General. When he asked me, I gave him my real name. It worked: he spoke briefly on the phone and then pressed a button. The electronic gate opened. I was admitted. I took the lift up to the fifth floor.

I got out to find Zetu waiting. He came towards me, his hands outstretched as if to clasp mine. I circumvented them. 'I want to get this over fast,' I said. I walked through the open door of room 504.

I was in an ante room occupied by men. Three of them sat at an oval conference table playing cards. Another, with his feet up on a glass table and his head against a long sofa, was snoring loudly. I wondered which one of them had put the scare on me the night before.

A fifth man was by the mini bar, rifling through bottles. As I entered, he looked up. It was my father's squat chauffeur. He nodded at me, and then at another door.

That must be where my father was. I went up to it and, for form's sake, knocked.

No one answered. I went in, closing the door behind me. The room was so dark, it took a moment for my eyes to acclimatize. When they did, I saw that the place was perfectly tailored to my father's pretensions. There was a king-size bed – empty – whose cover was a rich plum colour; a maroon three-piece suite, likewise empty; some long purple velvet drapes which were almost completely drawn and a huge mahogany desk. Behind the desk was an executive chair. All I could see of it was its high back.

Not for long, though. The chair swivelled round, revealing a once-familiar face. It was too dark to see how he'd changed. He switched on a table lamp. It was harsh and bright and it shone straight into my eyes. I looked away.

His voice was measured. 'Thank you for coming,' he said in Portuguese.

I spoke deliberately in English. 'Don't thank me. Just tell me what you want.'

For a man who couldn't hold a tune he had perfect pitch when it came to faking an emotion. When he said, 'I wanted to see you,' he sounded genuinely hurt.

Not that it fooled me. I held my tongue.

He switched to English and served up low sincerity. 'You are my daughter.'

There was a chair opposite his. I pulled it out and sat down on it. 'That's not how you put it the last time we met,' I said.

The light was blaring in my eyes, concealing his expression. 'Can you not let the past go?'

It was his kind of question. I didn't bother answering. I leaned forward, aiming for the light switch.

Either he misinterpreted my move or he'd been waiting for it, either way, his hand landed on mine. I felt his skin, soft and softly tremulous, an old man clutching for his daughter. The hypocrisy made me want to vomit. I snatched my hand back.

'Kate.'

'Let's not play games,' I said.

He moved the light so it was no longer blinding me. I looked across, seeing a face that was different from the one

93

I had so recently dreamed. Age had leached the hard almond colours from his eyes and had made his lips go slack. His cheeks, once dominated by strong aristocratic bones, now looked almost flabby.

He spoke. 'You're looking well.'

'Call off your dogs,' I said.

Age had taken none of the cunning from his smile. 'My dogs?' he raised one bushy eyebrow.

'You know what one of them did to me on the South Bank.'

'I do not know.'

'Tell him to stop. Tell him to leave me alone.'

He turned his hands over, a gesture of innocence. 'I sent a man to find you and to deliver a message. If he over-stretched the mark, I must apologize.'

Apologize! I was astounded by his audacity. I opened my mouth to laugh. Nothing came out.

He seized the initiative. 'I have thought of you often, my daughter,' he said. 'I have missed you.' He spoke the words clumsily, as if he were force-feeding them. When he reached their end, he coughed.

The cough started lightly but soon took hold, racking his body. I sat and watched him choking on his own dishonesty. He gave it all he had. When the spasm finally abated, he took a handkerchief from his pocket, spat into it and then, having folded it, threw it in the dustbin. He always had been wasteful with linen.

He'd found his voice again. 'I heard about your fiancé,' he said. 'You lost someone you loved. Just as I had.'

That was so bizarre, coming from him, it almost set *me* choking. I decided it was time to cut the crap. I made no effort to harden my voice. I didn't have to. It just came out like that. 'What do you want?'

94

'To see you. I –'

'No.' My voice was so loud it almost frightened me. 'Don't start that again. Just tell me what you want.'

His eyes were moist. 'I've told –'

I got up. 'Last chance.'

He looked at me and then away. The silence stretched so long that for one, crazy moment, I thought I might be wrong. But no. 'There is one thing,' he said.

I knew there would be. I sat.

'I want to sell the *palacio*.'

I was glad that I was sitting. 'No.'

'But, Kate, why not?'

I didn't owe him any explanation.

'You never go there,' he said.

Of course I didn't. I couldn't. It wasn't mine. It was his, like everything else. My mother had left all of her considerable fortune to him and then punished us both by making sure that I had joint control. He could use the income from her investments but, without my signature, he could never sell.

'You have never refused me before.'

With good reason. My mother's act of twisted revenge had been intended to tie my father to me, but I had found a way of cutting free. I had told him he could do anything he liked on condition that I did not have to see him. He had agreed and for many years our only contact had been our joint scrawls on the documents his lawyers had concocted.

'Why stand in my way now?'

Because this one of her investments was different. It was a huge, elegant, rambling and decayed pink-washed house in the Bario Alto district of central Lisbon, a home she had loved more than she had loved any human being. I couldn't let him sell; I wouldn't. And of course he'd known that this

95

was how I'd feel. That's why he'd broken our agreement and come looking for me.

'No,' I said again. 'Not now. Not ever.' I got up. 'And don't bother coming after me with your scare tactics. I won't change my mind.' I turned.

His voice pursued me – 'Kate?' – delivered with a perfect little flutter. But although I couldn't help admiring the technique, I didn't feel like staying for an encore. Speeding up, I got myself out of there.

Chapter
sixteen

As I pressed the button, summoning the lift, I could feel Zetu's breath licking at my neck. 'I'm glad you came,' he said.

I wasn't glad. I stepped closer to the lift.

'He told you?'

'Yes.' I wished the lift would hurry. 'He told me he wanted to sell the *palacio*.' Where the hell was it? I banged down on the button.

Zetu's skin made mountains of confusion on his forehead. 'He didn't say anything else?'

'Like what?'

Zetu shrugged.

I wasn't in the mood for mysteries. 'I won't let him sell,' I said.

He came one step nearer. 'Listen to me, Kate . . .'

He was far too close. I looked over his shoulder. At the corridor's end was an emergency-exit sign. There had to be stairs beyond.

'Your father does not always have the best approach.' Zetu's voice seemed distant.

'You're telling me.' I pointed at the sign, indicating that he was in my way. 'Now, if you don't mind?'

He reached into his shirt pocket and pulled out a long, thin key which he used to activate the lift.

It had been there, waiting, all the time. I heard a soft whir as it came to life. Then its metal doors opened. I stepped in.

'Kate.'

I turned to face him.

'Your father is seeing a doctor.'

So what? My father's list of psychosomatic illnesses was almost as long as his association with murderers and arms dealers. I hit the button that said it would take me to the ground floor.

'He's not well.'

It was awfully slow, the lift. I jabbed the button.

Through the closing gap, I could see Zetu's moist eyes pleading with me. I don't know what he expected – that I would put my foot out and stop the doors?

'He is old and very ill,' Zetu said. 'And all he wants to do is talk to . . .'

Two edges of metal met, shutting out his final word. No matter. I knew what it would have been. 'You', as in: 'All he wants to do is talk to you.' It was the kind of thing Zetu had always told me. That my father had done this or that, not to spite, but to please me. There had been a time when I'd longed to believe Zetu's fabrications. But I was grown up now and that time had gone.

If my father really wanted to talk to me, he should have gone about it a different way. The intimidation of the previous night was hardly intended to endear him to me.

The lift doors opened. I was at the ground floor. I stepped out. A buzz – the guard releasing the electronic catch. I pushed through the barrier and kept on going, walking straight out of there.

I drove to Hampstead Heath and walked for a long time.

Longer than I realized. When eventually I looked at my watch I found that the day had all but slipped away. I had barely time to go home, bath and change before Gavin Dowd picked me up. I drove through rush-hour traffic, concentrating on my route. I parked outside the house.

Spring had gone back into hiding: office workers trudged down the pavement, hunched against the chill wind that made litter whirlpools round their feet. An old man passed by, leaning heavily on a stick. All the time I'd been walking I'd put my thoughts on hold. Now I thought: What if it's true? The old man turned the corner. What if my father really were ill? What if he were dying?

I was halfway into the shower when the bell rang. I grabbed my watch – Gavin Dowd was ten minutes early – and a towel. Wrapping it round me, I went to buzz him in.

He came up fast, bearing a bunch of purple tulips. Seeing the state of me, he stopped abruptly. 'I'm sorry, I'm too early.'

'No problem,' I said. 'I'll soon be ready.'

He was wearing jeans and a green shirt that brought out the colour of his olive skin. He grinned. 'Can I come in?'

Silly me. I skipped out of his way.

He didn't need directions. He went, quickly, to the living room. I followed and found him standing in its centre. He looked completely at ease. I felt disoriented.

'Why not . . .?' He gestured at my towel.

Why not indeed. I was acting like a teenager. I should get changed. 'I won't be a minute,' I said. 'Drinks in the top right-hand kitchen cabinet if you want to fix yourself one.'

I showered and dressed. I took my time. I dried my hair

and looked at myself in the mirror. My gaze was steady – I could go. I walked into the living room.

He had found a vase, the one that had been Sam's last present to me, and had arranged the tulips in it. He'd seen to himself as well. He was sitting on the sofa, sipping iced Glenfiddich. There was a spare glass and some ice in a bowl in front of him. The TV was on, he was watching the news.

He got up as I entered. We stood, facing each other awkwardly.

He broke the silence. 'About the death,' he said.

I frowned, confused.

'James Shaw's.'

I didn't know how I could have forgotten.

His voice overrode my shame. 'Preliminary results suggest Mr Shaw died from a cerebral haemorrhage.'

I nodded.

He guessed what I was thinking. 'Don't worry,' he said. 'It will be investigated properly.' His voice was formal.

I didn't reply. I couldn't. I was too distracted by the television. The newscaster was talking about the Angolan peace talks but it was the pictures that had caught me. I watched, my eyes riveted by the sight of my father limping, amongst other dignitaries, up a set of official stairs. When he got to the top, I shut my eyes.

Gavin used the remote to cut the volume. 'I hope you don't mind me switching it on.'

'No,' I said. 'It's fine.' I poured myself a drink and sat down with it. I watched my father laughing at something Savimbi was saying.

The item had come to an end, replaced by pictures of starving children in another part of Africa. Gavin switched off and looked at me. 'Your father's quite a power-broker.'

That he was. I nodded. And raised my glass.

'They say he's vital to the settlement.'

A major malt rush nearly had me choking. I swallowed hard. 'You know what they also say: Blessed are the base in motive for they shall inherit the peace talks.'

His eyes were fixed on my face. 'You and he don't get on?'

This wasn't a subject I normally discussed with strangers. I opened my mouth, intending to deal out one of a number of stock phrases that would put an end to the conversation. But instead, 'We hate each other's guts,' came out.

I don't know why I broke my rule. Because he'd told me that he had an alcoholic in the family, perhaps, or because his tulips were drooping lazily over the edges of Sam's vase. Either way, I wished I hadn't. His gaze was too intense. I felt exposed.

He wouldn't let it go. 'Is there something the matter?' he asked, and, when I didn't answer, added: 'Did something happen?'

I thought about saying yes, as a matter fact, something did happen: my father, whom I'd cut out of my life, had come bursting back in. I didn't want to see him – ever – and yet I didn't know if I was ready for his death.

It sounded ridiculous. I couldn't tell Gavin that. I shook my head.

He misunderstood. 'I have to admit,' he said, 'that I also thought about cancelling tonight.'

Great, this was all I needed. I looked away.

'I was scared, I suppose. I know we've only just met,' he said, 'but I feel . . . I feel . . .'

Too much had happened. I wasn't sure I could take a stranger's declarations.

'Jesus,' he said. 'This is embarrassing enough without you pretending I'm not here.'

I had to look. I turned.

He wasn't so embarrassed that he couldn't raise a smile. 'You know, I almost forgot,' he said, his voice now flippant. 'I brought you something.' He held out a package, small, wrapped in tissue paper and tied with a light blue bow, which he nudged at me. 'Careful,' he said. 'It's fragile.'

I took it, turned it over. It was the strangest shape, lumpy in parts, smooth in others.

'Open it.'

I undid the bow and put it to one side. Then, gently, I removed the tissue paper. Inside was a chocolate policeman. A village bobby complete with hat and shiny blue foil clothes. I turned it over. On its bottom were the words, tiny on a square of white paper, 'Made in Britain'. I turned it back again. I looked at Gavin.

He was watching me. I smiled. He kept on watching. My smile stretched and dissolved into a giggle. 'Thanks.' I didn't want to crush it. I put the chocolate down. I started laughing: mirth and misery and a touch of mania, all coming together.

I wasn't laughing. I was crying.

I registered movement: Gavin getting up. I shifted to the left; he sat down next to me. His arm went round my shoulders and I buried my sorrow in the embrace.

Chapter
seventeen

I turned and saw him lying there, as still and as pale as death. Asleep he looked his true age: a man in his late thirties.

I didn't want to wake him. I sat up and swung my legs over the bed. I was reaching for my dressing gown when I heard him stirring. I looked back. His eyes were open; he was watching me. I should have known that there was no catching this man off guard.

'Good morning.' He pulled me to him.

What the hell, I thought. I didn't even know why I was getting up so early.

We were up and eating breakfast when the phone rang. Sometime between the first kiss and our moving to bed I'd switched the answerphone on to automatic and now the machine did its business. I lifted the coffee pot and looked questioningly at Gavin. He nodded and held up his cup.

I was pouring coffee when I heard a woman's voice: 'If you're still looking for Janet . . .'

My stirring the pot had worked – and faster than I expected. I grabbed the phone. 'Hello,' I said and again: 'Hello?' Silence. I cursed the answerphone. 'Hello!'

She spoke. 'If you're looking for Janet Morris, she said

she'd be at Francio's in Upper Street tomorrow at one.'

That was all. She hung up.

I made a note of what she'd said and then turned back to find Gavin watching me. His eyes were wary. I saw the policeman in him then. I came down off my high and started wondering whether sleeping with him was one of those crazy things I'd soon regret. He smiled then, so tenderly, that my doubts evaporated. I touched his cheek. He took hold of my hand and kissed it gently. I felt the warmth of his skin against mine, and I thought that I hadn't felt this comfortable with anyone since . . .

No, I wouldn't think it, not after just one night. I pulled my hand away.

He didn't seem to notice. His mind was elsewhere. 'You looking for someone?' he asked.

'Kind of,' I said, which was kind of true.

His face was serious. 'Someone who wants to be found?'

I wasn't sure of anything except that it was none of his business. I shrugged. I could tell by the stillness of his face that he was thinking of saying something more. I waited, unblinking.

He stretched then, languorously, as if the tension in the atmosphere was a product of my imagination. I thought he was about to rise. 'Time for work?' I asked.

'No.' He smiled. 'I've got the morning off. But if you need to get to work . . .?' He got up to show me how easy it would be to get rid of him.

I spoke. Without thought. 'Want to spend the morning with me?'

We went to Dulwich. We went in his car, him driving, me worrying about what everybody would say when we arrived.

They didn't say anything. Not at first, they didn't. Matthew, Sam's adolescent son, was too caught up organizing his school team to do more than wave a hasty hello. His grandfather, John Layton, Sam's father, also kept his distance. Nothing to do with Gavin: John and I had long ago agreed to restrict contact to the courteous minimum.

The only other person I knew at the event – Anna – didn't say anything either. Not to me, that is. To Gavin, she had, apparently, plenty to say. While her daughter, Kate, climbed up my shoulders and made me carry her from one part of the playing fields to the other, I could see them engrossed in conversation.

The game began. As we stood on the sidelines, watching, I stopped worrying about why I had brought Gavin. I was too entranced by the sight of Matthew, who, as captain of his hockey team, was dominating the game. He was fifteen, an awkward stage – half child, half adult – gauche and yet at the same time knowing. Or that's what I had thought. But now I watched him manipulating the ball with the kind of grace that made you forget the hints of acne on his face, with the kind of confidence that made his awkward attempts at conversation irrelevant.

I couldn't help my eyes misting over as I stood, wondering what Sam – whose reaction to public school had been to despise all team games – would have thought of his son. I flicked my eyes to the right and saw Gavin, watching intently, nodding in admiration.

As soon as the game was over, Anna had to go. She linked her arm to mine and told me to walk her to her car. With my other hand holding on to Kate, I went with her, waiting nervously for the stream of comment that I knew must be coming. But Anna was uncharacteristically silent. Only when she already had the car doors open and was leaning over, buckling in her daughter, did she say anything. A small thing: 'He seems nice.'

I don't know why I felt so relieved.

Anna straightened up. 'Who's nice?' came Kate's piping voice. Anna shrugged, kissed me on both cheeks and went to the front of the car. I closed Kate's door and then I stood and watched Anna driving off, hearing my namesake asking it again. 'Who's nice?'

He was standing by Matthew when I returned. They were talking hockey. I stood between them, listening to the exchange. When they had finally finished and Matthew asked us both to lunch, I knew that Gavin had passed some kind of test. I wondered whether he knew, but if he did, he gave no sign of it. Instead, when the time came, he drove me home, saying reluctantly that he had to go to work. Then he said something else as well: 'Doing anything tomorrow night?'

I felt positively light hearted. 'No, nothing I can't change.'

'Good. I'll come round. Same time?'

I told him yes and after we kissed I stood and watched him walking away. I kept on watching as he got into his Saab, saluted briefly, and drove off.

There was a man on my doorstep, a tall, thin man dressed in a grey suit one size too big for him. He was waiting for me.

'Miss Baeier?' He flashed me a dazzling white smile, reached into his breast pocket, pulled out a card and flipped it open. 'My name's David Newlands,' he said. 'Superintendent David Newlands.'

I saw his smiling picture stuck beneath some official writing and a Metropolitan Police badge.

'I'm from CIB2, the police Complaints Investigation Bureau,' he said. 'I'm in charge of the investigation of the death of Mr James Shaw. I need to go over your statement with you. Do you mind?'

I said no, I didn't mind and I led him upstairs. I took him to the kitchen where I made a pot of coffee. While I fussed around with filters and milk jugs, he took a file out of his briefcase and began reading through it. I handed him a cup: he smiled his thanks. He was completely at ease. Gavin also settled down this quickly, I thought, it must be part of the training. Then I pushed the thought away: I wasn't going to think of Gavin, not with this stranger in my kitchen.

'In your statement, you say you saw three officers in the cell area,' he said. 'Any idea who they were?'

'Not the men,' I said. 'Although I could describe them.'

'No.' He shook his head. 'That won't be necessary.'

'The WPC's first name is Gracie. I don't know her surname.'

He wrote that down. Then he took me through the rest of my statement, piece by piece, marking up the text as we progressed along it. I watched his hand moving lazily across the page and couldn't help feeling that the motion was purely diversionary. He had a kind of wired, thyroid feel to him and yet he sat, sipping coffee, as if he had all the time in the world to coax out answers that were already there in black and white.

He kept it up for quite a while. I hadn't had much sleep the night before and, despite my scepticism, I found my head drooping.

He hit me with it then. 'Miss Baeier,' he said. 'I have something to ask you.'

I was instantly alert. 'What kind of something?'

He closed his file. 'You're a journalist.'

I knew that already.

'We have a problem.' His tongue darted out, moistening his lips. 'There were three civilians in the cells on the night Mr Shaw died. We've managed to interview two of them but we can't get close enough to the third, a young man, name of Melville Adams, to ask him anything. We would like you to contact him.'

'Me?' I didn't care that I'd hit the upper register. 'Why me?'

'Melville has been in and out of trouble since he was ten. He sees us coming, he runs away. We need someone to pass a message on. To tell him we're not interested in him, we just want to hear what he has to say about that night. You're not connected to us. He might listen to you.'

Remembering Melville Adams's pose that night, I thought he was probably beyond listening to anyone. I said as much.

David Newlands nodded. 'But even so . . .' He let the sentence hang.

I sat there, meeting his gaze, pretending to be calm while an internal battle raged. Instinct – the thing I had learnt during my years away to trust above all other feelings – told me to say no. After all, letting Valerie bamboozle me into finding Janet Morris was what had got me into this mess. And if my morning's phone call could be trusted, Janet Morris was found. It was an absurd idea to branch out now and start working for CIB2.

And yet . . . and yet there was something not quite right about what I was being asked to do. And that intrigued me more than anything else. Curiosity, the thing that usually got me into trouble, was egging me on. If you say no, it whispered in my ear, you'll never get to the bottom of this.

In the end, I couldn't hold it back. I made myself a bargain which I tested with a question: 'How did James Shaw die?'

'I can't tell you. Not at this point.'

Which put an end to my dilemma. I smiled. 'Then the answer is no.'

He didn't miss a beat. 'Cerebral haemorrhage.'

Which confirmed what Gavin had told me. I went one further with Newlands. 'He was beaten?'

'It's a possibility. He may also have fallen down, either in the police station or before – there are reports that he was unwell when he came in. Or it could just have been years of drinking. According to most people who knew him, Mr Shaw was uncharacteristically aggressive during his last few weeks.'

Which my own memory confirmed. But still: 'Is there any evidence that he was killed in the police station?'

His answer was prompt. 'No.' And very definite. 'None at all.'

It really didn't make any sense. 'Why go to all this bother for a down and out?'

'It's no bother, Miss Baeier.' His voice was stiff. 'It's my job. Or do you think that, because Mr Shaw was homeless, we should investigate his death less thoroughly?'

No, of course I didn't think that.

He went in for the kill. 'So will you do it?'

I hesitated. I knew I should say no. But then I remembered James Shaw's waxen face. I couldn't say no. I nodded.

His eyes flickered and I wondered what I had done wrong.

Nothing apparently. 'Good,' he said. He laid a sheet of paper in front of me. 'That's Melville's address.' He put a card on top of the paper on which his name and number were embossed. 'Tell him he can ring me any time – reverse the charges – and I'll meet him at a place of his choice.' Another, identical, card went down on the first. 'This is for you. If you need me, give me a ring.' He smiled and got up. 'Thanks for your time,' he said. 'I'll show myself out.'

Chapter
eighteen

I put instinct on hold, grabbed an *A–Z* and headed out into Hackney's badlands.

Melville Adams's house, near Victoria Park, was one in a row of double-fronted semi-detached numbers that harked back to a time when traders had enough surplus to imitate bourgeois life. They'd set up home near Victoria Park, building small monuments to their success. All that private money had long since gone west, leaving behind houses spacious enough to attract a flood of small speculators. They'd zoomed in, divided the insides, shoved in heavy doors that were supposed to block out fire, bought job lots of cheap furniture and hideous carpets and, hey presto, they had that modern money-spinner – the bed and breakfast.

I walked along the line-up. They had names like 'Fresh Fields' and 'Meadowlands' that conjured up an altogether different, pastoral life. They all used a double-door system – one wooden, closed at night to keep out undesirables, and one glass, closed during the day to keep in the heat – which made it easy to look in. They were clones of each other: their halls had the same sort of cracked vinyl on the floor, the same kind of flock on the walls and the same desk where middle-aged men from the Middle East sat.

Number three, which Melville inhabited, was quirky; it was called 'Lands End' – perhaps because it was the last but one in the row. I pushed its glass door open: a bell tinkled. When I closed the door, it tinkled again. Neither ring roused the bouncer who was slumped over his table at the end of the hall.

I walked towards him. On my way I passed what must have been the lounge. Someone had taken an axe to its plywood door, reducing it to splinters. I looked in and saw a set of blue Dralon sofas, one stained by old vomit, one with methodical burn holes across its back. No Melville Adams. I kept on going until I reached the desk.

I tried speech. 'Hello.' Only the heaving of the man's shoulders told me he was still alive. I raised my voice: 'Excuse me.' To no avail. He kept on sleeping.

The place was big on bells; there was a small brass one on the table. I picked it up and rang it in his ear. That roused him, but only slowly. His bullish head came up, exposing first one bloodshot eye and then the other. When he yawned the fumes that seeped out of his mouth were alcoholic enough to give me a contact high. He mumbled something that I took as a request for information.

I supplied him with some. 'I'm looking for Melville Adams.'

Which produced a surly: 'What's he to you?'

'He's my first cousin once removed,' I said.

The man blinked, his eyelids falling like scales. When he finally winched them open again, he was scowling. He lurched into speech. 'Yeah. Funny. But if you wanna visit one of the residents, you gotta know which room he has. You don't know that, we don't know if you're wanted. We don't know if you're wanted, we don't let you in.' The strain of stringing so many words together was beginning to show. His head drooped down.

I was, in contrast, all sweet energy. 'I've got my own set of rules,' I said. 'They go like this. The council gets to hear your emergency exit is padlocked, the council gets worried. The council gets worried, it sends inspectors round. The inspectors come round and your bosses . . .'

'OK.' He was glaring now. 'Who are you after?'

'Melville Adams. Room number?'

'Twenty-seven.'

'Thanks.' I walked round his table. When I looked back I saw him opening a small hip flask, wiping its neck against the back of his hand, and taking a heavy gulp. I started up the stairs. They were steep and rickety. I made the mistake of trying to use the banisters for support and the whole thing wobbled precariously. I heard a bellow: 'Watch it, will ya?'

I watched it all the way up to the first landing and then on to the second. Number twenty-seven was at the end of a long, dismal corridor. As I walked towards it, I was assailed by sound. The same male voice that I had thought was telling me to watch it kept hammering on at his invisible partner. I wondered what I would do if the words turned into blows and then I wondered whether, if you were on the receiving end, there was much difference between the two. The rhythmic insults kept on coming; I went further down the hall.

Several of the doors were open. I saw a woman sitting listlessly on an unmade double bed while on the floor her little girl tried to grind jigsaw pieces into spaces that didn't want them. I saw an old man standing in the middle of the room, smoking as if his life depended on it, and a couple of teenagers necking in one of the communal bathrooms. As I passed by, the young man's foot stretched out and pushed the door shut.

I was by number twenty-seven. I knocked. No answer. I knocked louder. I heard footsteps, rapid fire, coming closer.

The door was wrenched open by the same youth I'd seen slumped in the cells. He was animated now, so eager that he was almost jumping out of his skin. Seeing me, however, his disappointment was extreme enough to bring tears to his eyes. He started to push the door closed.

I stuck my foot in the way. 'Melville Adams?'

He kept on pushing, cramming my sneaker against the door jamb. I pushed back. For a moment we were equally matched, straining against the wood. Then, suddenly, he gave up.

Momentum carried me lurching into the room. As I straightened up he started chewing on his little fingernail. 'What do you want?' His voice was an eerie, high-pitched whine.

I was still breathing heavily. I bought time by looking round the room. It was small and shabby but surprisingly tidy. Against one wall was a single bed. Although its top sheet was the kind of filthy that will never wash off, it was tucked in tightly enough to have satisfied the most stringent of sergeant-majors. The bed itself was tilting to one side, the books which supported its fourth corner being of a different height to the three surviving legs. Beside it was a small side table on which stood a kettle and a mug. To the right of this arrangement was a sink. The only other item of furniture was a clothes cupboard in the corner which was having the same kind of stability problems as the bed, although it was leaning in an opposite direction.

The room stunk of poverty and ill health; a second glance at Melville Adams showed just how far gone he was. His skin was closer to grey than brown, small ulcers clustered at the bottom of his nose, and there were murky specks floating where the whites of his eyes should have been. He'd already eaten his little finger raw; he moved on to the next. 'What do you want?'

I told him my name and that I had last seen him in the police station. He nodded – or at least I think he did. It was hard to tell since he went on nodding so long it could easily have been a nervous tic.

'Did you know someone died that night in the cells?' I asked.

His eyes flared. I don't know whether that meant he knew or not. He turned his wrist, looking at a watch that wasn't there. 'I'm in a hurry,' he said. 'I've got an appointment.'

I sat down on his bed.

He was jiggling in frustration. 'I've got to go.'

'Sure,' I said. 'Just hear me out.'

He had no choice. He showed me he was listening. I told him some of what Superintendent Newlands had told me. Halfway through I knew I'd lost him. His eyes were mobile, darting from one section of the room to the other, resting only occasionally on me before speeding off again.

What I was doing was ridiculous – even if Melville remembered what I'd said, he wasn't the type to talk to a policeman voluntarily. But since I'd made the journey, I gave it one last try. 'Look,' I said. 'You're in no danger. All they want . . .'

A rapping on the door put an end to my tale. That and Melville Adams's reaction. He jumped so high he almost took off. 'Shit, shit.' He grabbed my arm. 'Don't fuck me up. Please, I've been waiting.'

I wasn't sure what I was supposed to do.

'If they see you, they'll . . .' He didn't say what they'd

do. Instead he grabbed my arm and, hauling with all his might, hustled me over to the wardrobe. There was an ironing board just inside it. Working frantically, he pulled it out and threw it on to the bed. Then he tried to shove me in. I resisted.

Another knock – this one more impatient.

'Please. Please . . .' He was almost crying.

I climbed in. He tried to slam its door. I blocked the movement and stood there, holding it partially closed, which was good enough for him. I heard him moving away and then yanking the room's door open.

A soft, woman's voice: 'Took your time, didn't you?' was followed by Melville's jittery: 'I was in bed, man. I was in bed.'

'Sleeping, Mel?' She gave a seductive throaty laugh. 'Alone?'

He made a weak attempt at containing his impatience. 'Yeah. Yeah. Alone.' Then he gave up: 'You got it?'

'Sure, I got it.' Her voice had hardened. 'You're a lucky boy.' I heard rustling. 'But your luck's run out. He says this is the last. He says no more freebies for you.' There was a steel edge to the way she talked that made me shiver.

Melville Adams didn't seem to hear it. His 'thanks' sounded less like gratitude than an impatient bid to get her out. I heard high heels clicking against the corridor's linoleum. The door closed.

I came out of my hiding place. Melville was standing a few feet away, his teeth tearing at a small plastic bag. He was almost panting in his desperation to open it. When he did, his smile stretched as thin as a death mask. His movements were frenetic. He jiggled past me, went to the cupboard, stretched up and pulled a tattered wash bag from the top shelf. Then he started moving towards the door.

I grabbed him by the arm. 'Wait a minute.'

When he looked at me, his eyes were luminous with expectation. 'I have to go to the toilet,' he pleaded.

He was hell bent on one thing only; there was nothing to be gained by standing in his way. I let go of his arm and watched him running.

While he was gone I wandered through the room. I ended up by the sink, staring at the spray of tiny red-brown droplets on its tiling surrounds. I moved away, going over to the window and looking out.

There was a shiny BMW convertible double-parked directly opposite. Someone was in the driver's seat, speaking on a mobile phone. I heard a woman's tinkling laugh. I looked down and saw her stepping out of the house. Her blonde hair was tied up in a high pony-tail, matching her drainpipe jeans and high black shoes. She sashayed over to the car, said something to the driver, and got in. Without breaking his conversation, he moved off. You never know when the licence number of your local drug dealer will come in useful; I made a note of it.

That was about all I did apart from tuning into a shouting match coming through the thin walls. The words were spat out in accents far too thick for me to distinguish one from the other but I got enough of the general drift to tune out again. I heard a child's laughter, quickly stanched. I heard a couple making love – except it sounded like armed combat. In between all this, I kept looking at my watch. He was taking his time; I hoped he hadn't gone and overdosed in the bathroom.

He came in fifteen minutes later. His walk, in contrast to his previous physical jerks, was almost languid. His voice had changed as well, dropping a full tone. 'Sorry I was so long.' He was floating so high, he hadn't even bothered to clean himself up. I saw a spot of blood on the flesh of his upper arm where the needle had gone in. His smile was overdone. 'What was it you wanted?'

I didn't know how much he'd taken in before, so I started at the beginning. Halfway through my story, he wandered over to the bed, picked the ironing board off, and set it up. He pulled out an iron from under the bed and plugged it in. Then he took his trousers off.

I don't know what surprised me more – the unpredictability of the action or the blisters on his legs. I swallowed.

He put the trousers on the board, spat on to the iron's metal surface, and carefully began to run it down one leg. He didn't seem to notice that I'd stopped talking.

I went over to the board and laid Superintendent Newlands's card in the way of the moving iron. He looked up in surprise. 'You still here?'

'Yes.' My frustration made the word sound like a curse.

To which he reacted. 'Hey.' His smile was lazy. 'No need to be uptight.'

For my last try, I put my irritation on hold. 'Do you know anything about what happened in that cell?'

It had been long enough since his fix to get his thought processes clicking back into place. 'What if I do?' There was something knowing in the way he framed the question.

I was running out of patience. 'If you do, the police would like to talk to you.' I tapped the card. 'Do you?'

'I might.' His smile was crafty enough to show me he was working out what kind of profit he could make out of the situation. But that was none of my business. I had done what had been asked of me. I could go.

'Give Superintendent Newlands a ring,' I said.

'I will. I will.' Oozing the kind of charm that was beginning to make my flesh crawl, he took me to the door. 'Thanks for coming round,' he said.

Chapter
nineteen

Half an hour with Melville Adams left me in urgent need of my own kind of detox therapy. I drove home, dumped my car and walked to the nearest tapas bar where I ordered a selection of garlic infused seafoods and a beer that came with a wedge of lime stuck in its neck. This was all mere aperitif: I disposed of it before moving on to the hard stuff.

Every now and then I set out to get drunk and when I do, I'm committed. That evening I excelled myself. In the process I learnt that what they say about eating while you drink only works if you don't get so drunk that you forget to match the tapas to the tequila. I reached that stage at ten and kept on going.

I don't remember how I got home. All I know was that, for the second time in a week, I woke up fully dressed, although this time a full troop of Burundian drummers was playing in my head. I staggered out of bed, threw aspirins and gallons of water down my throat, and myself into the shower. Even so, by the time the hot water ran out, I was feeling only vaguely human. I wanted to go back to bed but I couldn't: I had a date.

I was waiting in Upper Street at one-fifteen when a panda car drew up opposite. Janet Morris got out on the passenger side. She was as I had remembered her, short and muscular with a pretty face somewhat overshadowed by a severe haircut. She didn't look in my direction. Her attention was on her companion, a tall policeman who got out of the driver's seat. From a distance they seemed a happy couple. Must be a friend, I thought, who'd come along for moral support. He smiled and said something to her. She tossed her head back and laughed. It was so exaggerated a gesture, I wondered whether it was for show. He pointed across the road, not at me, but at the sandwich bar behind. She laughed again.

They crossed the road. I moved towards them. Her eyes settled briefly on me and then kept on going. She said something to her companion. I couldn't hear what it was. Obviously funny: he was laughing loudly as they passed me by. I didn't try and stop them. Her glance and her phony animation had been warning enough: she couldn't talk in front of him.

I followed them inside and stood at the back of the shop wondering how I was going to separate Janet Morris from her partner. I watched as they reached the head of the queue. He handed her a piece of paper and she gave the order in a flattened monotone: 'Tuna,' 'Beef,' 'Cheese,' and 'Lay off the onion.' When she finished, she stood back, watching knives slathering bright yellow paste on to thick white slices.

Her companion was so tall he had to bend almost double to whisper in her ear. His smile showed he was tinkering with the jokes again but this time, instead of a belly laugh she only managed a weak smile. He said something else. That was better. She giggled, and then spoke – unnecessarily loud. 'I'll wait for you outside.'

I gathered this was my cue. I backtracked fast, moving

out and a few paces beyond the shop so that I was waiting when she emerged. She was no longer frisky; she looked tired and the depression that had settled on her features seemed there to stay. She didn't acknowledge my presence.

I called to her: 'Janet.' She looked in my direction, but I obviously looked nothing like a normal rape vigilante. Her glance went straight through me. I said it again, 'Janet Morris.' I went closer and offered her my hand. 'I'm Kate Baeier.'

Her face was a picture of bemusement.

'Valerie asked me to find you,' I said.

She looked even more confused. 'Valerie?'

I went fishing through my memory banks, looking for Valerie's surname, but alcoholic poisoning had driven it out. I gave up. 'She runs the Hackney and Islington Rape Crisis Centre,' I said.

Janet shifted round, keeping one wary eye on the shop. I moved to accommodate her. She didn't seem to have any words. She didn't speak.

'Valerie wanted to know if you were all right,' I said.

She blinked. 'Why would she?' She sounded angry.

'She was concerned about your phone call,' I said.

'Phone call?' Her face flushed pink. 'What phone call?'

Not only was I fed up with playing footsie, I was also worried that her policeman watchdog would soon appear. I junked the euphemisms. 'The one where you said you'd been raped.'

She was changing colour faster than a kaleidoscope. First pink and now a white so ashen, I thought she was going to faint. I took her arm.

She was far from fainting: she was furious. She knocked my hand off. 'Who the hell are you to talk about that?' She advanced on me, eyes bulging.

122

As I stepped out of her way, I tried to sound reassuring. 'It's OK. I'm a friend. The Crisis Centre sent me.'

She was still moving in on me. 'They had no right,' she hissed. 'No right.' A globule of spittle landed on my cheek. 'You tell Valerie to keep away from me.' She grabbed my wrist.

I was backed up so tight against the shop's glass window that one shove and I would have gone through. I felt her fingers digging into my bone, her rage pulsating. I tried to wrench my arm away but she was much stronger than I. I brought my knee up . . .

She let go. Suddenly.

She was quite an actress. Her smile was open and stress free. 'Got everything?' she asked of the policeman who'd come out the shop.

I rubbed my wrist.

'Yes.' His half-smile wrestled with a frown that showed he was trying to work out what was going on.

Nothing, apparently. 'Great.' She was better than good, she was superb, her voice a finely balanced combination of impatience and seduction. 'Shall we go then?' It worked a treat. He forgot that I was there and what he might have witnessed. He smiled and moved off with her and together they crossed the road, got into their panda and drove away.

I went back to my car and sat a while, waiting for my head to clear. It did eventually. I worked out what must have happened: some well-meaning friend of Janet's had sent me to her without asking permission. The kind of friend we all could do without. But it wasn't my problem. As far as I was concerned, my mission was accomplished. I could go to Valerie's. Straight to Valerie's. Without passing go. Without collecting nearly as much as two hundred pounds.

I pulled out into the traffic, thinking that my aching wrist was the result of my own stupidity. I should never have agreed to work for next to no money for Valerie – a woman I'd never particularly liked – on the suggestion of Carmen – a woman to whom I was no longer speaking. Oh well, I thought, easily remedied. I kept on driving. At the end of Essex Road I turned right, heading into Hackney.

The Crisis Centre was where it had always been, amongst a line of shopfronts in Homerton. Never the most elegant of places, the whole row had taken a battering since I'd last been there. The dry cleaner had given up and gone home to Italy, the off licence was trying to stay solvent by diversifying into the sale of pornographic videos, and the wrinkles on the apples which were the fruiterer's only display showed they'd long passed their sell-by date.

The Crisis Centre was, in contrast, a haven of organized respectability. Its sign, welcoming all needy women, was freshly painted and firmly battened down and the metal shutters which covered everything but the door had been polished until they gleamed. The place was sealed tight: there was no way of looking in. The notice on the door said it was open each weekday evening between six and ten. I didn't let that worry me. Even when it was officially closed, Valerie would always be inside, doing admin, answering the phone, plotting the next phase of a succession of ambitious campaigns.

I pressed the bell and stood listening as it repeated in the distance. No answer. I knew how complete Valerie's concentration was; I rung again and then a third time and, just for good measure, I banged my knuckles against the shutters.

Again no luck. If there was anyone inside, they could not possibly have missed me. Which meant that there really was no one there. I turned away and began walking back to my car. I passed a young man coming out of the fruiterer's. I nodded to him and kept on going.

'Excuse me.'

I was the only one in sight. I turned.

He was smiling shyly in my direction. 'You Valerie's friend?'

I supposed I could just about call myself that. I nodded.

'She left this for you.' He was holding out an envelope. I plucked it out of his outstretched hand and opened it. I found a note and a set of keys. I left the keys in the envelope and pulled out the note. It was written to a Moira. *Moira*, it said, *it's easier if I meet him at home. Go inside and I'll call you when it's all clear. Val.*

Him? The Valerie of old would never have dreamed of letting a man in her home. How things had changed. I refolded the note. Not that it was any of my business. I put the note in the envelope.

The fruiterer was still standing close by. 'Wrong friend,' I said. I gave him back the envelope and went to my car. I wasn't going to let a small change in Valerie's routine stand in my way. If she was at home, I would go there.

That left me with only one small problem: I didn't know where she lived. I rolled down my window. 'Is there a phone around here?'

The fruiterer lifted his shoulders in expressive uncertainty. 'You can try the first on the right.'

'Thanks.' I drove in the general direction of his pointing hand.

I understood what he'd been shrugging about when I got to the phone box. It had been vandalized beyond redemption: all that remained was its metallic skeleton and black connecting wire. There was nowhere to put your money. Not that it mattered: there was no receiver either.

I got back into my car and continued driving, twisting in and out of the Hackney streets. I ended up in familiar territory, near the place where Rodney Ellis had nearly got first-degree burns. I thought about that time, only a few days ago, yet it felt so distant. I was even slightly nostalgic for the memory. I wasn't in any hurry. I found the street and drove down it. Normal life continued behind grubby net curtains, except at the house in question. Even before I reached it, I knew I shouldn't have bothered: the way they'd boarded up the house, I couldn't see inside. I wondered how the baby was doing and whether he and the policeman who had saved his life would ever meet again. I smiled ruefully. Given the crime rate in the area, the odds were that they would.

I found a phone box that was in working order. I dialled Carmen's number. As it started ringing, I had second thoughts. There's no hurry, I told myself, I can get to Valerie another day. I was about to hang up.

Too late. '3471, Carmen Jones speaking.'

'Carmen.' I didn't say my name. There was no need: since we'd spent years in the same office working against a background of each other's voices, she would know me instantly. 'I need Valerie's home address.'

She didn't ask why I had never returned her call. Instead she said, 'A moment.' I waited for a moment, then she came back on line. 'Valerie lives in Islington,' and read out the street name and number.

'Thanks.'

No one could say Carmen wasn't efficient. She gave me Valerie's telephone number as well.

'Thanks,' I said again.

'Anytime.' She hung up without saying goodbye. It didn't bother me. On the contrary: I was pleased. After the series of rows that had marked our recent encounters, it was progress to find that we were on speaking terms again. I pocketed the spare twenty-pence piece that I'd fed – just in case – into the machine and went back to my car.

Chapter
twenty

Valerie lived in a council block in Islington. It was one of those inter-war constructions that five years earlier had reached the bottom of a slide into dilapidation. But the inhabitants of this place had been lucky: the council had done one of those conversion jobs that, from the outside at least, had turned a concrete disaster into a set of almost bijou residences. Not that Valerie would care: housing had never been one of her priorities.

Anonymity had. One of the ways the council had made the place safe was by putting up wrought-iron doors between each section so as to prevent undesirables wandering through. I searched the list of names beside the bells. I couldn't find Valerie's. There was only one without a name attached: I rang that one.

Above me, I heard a window opening. I looked up to find Valerie, her substantial breasts packed in cerise, leaning out. I had expected surprise at my appearance, but what I got was speechlessness. Her mouth gaped open, closed and then drooped again.

I filled the silence. 'Hi.'

Her head jerked round as if she were looking at someone in the room. When she turned back to me again I thought that I'd never seen her so ill at ease.

I carried on. 'I came to tell you that I . . .'

'Hold on a minute.' The window closed.

It wasn't long before I heard her footsteps thundering downwards. The door opened. I assumed I'd be invited in and I took a preparatory step forward. Apparently not: she filled the space, blocking entry. Her lips were the same shade of pink as her blouse; I wondered again about her visitor.

I told myself again that it was none of my business. And if she didn't want me in, that was fine by me. All I'd come for was the short report followed by the long goodbye. I set to it. 'The good news is that I found Janet Morris,' I said.

'I knew you would.' She didn't sound pleased; she didn't sound anything. 'And the bad news?'

'She wants to stay lost.' I turned my wrist to reveal the beginnings of a spreading purple bruise. 'This is how strongly she feels about her privacy.'

'Oh.' Valerie's voice was still strangely flat. 'She hurt you.'

'It's OK.' I smiled bravely before I went in for the kill. 'But it does prove that, no matter what she said on the phone, she is not interested in any kind of counselling.'

Valerie served up another, flat 'Oh' and then, as if this was too miserly, tacked a 'Well, if that's how she feels' on to its end.

It was my turn to gape. When Valerie had come to me she'd been desperate to find Janet Morris. Two days later, when she'd phoned, the pressure had still been on. And now she, who always knew better than other people, was accepting how Janet Morris felt? It made no sense.

'Look' – she wasn't about to explain – 'I'm sorry. I've got somebody upstairs.' She stepped back pulling the gate with her. 'I have to go.'

I'd come prepared for a ferocious argument: I was so stunned, all I could say was, 'I'll send you my bill.'

She glanced briefly back. 'You do that. And thanks for all your hard work, Kate,' she said. 'Please, don't worry about it any more.' That was it. She left.

Her words echoed in my brain. *Don't worry about it!* This from the woman who could worry spilt coffee back into a paper bag? There was no doubt about it. Something wasn't right.

Something, I wondered, or someone? I looked up. I saw her face appear briefly at the window and then fade back. I told myself to cool it. I didn't know what I was doing standing there. I'd got everything I'd wanted: I'd got out. I waved in case she was still watching and then I walked away.

The sun came out as I drove away from Valerie's. I didn't feel like going home. My hangover had finally deserted me and for the first time that day, I felt alive.

Alive. So what did I do? I went to Highgate to where Sam was buried.

I parked my car outside the cemetery and used my pass to get in. Then I walked down the narrow paths, by decaying brambles and the stirrings of spring, towards Sam's grave. I rounded the corner and there it was, that symbol of Layton wealth – a mausoleum which was a mismatch of clashing styles, of Greek columns, a round window or two, and a come-hither name plaque stuck above a set of high railings. You needed a key to get any further. I had one. I didn't use it. I walked round the monstrosity to the place where they'd planted a scented jasmine, a clematis and a climbing rose. White flowers thrust their way out of the clematis's tangle of green. New life: it made me smile. A first. I'd never felt like smiling here before.

130

There was a bench close by. I went to sit on it. I didn't think of Sam. I didn't feel the need to. I sat, cherishing the sun's warmth, letting my thoughts wander free. Half an hour later, as spring lost the battle of the seasons, watery sunlight gave way to clammy cold. I didn't really mind – I'd been there long enough. I got up and began walking out.

I was almost at the entrance when I saw him. I looked away, sure that when I looked back again he would have transmogrified into some other grey-haired, limping man.

I looked back again. It was him – my father – a bunch of daffodils in one hand, the other clasping a heavy walking stick. He was making his way slowly towards me.

When he saw me, he said, 'Kate!' His smile was a consummate mix of pleasure and surprise.

I was flabbergasted. How did he know that I'd be there?

He was coming closer. 'John Layton told me where his son was buried. I wanted to pay my respects.' He hesitated and then added: 'I wasn't expecting to see you here.'

Oh yeah? He was a shrewd old bastard. He would have guessed that I'd eventually turn up. In fact, I thought, he'd probably left one of his underlings in a car to wait for when I did.

'Isn't it strange that we've met twice in as many days.' He was beginning to sound nervous. 'After all this time. I hope you don't mind?' His liquid gaze was fixed on me.

I shrugged. It was all I could bring myself to do.

'Well . . .' His glance said he was ready to move off.

Which suited me. I made it easy. I stepped out of his way.

He did something then he'd never done before. He apologized. He stuttered it out but still I heard it clearly. 'I'm sorry . . .' And then again. 'I'm sorry.' The hand on the walking stick was shaking. 'I was taken aback when you came to see me. I handled it all wrong.'

Wrong? My father was never wrong!

'Please, hear me out. It would make me so happy.'

He was never happy either. I looked again at him. I could see how pale was his skin, how puffy his face. That at least was no trick. He did look ill.

He glanced briefly at the bouquet in his hands. Then he looked at me. 'Will you accompany me?'

I wasn't going back, not with him. I shook my head.

His smile was understanding. 'Will you wait for me then?'

I hesitated. I was cold.

'There is a café, I think, in the park next door. Will you wait there?'

I sighed.

It was all the answer he needed. 'Thank you,' he said, 'I will join you soon,' and then he turned and walked away as fast as his gammy leg would allow.

I was the café's only customer, sitting in the corner nursing a cappuccino when he turned up. He waved briefly in my direction, went up to the counter and said something to the waitress. I couldn't hear what it was but I could see by the way she was smiling that he still knew how to charm strangers. His instructions over, he joined me at my table, making a big performance of lowering himself gingerly into a chair. I took another sip of coffee.

The waitress brought over a cup of hot water and, on a side plate, a slice of lemon. He used a fork to empty the lemon of its juices and pulp. I found myself mesmerized by the familiarity of his hand's movements.

He caught me looking. 'It used to be strong black coffee,'

he said. He brought the cup up to his thin lips, swallowed and then returned it to its saucer. 'Unfortunately my gastric juices will no longer tolerate the caffeine.'

I didn't know what I was supposed to say. I tried 'Oh dear'. It didn't come out right.

Not that it bothered him. 'My health is not all it ought to be,' he said.

'Yes. Zetu told me.'

'He did?' Displeasure flitted across his face. He swallowed it down. 'I am putting my affairs in order,' he said. 'In case . . .' He didn't say in case of what. Instead he veered off into uncharted territory. 'I have wronged you, Kate,' he said.

This was really unprecedented!

His voice was gentle. 'I did not help you enough when your mother died.'

I couldn't let that go. 'No,' I said. 'What you didn't do was help her when she was alive.'

It was the kind of thing which, if I'd said it in the past, would have incited him into a long rant. But not this time. This time, the shake of his head was sorrowful. 'When marriages go wrong,' he said, 'sometimes only hate survives.'

A truism that brooked no reply. I sipped my drink and he sipped his until eventually I was ready. I looked at him straight. 'What are you up to?'

He didn't answer. Although he hadn't finished his drink, his concentration was taken up in fumbling for his walking stick. I couldn't stop myself – I reached out to help him.

'I have said enough. I will leave you now.' He leaned heavily on the stick, pushing himself up. 'Please ring me, whenever you wish. We can spend some time together.'

He bent as if he was going to kiss me on the forehead. I

shifted out of the way. He turned the gesture into forward motion. I watched him going. I watched the waitress spring to her feet and open the door for him. He turned. 'I hope you will call,' he told me.

I continued watching as the waitress helped him down the stairs. They stopped for a moment at the bottom. When he spoke to her, her face lit up. She offered more help, but he shook his head.

She came back into the café. 'Nice man,' she commented.

Nice? Well, perhaps he was. As long as he wasn't your husband, your father, or your political opponent.

She wouldn't let it alone. 'A real old-style gentleman,' she said. 'Don't you agree?'

'He's certainly an old-style something,' I said. I got up. I noticed her gentleman had not paid for the coffee. I handed her the money and then I left.

Chapter
twenty-one

All the way back home, I wrestled with myself. I repeated what I had always known: that my father was a user. He'd used my mother and, in the past, he had used me. Just because I couldn't work out what he was up to now, didn't mean he wasn't up to something.

Which is when a second voice took over. It told me that my father was ill. He had always acted as if he was more than mortal, perhaps the prospect of death was enough to force a change, to make his plea for reconciliation genuine.

The first voice came surging back. It said that my father was never genuine, that he always had a game and he always played for keeps. Nothing, not even death, would change that.

As I drove, I shuttled between these two conflicting versions. When I finally arrived in Camden Town, I decided to stifle both. I parked the car and went up to my flat. I wasn't going to think about my father, not any more. I had other things to occupy my mind – like what I was going to wear, and how it would be seeing Gavin again.

It was strange, seeing him. At least it was at first. He arrived on time and rang the bell. I buzzed him in and stood at the top of the stairs waiting.

The climb took much longer than I'd expected. When finally he turned the corner, he was looking at his feet. I said hello.

He glanced up. He didn't smile. He just kept on looking.

I frowned. 'Is there anything the matter?'

'No.' He shook his head. Then he added aggressively: 'What did you do today?'

Since I didn't know what kind of question that was, I couldn't answer it.

He was alongside me now. 'May I come in?'

I stepped out of his way and watched him heading into the living room. It was just like the last time except that he was no longer at ease. I followed and found him standing by the window, staring out. Although he must have heard me coming in, he didn't move.

I had a bad feeling about this. 'Gavin,' I said.

He turned, his expression so fierce that I took an involuntary step backwards. All that had gone on between us was instantly annihilated. To think I'd actually believed we had something special going! It was so pathetic it was almost funny.

Except I didn't feel like laughing.

He smiled. 'I'm sorry.' His face was no longer belligerent. He started walking towards me. 'I've had a hell of a day.' His voice suddenly softened. 'Will you forgive me?' He didn't wait long enough for me to frame an answer. Instead, he took me in his arms. After a while, neither of us felt like speaking any more.

I learnt a lot about Gavin Dowd that weekend. I learnt that he had a capacity for tenderness that astonished me, that the kitchen was always clean after he'd finished cooking and that, when his job got too much for him, he sailed his dinghy through the Essex marshes. He was not always an easy companion. Once in a while he seemed to disappear, withdrawing to an inner place I couldn't reach. But those brief times aside, we spent hours talking, laughing, making love. We fitted together, he and I.

And then Monday came: time for normal life. I walked him downstairs. Our parting kiss was strong enough to produce a catcall from an envious stranger. When eventually we separated and Gavin had driven off, I went to buy my morning fix of printed news.

Back at my flat, my answerphone was blinking. I rewound the tape and stood listening to an unfamiliar voice reeling out a message I didn't want to hear: 'This is Claire, a member of the Rape and Battered Wives Crisis Collective. Valerie needs to meet you. At the Centre. She's there now and will be until you turn up. She says it's urgent.'

Wasn't it always urgent? I dialled the number of the Crisis Centre. Five rings in, an anonymous voice gave me its opening hours and a number I should use if I was desperate. It suggested that, if I wasn't desperate, I should leave a message. I hung on until I heard the bleep.

'Valerie,' I said. 'If you're there, pick up the phone.' No response. I tried it again: 'Pick up the phone, Valerie.'

She didn't. She wouldn't, would she? If she wanted to talk to you in person, then that's what she got. I dialled her home number. The phone rang and rang but no one answered. I knew what the bloody woman was doing; sitting in the Centre, ignoring the phone, waiting for me to drop everything and come by. Well, that's what I would do, but when I got there I would tell her precisely where she could stick her unending string of urgent demands.

It was raining heavily when I got to Homerton. The wet

did nothing for my mood. I pulled up my collar as I walked past the fruiterer's mouldy apples. The man himself was nowhere in sight. I kept on going, over the soggy trash that had stockpiled by the defunct dry cleaners, and past a set of video display boxes where buxom women pursed their mouths in coquettish come-ons. I didn't think it was legal to display soft porn, I wondered why the Crisis Centre hadn't done something about it.

I wasn't dressed for rain. Despite the collar, water was already dripping down my neck. I hunched into my clothes and went faster.

I reached the Centre and pressed the bell. I heard it ringing, hard and sharp. I kept my hand there. Inside the noise would soon grow painful. It was childish, I know, but I got pleasure from imagining Valerie jumping up and striding hurriedly to the door.

That's all it was – my imagination. There were no footsteps and no Valerie. I tried a few short jabs at the bell. Still no reply. I was cold, wet and furious. Bloody Valerie – she'd always been impossible. I was so angry, I hit the door.

It swung open. I shouted, 'Valerie!' She didn't answer. I stepped in and called her name again. The dingy hall had an empty feel about it. I didn't expect a response. I didn't get one.

I looked out through the open door at the rain pelting down. I didn't want to get any wetter, so I decided to wait it out. I could see a toilet at the end of the hall. I thought there might be a towel there. I started walking towards it. Halfway down, I started walking slower. I was entranced by the posters that lined the hallway. All the old favourites, some dating back to the early seventies, posters that told of 'Reclaim the Night' marches and abortion conferences and crèches run by sympathetic men were there, and alongside them their less abrasive, glossier, modern versions. It was like a stroll down memory lane: despite my irritation I found that I was smiling. I knew that there was only one person with the staying power to preserve this little bit of history and that was Valerie.

What I had thought that night when Valerie had come storming back into my life repeated on me: she might be a pushy, stubborn, abrasive zealot, but she was also one of those unusual people who pledged their lives to a cause. I would never agree to work with, or for, her again – she wanted too much to be in charge of everything – but I couldn't help admiring her unshakeable convictions.

I had reached the toilet. I corrected myself: Valerie wasn't in charge of everything, certainly not of the Centre's supply of hand towels. Her style would have been abrasive grey, while the one hanging on the rail was fluffy, white and smelt of flowers. I used it to dry my neck and hands and then I rubbed it all over my wet hair. That done, I put the towel back and started retracing my steps.

Apart from the toilet, the Centre was made up of two ground floor rooms. I looked in both. In the first was a set of easy chairs, the low, durable kind you can find in most institutions, arranged in a rough circle. There were ashtrays dotted about, all of them wiped clean. By the side there was a table on which stood a kettle, an industrial tin of instant coffee, a half-empty box of Red Label T-bags, an unopened bag of white sugar and a dozen or so clean mugs. I toyed with the idea of making myself something hot to drink but, looking out of the room's high, barred window, I saw that the pressure of rain had already lifted.

I decided I'd leave a note and go. There was no paper visible in the room, so I moved on to the next. Because of its metal shutters, it was pitch black. I fumbled around until I finally managed to locate and switch on the overhead light. I was in the office; I knew there would be writing equipment there. I moved to the first of the two large desks.

Whoever cleaned the Centre was quite compulsive: there were three phones lined up in a neat row beside a small pot holding pens, a few message pads and a large white blotter. I picked up one of the receivers and rang Valerie's home number. Nobody answered. I tore a sheet of paper off the message pad, stood for a moment wondering how rude I should be, and settled for a curt *Where the hell were you?* before signing my name. I put the note centre stage on the white blotter, switched off the light, and left the room.

When I opened the front door, the storm had almost drizzled itself to a standstill. I stepped out and thought, momentarily, about leaving the door open. I decided not to: even though I'd found it that way, I didn't want a break-in on my conscience. So I pulled the door to, and then I made my way home.

The drizzle never did let up. I didn't really mind. I spent the rest of the day indoors, putting the finishing touches to a piece on my adventures as a war correspondent which I'd managed to sell to an up-market weekly. I kept expecting Valerie to phone. She never did. I was also waiting for another call, this one from Gavin. We'd made only half a date: he'd said he was on the move all day and that he would ring me.

He didn't. He'd warned me that it might be difficult so I wasn't really worried. He'd also warned me that he might be working late. At eight-thirty, when the door bell rang, I knew it must be him. It had to be – I wasn't expecting anyone else. I felt a thrill of anticipation. I decided to go downstairs and open the door myself.

I went downstairs. I opened the door.

It wasn't Gavin. It was, however, a policeman. Or, to be more precise, a mass of policemen. The men in front were wearing suits but behind was a group of uniforms and a couple of vicious-looking dogs straining at their leashes. I had time only to open my mouth before a badge was shoved at me. It was closely followed by a quick glimpse of a search warrant.

My reflexes were far too slow. I didn't even have time to wonder out loud whether they'd got the wrong flat before the officer in charge's brusque, 'Out of our way please, Miss Baeier,' told me this was only wishful thinking.

Chapter
twenty-two

There were six of them, three in plain clothes and three in uniform. Two I'd met before: one was Brian Turner, the man who had interrogated me on the night of James Shaw's death, and the other the man who'd been behind the desk that night, the one I called Action Man. He was followed in by the dog-handler and, finally, a WPC whose brief was to watch me. As the others began stamping up the stairs, she stayed put. I thought about asking her what was going on, but one sight of her zipped-up lips and I knew there was no point.

I followed the men. They went straight past my first-floor neighbour who'd come out of his flat to find out what was going on. His face was a long cold letter box of disapproval. As I came closer to him, he beat a quick retreat. I heard the sound of security bolts slamming into place.

My escort's breath was fetid on my neck. I climbed the final flight of stairs. By the time I reached the flat, the men had already peeled off. One was in the bedroom, one in the kitchen, another heading for the living room and a fourth just about to switch on the bathroom light. The dogs, it appeared, were entirely for show. They sat at their handler's feet, panting peacefully.

I found my voice. 'What are you looking for?'

'As if you didn't know.' This from Action Man, who was in the process of moving from kitchen to bedroom.

I headed for the living room. The policewoman beat me to it. As I moved to the phone she put her hand down, flat down, on the receiver.

'I want to make a call.'

Her mouth stayed sealed.

I raised my voice. 'Are you saying I can't?'

The man who'd had the search warrant was by the bookshelf. He turned. 'We don't want you warning anybody,' he said.

'Warning who? About what?'

He shrugged and went back to rooting through my books. I got the message. I was outnumbered six to one and they knew what they were doing. Trying to break through their silence was a waste of time. Which didn't mean I had to be entirely passive. I walked from room to room, seeing what they were up to. My shadow followed close behind.

I stood in the bedroom doorway, watching one of the uniformed men rifling through my underwear. A few minutes of that and I revised my earlier decision. I took myself back into the living room and sat down on the sofa.

Fifteen minutes went by. I kept on sitting. Another five. I wondered what had happened to Gavin. I stopped wondering when I heard a shout: 'Hey, skip. Come and look at this.' I heard movement in the background and an exhilarated exclamation. I'd never thought my underwear was that exciting – maybe all that enforced overtime was taking its toll.

'Miss Baeier.' One of the plainclothes men was standing at the door. 'Would you come this way, please?'

'This way' turned out to be into the kitchen. It was

crowded in there; I and my silent partner made it seven. We were the VIPs – they gave us a ringside view.

'Miss Baeier.' Centre stage was the officer that they called 'skip'. In his hand, a plastic bag filled with white powder. 'You ever seen this before?'

'No,' I said. 'But I have seen the movie, so I know the lines. Isn't this where I tell you it's either sugar or flour?'

He licked his index finger, opened the bag, dipped the finger in, took it out and touched his gums. He smiled. 'It's certainly not sugar.' I could tell by the way his face lit up that it wasn't flour either.

I narrowed my eyes, remembering how when I'd arrived one of them had been moving out of the kitchen.

An officious voice rolled over my thoughts. 'Kate Baeier,' it said, 'I am arresting you on suspicion of being in possession of a controlled substance, namely heroin . . .'

The light was very bright. I hated standing there for the photo but found I hated being fingerprinted more. Neither of them prepared me, however, for the indignity of the body search. They were very thorough about it: a gloved hand went up places that nobody except the occasional lover had ever been. Finding nothing they fast forwarded me into one of the tiny interrogation rooms.

It was like old times – Sergeant Brian Turner at the table, a thick manila file laid out in front of him. He gestured at the only other chair. 'Sit down, Miss Baeier.'

The uniformed policeman who'd led me in was standing by the door, arms folded. I sat.

Brian Turner unsealed and unwrapped two blank tapes. He put one into each side of the double-fronted tape recorder, hit a switch, and read in all the relevant information including date, time and the names of those present. Then he looked at me. 'Dealing heroin is a serious offence,' he said.

'No!' I raised my eyebrows. 'Really?'

His mean lips disappeared into a non-existent chin. 'This is no joking matter, Miss Baeier.'

'No,' I said, 'it isn't. Especially since we both know those drugs came into my flat in somebody's blue serge trousers.'

His smile was more than halfway to a leer. 'You're not going to blame it on Postman Pat, are you?' He thought this was so funny that he rocked his chair back until it was leaning against the wall. 'Won't go down very well with the judge, will it?'

I wondered whether, if I kicked my foot out, I could knock him off.

'Face it, Miss Bacier. We caught you bang to rights.'

I scowled. 'Aren't you supposed to offer me a phone call before getting into the clichés?'

'All in good time.' He opened the file in front of him. My passport was lying on top. He began turning its pages, reeling out the names of the places I had visited. 'Columbia, Bolivia, Peru . . .' He looked up. 'A who's who of drug-producing countries.'

'Of local wars,' I said. 'I was a war correspondent.'

'Sure you were.' He turned another page. 'Oh.' He seemed amused. 'And look what we have here.'

He picked up something. All I could see was its slinky white underside, the kind you get in a glossy print photograph. I frowned. There'd been no photo in my passport when I'd last used it.

Brian Turner's hand moved so fast I thought he was going to hit me. But no, he tossed the photo over. Good aim: it landed right side up. I couldn't help myself. I was curious. I looked down.

While Brian Turner told the tape what I was doing, I kept on staring. I was stunned. I don't know what I had expected. Certainly not this.

It was a picture of Melville Adams. He was sprawled on his back, his head tilted awkwardly to one side. His eyes were half closed. Beside him there was a pool of what was almost certainly vomit. He'd looked ill when I had seen him but this was different. Now he looked dead.

I heard distant words. 'Do you know this man?'

Shock squeezed an answer out of me. 'I saw him here on the night James Shaw died.'

'Did you speak to him then?'

'How could I?' I couldn't tear my eyes away. 'He was in a cell.' I remembered how I'd sat on Melville's bed, thinking that he'd been so long he must have gone and overdosed. Looking at him now, I felt sick.

'Miss Baeier . . .'

The voice was loud and domineering. My head snapped up.

'I asked you a question. Did you see Mr Adams after that night in the cell?'

As the first wave of horror receded, my mind snapped into focus. It was plain that I'd been had. What I didn't know was how far the frame-up extended. I thought back to how this had started, to a man who called himself Superintendent Newlands and who had sent me after Melville Adams. Now Melville was dead. I looked at the picture. 'How did he die?'

'How do you think?'

A drug overdose, I bet. And I'd had drugs planted in my flat.

'You arranged to meet him, didn't you?'

Him? Not Newlands, surely? I looked across the table. 'I don't know what you're talking about.'

146

'Oh yeah?' His voice was deadpan disbelief. And then it hardened. 'Come on, Kate, let's stop playing games. We already have a witness who will testify that you met Melville. He saw you going into the Centre . . .'

The Centre?

'. . . and he saw you coming out. Said you were in a hurry. Said you looked furious. What happened, Kate? Did Melville get greedy?'

'What Centre?'

He'd been waiting for that. 'The Hackney Rape Crisis and Battered Wives Centre.' His smile was gleeful. 'The place where you gave Melville Adams his last fatal fix.'

Wait a minute – there'd been no Melville Adams when I'd been there.

'You've been, stupid, haven't you, Kate? You left your fingerprints all over the Centre.'

'I was called there.'

'That's not what Miss Watson says.'

Miss Watson? Of course. That was Valerie's surname: Valerie Watson. Was she also part of this?

'She denies that she asked someone to ring you and request a visit.'

Valerie and the police? It wasn't credible.

'In fact, I wouldn't be surprised if Valerie Watson wasn't furious with you. Using the Centre to dispose of Melville Adams. It's not what you call a friendly act, now, is it?' He blinked, punctuating his sneer, and then moved on. 'We have an eye witness who will testify to seeing you outside the Centre, a note with your name on the bottom, and a set of fingerprints that forensic is working on now. You're in trouble, Kate, big trouble. What have you got to say to that?'

There was only one thing to say. 'I want my phone call.'

His eyes flashed. 'Come on, Kate . . .'

'I want my phone call,' I said.

I kept on saying it until he got bored with me. Eventually, he decided to take me to the cell. He grabbed me by the arm and hustled me out. I was propelled past a group of policemen sitting by the custody desk. 'I want my phone call,' I said. The hand on my arm was dug in. 'I want . . .'

I never got to finish. I heard a voice. 'Let her use the phone.'

My escort cursed, but stopped. We both turned, together, to find Sergeant Tom Harrison, the policeman who had once left me in the witness room, coming towards us. He smiled at me, a sympathetic smile. My first impression of him as an ideal father figure, strong but open, came back to me.

'This way, Miss Baeier,' he said, ignoring my escort's glare.

Then he showed me to the phone.

It was already past one o'clock in the morning. Too late for Anna. I dialled Carmen's number. The ringing went on for a long, long time before I heard her drawl out, 'Hello.'

'Carmen,' I said. 'It's Kate. I need a solicitor.'

She was half asleep. 'You writing a will?'

'I might have to. I'm in the Parchment Road nick.'

Her voice flashed into focus. 'They charged you?'

'With possession of drugs. White powder – heroin, maybe, or cocaine. I don't know which it is. I do, however' – watching Action Man swanning past – 'have a pretty good idea how it got there. I'm being set up. For a death as well. I need someone top rate.'

I expected questions but only because I'd forgotten how Carmen operated. 'I'll get you someone,' she said, and then the phone went down.

Chapter
twenty-three

They put me back in the interview room alone but for my silent guard. I was there an hour before an apparition in blue and white – light blue skirt, white shirt, blue shoes, blue briefcase – came sweeping in. Her voice was anything but pastel. 'Miss Baeier. I'm Erica Cadogan. Cadogan as in the square.' Her accent was Roedean and Cambridge. Or maybe Oxford. I couldn't be sure. 'I gather that the wonderful Carmen is a mutual friend.'

I gathered that Carmen was moving in different circles these days.

'If you don't mind?' This to the guard who took his cue and left. 'Now.' She settled herself down. 'Why don't you tell me what's been going on?'

I told her – not what I suspected, but the bare bones of what had happened. She was a class act. She listened to my tale of planted drugs and dead drug addicts as if it were all routine. She wasn't stupid, either: she knew I was holding something back. When she was sure that I had finished, she lined her gold-inlaid fountain pen carefully by her pad and then looked at me. 'Anything else you want to say?'

I had plenty to say. But not there. 'I just want you to get me out of here.'

She carried on looking. Her eyes were cornflower-blue to

match her outfit. Her strawberry-blonde hair was held up in a bun. I shook my head to show her I wasn't going to speak. Her polished nails tapped the table. 'Carmen said you would not be the easiest of clients.'

I didn't blink. 'Takes one to know one.'

She dealt up a light, delicious laugh. 'Yes, Carmen can be quite ferocious.' And stood. 'Why don't I go and see what they're planning to do with you?'

In the twenty minutes that she was gone, I put my mind on hold. There was one thing and one thing only on which I must concentrate my energies: getting out.

A tap on the door. Erica Cadogan re-entered. She did her quick one-two with the guard again before: 'I've got good and bad news,' she said. She didn't ask me which I wanted first. 'The bad news is that what you were told is correct. Your' – she coughed discreetly – *'friend* Valerie Watson disclaims any knowledge of your visits to the Centre. She says that the woman' – she looked down at her notes – 'Claire, who you say phoned to tell you to meet Valerie there, does not exist. And it gets worse, I'm afraid. Apparently Miss Watson also said that she had previously left a note to a nameless friend, along with the keys to the Centre, at the fruiterer's. She says, however, by the time the friend turned up, the keys were no longer in the envelope.' Erica Cadogan was a mistress of the straight face. 'I gather you had hold of this envelope at some point,' she said, dead pan.

I nodded, remembering how the key had lain snug next to Valerie's note when I had handed the envelope back. I put the memory into the 'to-be-dealt-with-later' section and then, matching my expression to my lawyer's, said, 'So what's the good news?'

'They're not going to charge you in connection with Melville Adams's death – at least not at the moment. They have connected you to a drug source, and to the Rape Crisis Centre, but I should think the question of motive and the fact that Mr Adams seemed intent on destroying himself is holding matters up. My estimation is that they'll never press that charge.'

I couldn't afford a moment's relief. I went straight for target. 'Can you get me out?'

She sighed. 'That's up to a magistrate, I'm afraid. The police will certainly try and oppose bail but if we volunteer your passport and can raise a substantial sum . . . Not from your own account: they will have frozen that.' She ran a hand wearily along her forehead – the first hint that she might have found being hauled out of bed in the middle of the night stressful – and said, 'I just hope you have some very rich friends.'

The bail was set at £200,000. There was nobody I knew who could raise that. I turned to look at Carmen who was sitting in the front row of the viewers' gallery. She didn't catch my eye: she was too busy nodding in Erica Cadogan's direction.

Somebody, somewhere, who could prove they had that much liquid cash, was prepared to risk it on me. I got bail. I was out. I walked – minus my passport – into the court's ornate entrance hall. Erica Cadogan muttered something about us meeting later to discuss strategy and then wafted off. I saw Carmen waiting by some ornate wood panelling.

She was as beautiful as she had always been. Her hair was pulled back tight against her scalp into dozens of little plaits, which left her face alone. It didn't need any support:

her high cheekbones, her long nose, her deep brown eyes, her full lips, all found a perfect symmetry on that mocha skin. She was not a woman who smiled easily and she wasn't smiling now. She looked at me, waiting for me to make the first move.

I knew something of what she was thinking. I was thinking it too. When last we'd met, the past had come between us, severing what had been not only a good working relationship but also one of my most important friendships. I remembered the pain of our misunderstanding and the way it had ended. Part of Carmen's charm, and part of her nonsense, was that she never admitted to frailty; she hadn't been able to apologize for what she'd done and, because of that, I could not forgive her.

But that was then. Now I went up to her. I smiled. 'Thanks.'

She nodded. I wasn't fooled by the austerity of the movement. I could tell she was pleased. 'You haven't changed, have you, Kate? Erica says you're still skimming through minefields.'

From Carmen this was a compliment. I linked my arm to hers. 'Come on. I've had enough of officialdom to last for ever. Let's get out of here.'

We walked, together, past the policemen searching people's bags, to a swing door. As we parted, each to go through separately, we grinned at each other. Carmen shunned anything approaching self-analysis: I knew this was the closest we would ever come to acknowledging that we'd buried our differences. It felt good.

Except, when I emerged blinking into the sunlight, our tenuous truce almost broke. I had turned to her. 'You never told me who paid the . . .'

She didn't need to tell me. Her gaze was concentrated on

the space beyond. Following it, I saw what could only be my father's smoke-black limousine parked at the edge of the road. I turned to Carmen. Her voice was all strained defensiveness. 'The Portuguese embassy located him for me. He was the only person with access to that kind of money. And Erica said you had to get out.' She shifted into defiance: 'You think I did wrong?'

I thought about the pounds of flesh that my father would extract in exchange for his generosity, and I frowned. But then I thought about what would have happened if I had stayed in gaol. I had no idea what was going on but one thing I did know: if I wasn't out and acting for myself, my chances of finding a way through the chaos were zilch. I converted my frown into a smile. 'No,' I said. 'You did right.'

Her face relaxed and I remembered how contradictory she could be, how her fierce exterior hid a softer, less confident side. 'Thanks again,' I said. 'For everything.'

She squeezed my elbow, which was as demonstrative as she ever got. 'You need any more help,' she said, 'you get in touch.'

'Don't worry. I will.' I reached up and lightly kissed her unresponsive cheek. 'And now' – taking a deep breath – 'into the beast's den.'

I walked over to the black limo. By the time I reached it, its hulk of a chauffeur was holding the back door open. I took another deep breath and got in. The door closed.

There were two of them in there: my father beside me in the back seat, Zetu in front. Zetu smiled and, turning, clasped my hands. I felt myself warming. It had been like this throughout my adolescence. Whenever I had got into trouble, Zetu had been there to hold my hand and tell me that it would be all right.

My father coughed. I knew I was in for one of his lectures. I turned to look at him. 'You bailed me out,' I said, thinking I was an adult and I didn't have to sit out the speech. Nevertheless I owed him something. 'Thank you,' I said.

He smiled.

I hadn't slept all night. Perhaps I was hallucinating.

But no. He was really smiling! And more than that. He reached out and lightly touched my knee. '*Da nada,*' he said, adding: 'Isn't that what money's for?'

No! I didn't believe it. To my father money was a way of buying power, or at least guns. My lower jaw dropped down.

'You look tired, Kate,' he said. 'We will drive you home. You can tell us what is going on when you have had adequate rest.' He paused. And added: 'Only if you want to, of course.'

Only if you want to? My world turned upside down. *Only if you want to,* from a man who, throughout my childhood, had forced me to tell him everything; literally everything: what I ate; the exact contents of my dream; whom I'd sat next to in the bus; whom I was going out with. I looked at him.

In the blurred light that issued from the tinted windows, his complexion was sickly green. I turned my gaze frontwards, making a quick comparison. My father came out badly. Although Zetu's face was lined and mottled, my father's skin was ancient, flaking, parchment-like. He was sick. Really sick.

'Don't worry, my daughter,' he said. 'They will never get away with it.'

'They?' I was completely discombobulated.

'Whoever set you up like this.' A pause. Then he went

one further. 'I know you were set up. You would not smuggle drugs.'

The father I had known would never have dreamed that, in a contest between myself and the authorities, I might be right. That did it. I was convinced. He had changed.

'Your Miss Cadogan seems efficient,' he said. 'We should now, of course, start looking for a barrister. Your decision, naturally. You just let me know' he touched my knee again – 'if there's anything that I can do to help.'

He went on in that vein for as long as the journey lasted. In that time he didn't ask me a single question – which was just as well. Fatigue and disorientation had tied my tongue in knots. It was only after we had arrived, and I'd got out of the car, that I thought of something to say.

Zetu, who had said he'd escort me upstairs, was waiting. 'Won't be a minute,' I said. I went back to the car. My father pushed a button and the window rolled down. 'Who wants to buy the *palacio*?' I asked.

He shook his head. 'It's a minor matter. No need to concern yourself with it at this moment.'

'I want to know. Who is it?'

He shrugged. 'A rich man. A man who collects books. He is looking for a fitting place to store his collection.'

'He'll preserve the building?'

My father nodded. 'He wants to buy it because he's fallen in love with it.' His hand stretched out and took mine. 'Go, Kate, get some rest. We can talk about this another time.'

155

Chapter
twenty-four

One look at the mayhem in my flat and Zetu offered to help clear up. The behaviour of old men had been uncharacteristic enough for one day: I told him I'd be fine. I also told him that I thought he was right, that my father had changed. He liked that. There was a spring in his step as he made his way downstairs.

I went over to the living-room window and watched him walking from the house. He got into the car. I kept on looking, long after the car had driven off. Fatigue and the effort to keep despair at bay had made me sluggish, but I couldn't suspend time indefinitely. I had to face the chaos. I forced myself to move.

Every book, every piece of clothing, every item of food had been taken from its resting place. I started with the worst – the kitchen – where a fine dust of white powder covered all the surfaces. I took a lick of it. It was flour: they must have planted their poison in the flour bin.

No. I shook my head. I wasn't going to think of it. I got out a cloth and turned the powder into a paste which I could wash down the sink. That done, I set to refilling my shelves. I had myself under tight control. My thoughts moved with my eyes, concentrating on restoring order and on nothing else. When the kitchen was clear, I moved to the bathroom and then on to the bedroom. The only concession I made to the rage, which kept welling up unbidden, was to throw my underwear, in its entirety, into the washing machine. Other than that I was completely disciplined.

But I was also running out of steam. By the time I reached the living room, I had no energy left. I slumped down in the easy chair. All that labour had helped calm me down: I was ready to make a call. I stretched over, grabbed the phone, and dialled the number that Superintendent David Newlands had given me.

The phone rang and rang but nobody answered. I hung on long enough to wake the dead and after that as well, but to no avail. In the end, I had no choice. I hung up. As I put the receiver down I saw the answerphone's light blinking crazily. I ran the tape back, closed my eyes, and listened to the messages.

There was a succession from Gavin interspersed only by a couple of heavy breathing hang ups. Gavin's messages told a story. His first was a mild 'Sorry I'm so late', his second a concerned 'Where are you?' and his third, an outline of the fact that he was going to bed and would call me in the morning. Which he duly did: the fourth phone call was a rather glacially delivered account of his day's plans which included the fact that he would not be on the end of a phone. 'I'll ring you later,' he said, just before the bleep sounded.

Perhaps the hang-up that followed the fourth message was his. I looked at my watch. Three o'clock. I wondered whether he would call again and why he hadn't ever given me a number so that I could reach him at work. I wondered whether it was really work or something other. Something personal.

I was heavily into censorship, so I shoved that thought

away, too. I turned my suspicions into action, sinking myself into a long hot bath and, eventually, scrubbing myself clean. That done, I stumbled off to bed.

The next thing I knew, I was squinting at my watch. This time it said six o'clock. I was disorientated: I had to look outside to see which six it meant. There were people out in plenty, strolling in the springtime sun: six in the evening then. I felt as if I'd been on a bender: my mouth was dry, as if I had been eating ash. Which reminded my stomach that I hadn't eaten anything for a very long time.

I put some pasta water on to boil and used the best olive oil I could find to make a simple tomato sauce. Three helpings later, just as I was beginning to feel almost human, the phone rang. I picked it up. 'Hello.'

'You're back,' Gavin said.

I liked that. No 'Where the hell have you been?' or 'Were you sleeping with someone else?', just a simple 'You're back', followed by an equally simple, 'Want to meet?'

'Sure,' I said. I yawned. I reckoned I'd managed three hours sleep in the last twenty-four. 'Will you come here?'

'No.' A beat and then: 'It's a lovely day. Why don't we meet somewhere else?'

I stiffened.

He'd gone repetitive: 'It is a lovely evening.'

Yes, of course it was. I reigned in the paranoia. And, anyway, I'd been inside enough. 'How about a park?' I suggested.

His reply came fast. 'Alexandra Palace.' Alexandra Park. An odd choice. 'I'll meet you outside the main hall in an hour,' he said before briskly hanging up.

One hour later, I sat on the pub bench and looked at the

unfolding drama. Their shoulders rubbing, the two chunky white horses heaved an ornate cream-and-white carriage up the hill. Behind them, up high, a man and a woman in eighteenth-century court dress playacted their part to perfection. Their skin was powdered pale ivory, perfectly matched to the cream ruffles around their necks. Dashing hats sat on pompadour wigs as the setting sun sparkled against black court shoes. A growth industry – make-believe weddings for a crisis-ridden country.

I could feel Gavin close beside me. I could smell him too. Funny how quickly someone's odour can grow familiar. I turned to him. 'You know,' I said, 'there's a lot you never told me. Like whether you've been married.'

'I'm not married.' He was quite serious. 'Not any more. Anything else?'

'As a matter of fact there is.' I thought about his choice of Alexandra Park – about as clandestine a public meeting place as could be found – and about his continuing and uncharacteristic reserve. I knew what I was thinking wasn't paranoia. I put it to the test. 'How did you find out that I was arrested?'

He'd been expecting that. 'Page five,' he said, handing over the *Standard* he'd been holding.

I turned to page five. There, somewhere in the middle, an account of my arrest and appearance at the magistrate's court. I scanned it quickly. I didn't read much: the words kept blurring. I gave up, in the end, and tried to hand it back to him.

'Keep it,' he said. His voice was carefully neutral.

Putting the paper down, I took another sip of my bloody Mary. The fairy-tale carriage was drawing closer to the Palm Court steps. Lips framed oval gasps of anticipation

159

as, amongst the confetti-mix of taffeta, diamond paste jewellery and rustling silk, guests skirmished to get a better view.

'There's no way I would ever believe that you've been dealing drugs,' I heard Gavin saying.

Relief washed over me. I turned to look at him.

He wasn't smiling. 'But they found something,' he said.

'Heroin.'

He swallowed.

Out of the fairy-tale carriage stepped the fairy princess. I watched her cappuccino-clad bridesmaids twitter round her overflowing white gauze.

'Happy days,' Gavin murmured.

There was irony in his voice. 'You're a cynic,' I said.

'Perhaps.' His eyes flashed. 'Whereas you,' he said, 'you're still a sucker for the myth aren't you?'

'The myth?' I didn't think we were talking weddings any more.

We weren't. 'Of the lone cowboy,' he said. 'Who rides in to clean up the town. You still believe in that, don't you?'

He'd lost me. I gave an indeterminate shrug.

He changed the subject. 'Who planted the heroin on you?' he said.

'I don't know exactly,' I said. I took a deep breath. 'I think it was a policeman.'

His face was strangely blank. 'That's quite an allegation.'

I turned back to the wedding party. The bride's smile was radiant, lips painted red-brown against a dark olive complexion. As her groom came down to join her, she tossed her raven hair.

Gavin's voice pulled at me. 'Why a policeman?'

'I saw him coming out the kitchen.'

'Do you have any other proof?'

'No.' I didn't bother hiding my irritation. 'I don't have any other proof.'

'It's a dangerous allegation to make. It could get you into trouble.'

My smile turned into a thin grimace. 'You don't think I'm in trouble now?'

'You should tell the police,' Gavin said.

I don't know why I'd hoped for something different. I should have known. Gavin was a policeman. And not just any policeman, a Chief Superintendent. He wasn't only part of the system, he was the system.

"This should be put in the hands of the complaints investigation authorities,' he said. 'Like CIB2.'

Thinking of David Newlands, I nodded unconvincingly.

'Cowboys belong to the good old days, you know,' Gavin said. He reached over and tucked a stray piece of hair behind my ear. 'And you know something else, don't you?'

Yes I knew.

I turned to watch the bride and groom make their way laughingly into the glass-domed Palm Court.

Gavin waited until they were gone before giving it to me straight. 'I can't see you any more,' he said. 'Not until this is cleared up.' He turned and stared into the distance. I did the same; the two of us sat side by side and watched the horizon darken. He spoke eventually. 'If word got round that I was . . . that I was involved with a suspected drug-smuggler, I'd be drummed out of the force.' When he turned to face me, he looked so sad. 'I'm sorry,' he said and, leaning forwards, he kissed me, lightly, on the lips. It came again: 'I'm sorry,' and then he got up and quickly walked away.

I looked down at the steps. The wedding crowd had gone in; I could hear laughter from inside. I didn't move. I thought I would wait until Gavin had left the park.

Chapter
twenty-five

I didn't feel like going home. I didn't know what I felt like. To help me make up my mind, I bought myself another bloody Mary. I didn't want to get drunk – not then I didn't. I sipped slowly watching the light on the top of Canary Wharf's finger blinking on and off at me. I thought about the men in my life, about Gavin and my father. Win one, lose one. Which didn't make me feel any better. I took another sip. That didn't help either. I was shivering from cold. Leaving my drink to one side, I got up and went slowly down the hill.

I did everything slowly. I got into my car and drove, slowly, back to Camden Town. I parked, got out, saw that the car was at too much of an angle, and carefully reparked it. Then I began walking down the road.

I was in no mood for the glitz of a tapas bar. I needed serious drinking. I found it in the back streets of the market where middle-aged men sat, shrouded in smoke, downing pints. I got myself a table in the corner and, dispensing with the tomato juice, bought a vodka straight. And another after that.

By my second drink, the men had stopped sending sideways glances my way. By the third, I had stopped eavesdropping on their conversations. I had also stopped counting drinks. I bought another. At first I drank away the memory of Gavin's face close to mine. After that I moved on to more external things: to the sight of a policeman's triumph when I had been charged with possession of drugs, and to the feeling of being incarcerated, the powerlessness of being unable to get up and walk out. That provoked me into another solitary round.

By the time the bar man called 'Time', I was no longer thinking about anything. I got up. I could stand – that was a plus – and walked, still slowly, to the door. Opening it proved more difficult than I'd anticipated, but one of my fellow drinkers helped me out, pushing what I had been trying to pull.

'Story of my life,' I told him as I stepped into the night. Outside seemed very cold. Unprepared for the contrast, I took in an inadvertent lungful of air. It made me gasp: I spat it out. I stood, looking round.

I was standing in the middle of the pavement of a dirty Camden street. My rental was close by. I knew that. The thing I didn't know was which direction. I thought that going right might bring me to it, but then I changed my mind and opted for a left. I ended up on Camden High Street. I hadn't meant to be there. But what the hell, I didn't feel like going home anyway.

'Not that it is home,' I said. Out loud. Just for the hell of it.

There was a taxi passing by. Its light was up. I love London's black taxis. I raised my hand and hailed it. By dint of sheer concentration, I managed to get in and even to close the door. That's when I ran out of steam.

'Where to?'

Good point, I thought. Where to? I put an index figure in my mouth, sucking on it for inspiration.

I could see the driver's expression changing from boredom to exasperation. 'Where to?'

I didn't have my passport. Which meant that going to an airport was a waste of time. A hand stretched out, reaching for the back door handle. I had to think of somewhere else. I saw him grasp the handle and push down. 'Finsbury Park,' I said. Of course. Brilliant. I gave him Carmen's address and slumped back in my seat.

I wasn't really asleep. I was just day-dreaming. I wanted that understood.

'Sure, darling. Anything you say,' the taxi-driver said. He was grinning. Which meant I must have paid him. 'You want me to give you a hand to the door?'

I said no. Or yes. I don't remember which. I do remember that he got out anyway, and helped me up the stairs. I could have done it on my own. Probably. Just like I could have found Carmen's bell on my own. Maybe with one or two mistakes.

I heard a window opening. I didn't look up. Too much air that way.

She came to get me. She opened the door and took my arm. I was midway between my two supports. I staggered forward and used the wall to stop me from falling. I turned my head. 'Thanks,' I told the taxi-driver. Except I needn't have bothered. I was facing a closed door: he was gone.

I was facing another closed door. A different one. I was upstairs. Somehow.

'Come on, girl.' Carmen was leaning over, hauling at me.

'I'm all right,' I muttered.

She didn't say anything. She heaved again. She was strong, was Carmen. She got me to my feet. And, between gritted teeth, spat out one word: 'Walk.'

She was taking me to bed. What a great idea. I walked. 'I'll sleep in my clothes,' I said.

Carmen led me into the bathroom.

Which was unnecessary. 'I think I'll give my teeth a miss,' I said.

She began pulling my jumper over my head. The neck hole had shrunk. Either that or my nose had got bigger. Either way she couldn't get it off. She didn't try for very long. She pushed me forwards.

'Hey,' I said. 'This isn't . . .'

Sharp needles of cold water stung my face. I cringed, and tried to get away from them. Carmen pushed me back, turning up the water pressure. I flailed around in it, succeeding only in pulling her in with me. We slid down to the floor, both of us cursing as cold water gushed over.

'All right,' I was shouting loudly, 'I get the point.'

She turned off the tap. I staggered out of the shower and grabbed a towel.

I was dressed in a towelling robe, sitting on Carmen's bed, drinking coffee. I took the last sip of the strong brew and put the cup down. Carmen immediately refilled it. I shook my head. 'Not another. Not if you don't want me to be sick.'

'I want you sober,' she said.

'I'm sober. Look.' I got up. 'I can walk a line.' I followed the weave of her striped grey carpet. I ended up by the wall, smiling proudly. 'You see.'

Her face rebuffed my smile. 'What are you going to do now?'

'Sleep,' I said.

'You know what I mean.' She was always tenacious, was Carmen.

166

I leaned against the wall. 'I don't know.' My legs were hurting. I slid my back down, all the way down, until I was sitting on the ground. 'If I had my passport . . .' I said.

Carmen glared at me.

I pulled my legs up and hugged them tight. 'What the hell do you expect me to do?'

'Fight,' she said.

That's what I should have guessed she'd say. Carmen was pure fighter. No matter what happened, she never gave up. I'd been like that. Once. All those years I had battled – to escape my father's tenacious grasp, to make a living in a strange country, to come to terms with life without Sam, to become a war correspondent. But I wasn't like that. Not any longer. I no longer had the energy. 'I'm tired,' I said.

'Good,' was Carmen's instant response. 'Because you're in for a long rest. Ten years, according to Erica, for having that quantity of heroin in your possession.'

'It was planted on me,' I said.

'I know,' Carmen said. 'But if you think that all the jury needs is to look at your honest face and let you off, then you've gone further down your mother's path than I would ever believe you could.'

My mother's path? That was a low dig. I glared at her. 'Just because I got drunk?'

Carmen shrugged. 'That and' – her gaze was relentless – 'and your general air of self-pity.'

Chapter

twenty-six

I was in a corridor of corpses. They lay there, decomposing. I held a handkerchief against my nose. I was the only live person in the corridor, the others had already gone. I knew I should follow them out. But I didn't. I stopped. I couldn't help myself. I stopped and reached down.

There was a sheet covering a body. I reached down and moved it off. I found myself facing James Shaw. His eyes were open. So was his mouth. His skin was thick, like waxen peel. I looked down the length of him. He had no trousers on, only a pair of dirty boxer shorts. His legs were splattered with blood which had leaked down on to a bed of white powder.

As I looked down on it the blood kept spreading, sticky strawberry on a bed of icing sugar. I was filled with horror. I needed to get out. But I couldn't, not yet. I couldn't leave him uncovered, it wasn't respectful. I reached down to grab the sheet.

A rubberized tentacle shot out from James Shaw's arm, grabbing me. I screamed. I was falling. The tentacle was sharp, digging into my flesh. I kept on screaming.

And heard another sound: 'Kate.' It brought me to consciousness.

I was awake. In Carmen's bed. She was by the door. 'Bad dreams?'

I nodded. Although the dream was fading, James Shaw's lifeless eyes seemed still to be watching me. I closed my eyes. When I opened them again, I saw Carmen coming closer. The dream had gone entirely. I sat up. Too quickly – my head lolled awkwardly to one side. It was almost unbearably heavy. I groaned.

Carmen handed me a cup.

The smell was enough to make me gag. The sight, a thick reddened brew, wasn't any better. I held it at arm's length. 'Don't tell me,' I said. 'Famous Caribbean hangover cure.'

'Albanian,' she said.

'Albanian!' I pinched my nose. 'In that case . . .' I tipped the foul concoction down my throat.

It was simultaneously glutinous and incredibly fiery. It repeated on me, taking my breath away. I swallowed down nausea. 'It wasn't really Albanian, was it?' I said.

She shook her head. 'Learnt it when I was living in Brixton. From a Brummie.'

'And the chili pepper?'

'That's the Caribbean bit.'

'Oh.' I swung my legs on to the floor. They seemed to be in working order. 'Where did you sleep?'

'On the couch.' She took the cup. 'What you going to do?'

Her question brought me to earth. I thought about two deaths that might have been preventable. I wondered how much of the responsibility for them was mine. I thought about what Gavin had said. I wondered whether he was right. I looked at Carmen. 'Do you think I'm an unreconstructed loner?' I said.

I should have known better. Carmen merely looked back.

'I'm afraid I'm responsible for a death,' I said.

Carmen's answer came fast. 'People like you always feel responsible,' she said. 'That's your burden.'

That was the Carmen of old, dealing out barely comprehensible homilies. I thought about the years, and about the misunderstanding, that had separated us, and about the reasons that had made me decide, the previous night, to go round to her house. 'Despite my mother,' I said, 'I sometimes think I have more sense drunk than sober.'

She knew what I was saying. She smiled, reached out and touched me on the hand. The contact was soon over; her hand lifted off. Even so, knowing of Carmen's physical reserve, I felt honoured.

She moved away from the emotion fast. 'What are you going to do?'

I stood up. Maybe her brew had worked: my head stayed on. 'I'm going to get even,' I said.

Carmen frowned. 'Ambitious.'

I pushed the door open. 'Yeah, well, if not even, then at least out of this mess.'

I went home and changed. I chose a red skirt, a bright yellow silk shirt, and a matching pair of high-heeled red shoes. I looked in the mirror. Maximum impact, which suited me fine.

I spread butter on a slice of wholemeal toast as I dialled Superintendent Newlands's number. I ate it while the phone rang uninterrupted, just like it had the day before. I hung up and made another slice of toast. Fifteen minutes later, I tried ringing again. And fifteen minutes after that, and then again on the quarter-hour until it was gone eleven.

By that time I was beginning to think that David Newlands was a figment of my imagination. Either that, or the bastard had lied about his number. My hand dropped down.

At that moment I heard a distant, garbled hello. I shouted my own version of a greeting into the receiver. There was a woman on the other end. 'Can I help you?' She sounded as if she'd just run round the block.

'I'd like to speak to Superintendent Newlands,' I said.

I half expected her to say I'd got the wrong number. But no: 'He isn't in.'

Which meant he did exist. 'When can I get him?'

'You can't. He's on leave.'

On leave? 'For how long?'

'A few more days. Can I help?'

I answered with a question of my own. 'When did he go on leave?'

The storm of her heavy breathing had lifted, giving way to edgy mistrust. 'Who is this?'

'I wanted to speak to Superintendent Newlands,' I said, 'of CIB2.'

'He's on leave.' She'd turned glacial on me. 'If you'd just tell me your name, I can transfer you to another officer.'

I put the receiver down.

My head was pounding.

I needed clarity. But for that, I needed to work out what had happened. I started at the beginning, counting it all up in sequence. I got a reported rape, a death of a tramp in custody, a visit from a man who may or may not have been a genuine policeman, a junkie overdosing in a place where he should never have been, a small package of instant death finding its way on to my kitchen shelves – all of them somehow connected. The trouble was, I didn't know how.

Time to use the same tactics that had rooted Janet Morris out: time to stir the pot.

Carmen was working on the Adams family. That left me with two other possible starting points: Valerie, who had lied about Claire and the keys, or Rodney Ellis, who must, surely, know what was going on in his police station. I didn't know which to choose first. I tossed a coin: heads for Valerie, tails for Rodney Ellis. It came down on heads. Which suited me fine. I grabbed my keys and left.

I leaned on Valerie's bell. An effective strategy. 'Who on earth?' I heard, coming over the speaker.

When I told her who, she buzzed me in.

The stairs were concrete lined with dingy maroon vinyl which must have been put on this earth so it would clash with the garish orange walls. Putting my taste buds on hold, I made my way up to the first floor. Valerie was waiting on the landing. She was decked out in a pair of long black shorts with matching black T-shirt. They made her look both sloppy and funereal.

Unexpected anger clutched my throat. 'So this is how your modern activist dresses after a death in the Crisis Centre,' I said.

'It isn't funny, Kate.' Her scowl had distaste and disapproval nicely mixed.

'You're telling me it isn't.' I met her gaze full on. She looked away. 'How about letting me in?' Her move to one side was half hearted: as I walked through I brushed against her. She jumped back.

I was inside. I stood waiting. She shut the door. We were in a small box of a hallway, half of which was occupied by an ageing bicycle. For the first time since I had known her, Valerie looked uneasy.

I raised an eyebrow. 'This way?' I asked, pointing in the direction of what I assumed was the sitting room.

'Y . . . yes . . .' It came out as a stammer. Another first. The Valerie I knew was always brazen in her certainties.

Perhaps her conscience is troubling her, I thought.

I walked into her sitting room. Like the hall, it was all flat, concrete angles. Anyone else might have found ways of softening the whole; Valerie hadn't bothered. Her only concession to furniture was an old armchair opposite the television, a sagging sofa against one wall and a huge unwieldy dark wood desk in the corner. By the sofa was a pile of tabloid newspapers. That was all save for a set of ragged, dirty brown curtains – there for reasons of privacy rather than for any aesthetic considerations. It was a room designed for a monastic life. Except Valerie was no monk. She stood in the doorway, a huge, overblown, awkward, impossible figure of a woman whose expression wavered between rejection and hospitality.

She opted, temporarily, for the latter. 'Tea?'

I shook my head. 'No thanks.'

She blinked. 'I want some.' And left the room.

Losing my temper would get me nowhere. I lowered myself into the armchair.

When she returned, she was carrying water in a glass which was smeared with dirt. She saw me looking at it. She said, 'I didn't want to keep you waiting.'

'That's big of you.' I watched her lowering herself into the sofa. 'Tell me about Melville.'

The hand that brought the water to her lips was shaking. 'Melville?'

'Melville Adams,' I said. 'Your Centre's resident corpse. You haven't forgotten him, have you?'

A moment's silence while she looked as if she were

deciding between emotions. She chose anger. 'How could I have forgotten?' Her hand reached down, picking up the uppermost tabloid. 'Look at this.' She waved it at me, showing a sensationalist front page which allied drugs, death and the Hackney Crisis Centre. 'We were up for a council grant. This morning, because of this' – her fist closed over the paper, scrunching it into a ball – 'we were told we wouldn't get it. The Centre will have to close.' She was yelling now: 'How do you think that makes me feel?'

I raised an eyebrow. 'Not as bad as Melville Adams,' I said.

As moisture squeezed its way out of her eyes, Valerie seemed to crumple. She lowered her head and spoke softly: 'You don't know how upsetting it's been.'

'Oh, but I do,' I said.

A tear splashed down on to her knee. 'I found him. He looked so . . . so . . . so dead.'

I felt like squeezing my hands round her soft neck. 'How did he get in?'

She swallowed. 'I don't know.'

'The door was locked?'

Her nod came courtesy of more tears. 'It always is. We're very careful about security.'

'Sure you are,' I said. 'That's why you left the keys in an open envelope for your friend Moira.'

She wiped her eyes with the back of her hand. 'Not Moira,' she said. 'Mona. Mona Phillips.'

Mona? Moira? I must have misread Valerie's undisciplined scrawl. Not that it mattered. 'And what exactly did Mona Phillips do with the keys?

'There weren't any.' There was something not quite right about Valerie's voice. 'She . . . Mona . . . swears to it.' She sounded as if she was trying to convince herself.

I glared at her. 'Who is this Mona?'

'A friend.'

'A friend and lover?'

'No.' She was quite definite. 'Just a friend.'

I didn't bother concealing my scepticism. 'Oh yeah?'

'She's just a friend.' Valerie's chin quivered.

I didn't want to start another crying jag. 'How can I get hold of her?' I asked.

'You can't.' She blinked. 'She's on holiday.'

Great, I thought: she's probably eloped with Superintendent Newlands.

Apparently not. 'She took a tent,' Valerie said, 'and headed off to Scotland. She's like that, is Mona. She likes to travel. She always carries her passport with her. For all I know, she went abroad. You never know when she'll be back.'

She was talking too fast, too much. She had to be lying. 'Come on, Valerie,' I said. 'Don't give me the runaround.'

'I'm not.' As she tried to meet my gaze, her eyes filled with liquid. She dropped her head. 'I'm not.' Sobs shook her massive frame.

Her neck was so tempting. My fingers twitched. I held them in check – but only just. I had to get out of there. Either that, or risk getting charged for a murder that I would have committed.

I stood. 'One more thing.' The face that looked up was streaked with tears. 'Where can I get hold of your colleague Claire?'

'There is no Claire.' Valerie's voice was soft.

'She phoned me.'

She shook her head. 'Ask anybody,' she said. 'There's no Claire in the Collective.' Her doe eyes latched on to mine.

175

To stop myself from hitting her, I went over to the mantel-piece. 'I promise you, Kate. I wouldn't lie.'

That was rich. I knew she was lying about something. The only problem was, I didn't know what.

'It's the truth,' she said.

My hand went out, sweeping across the array of objects that lined the mantelpiece. Amongst them was a small blue vase. When it hit the floor, it broke. I heard Valerie gasp. I looked at her. She was halfway out of her seat. When I turned to face her, she sank back down.

I couldn't take her. Not any longer. I had to go. I walked past her, to the door. 'I'll be back,' I said, as I pulled it open.

Chapter
twenty-seven

I stood outside the building thinking about what Valerie had told me. What I had thought upstairs came back to me: I knew that amongst the pathetic strands of information she'd fed me was a lie. And even if I didn't know what it was I was pretty sure what had motivated it. With Valerie it was obvious – a woman. A woman who was more important than I was. A client that Valerie was intent on saving.

I'd have to find out who. I walked to a phone box and got hold of Carmen. I'd already asked her to check out the Adams family, now I told her I had another job for her.

She listened in silence. When I had finished, all she said was, 'Tonight?'

''Fraid so,' I said. 'And if that doesn't work, we try something else tomorrow night. And if that doesn't work . . .'

'The night after that. Yeah. I got the message. Nine o'clock. I'll be there.'

I hung up and walked back to my car. All this tracking down of phone boxes was using up valuable shoe leather. If things went on like this, I'd have to get a mobile. Which got me wondering: Gavin was always on the move, why didn't he have one? I cut the thought right off. I wasn't going to think of Gavin. I got into my car and drove to Homerton.

It's not that the sun never shines on Homerton. It's more that when it does, Homerton's limitless supply of desolation absorbs the warmth. I stopped, for the third time, by the same tawdry row of shops. I got out of my car. What before had been a bright spring day seemed, with each footstep, to be turning insipid grey. Nothing changes, I thought, as I walked down the line-up.

I was wrong. Something had changed. The apples had gone, and metal shutters now sealed the fruiterer's glass front from view. I needed to speak to him. I saw a door leading to the flat above the shop. I went up to it. No bell. I used my fist.

I heard footsteps and then something creaking but the door stayed shut. I raised my hand.

A voice came from behind. 'What do you want?'

I turned to find that there was now a small opening in the metal shutters. I could see the fruiterer's head peeping out of it. He was frowning, trying to work out who I was. I went a step closer.

He placed me then. And panicked. He pawed at the metal, trying to push it closed. I was faster than him. I shot my hand into the narrowing gap. As one sharp edge went to join the other, both bit into my flesh. I shouted out, telling him to stop.

He hadn't meant to hurt me. He let go of the makeshift door. As I reclaimed and started rubbing my hand, he stepped out. 'Lady,' he said. 'I'm sorry. I'm sorry, lady.'

'It's all right.' I tried a smile.

It brought me back to square one. As he skipped back into the shop, there was no mistaking the fear in his eyes.

'I'm not going to hurt you,' I said. By the way the door started closing, I knew he didn't believe me. I thrust my foot out – it at least was protected by a shoe.

He stopped pushing. 'Please.' His voice was a high-pitched whine. 'I had no option. They asked me questions. I had no choice. Please, lady.'

I programmed my voice to be reassuring. 'I'm not here because you identified me. I just want to ask you something.'

'I know nothing.' He bent down. His thin hand started scrabbling at my shoe, trying to shove it out of the way. 'You have no right.'

'Don't worry,' I said. 'I'll go. But only if you tell me something.'

He looked at me. 'Anything. Please, lady, but be fast.'

'You told the police I was at the Centre.'

'I had to, didn't I?' They showed me your photograph. I had to tell them.'

'So you told them you'd seen me twice?'

'That's right.' He'd swung from anxiety to defiance. 'I told them the truth.' It was a passing change, he was getting nervous again. 'I had to.'

I nodded, of course he had to, and moved on. 'Was the key still in the envelope when you gave it to Valerie's friend?'

He pushed the door. 'I don't know. I already told the police. I am a neighbour. I am asked to give an envelope, I give it. I do not look inside. I know nothing of keys. Nothing. Now go away.'

'Did you give the envelope to a woman?'

'Yes, yes. To a woman.' He'd stopped worrying about hurting me: his full weight was bearing down. 'You said one question. If you don't go away now, I'll call the police.' He sounded determined.

I pulled my foot back. The door clanged shut. I could almost feel him breathing behind his metal barrier, waiting for me to go. There was no point in hanging round. I did as I had promised. I went away – but only as far as the Crisis Centre. The police had done their job – quickly: there was no sign that the place had recently been the site of a murder.

I rang the bell. Third time lucky. I heard footsteps and the door was opened by a woman in her late twenties, whose frizzy brown hair framed a wan face. She blew smoke at me. Not deliberately – when I winced she waved her hand about, trying to disperse it. 'You here for the workshop?'

Workshop? Why not? I nodded.

'We've had to move it,' she said. 'But don't worry, it's not gone far. Hold on a mo', I'll get you a map.' She clicked her way back into the office. She wasn't gone long. When she returned she was holding a duplicated map which she handed on to me. 'There.' One chipped red fingernail tapped a huge pencil cross. 'Ring the bottom bell. I'm sorry we had to change it. We've had some trouble.'

I was all concerned sympathy. 'Trouble?'

'It's fine now.' She smiled. 'Nothing to worry about.'

'Oh good.' My smile was vaguely perturbed. 'Is Claire all right?'

She looked uncertain. 'Claire?'

'The Claire who works here.'

Her bewilderment was utterly convincing. 'There's no Claire here.' She took another long, deep drag on her cigarette. 'You don't mean Cathy, do you?'

I shifted to the right, giving her inhaling room. 'No,' I said. 'Not Cathy. Oh well.' I served up another smile as I thought that Valerie had been telling the truth – at least about Claire. 'Mona must have given me the wrong name,' I said.

'Mona?' A stream of dove-grey smoke issued from each nostril. 'Mona Phillips?'

I nodded.

Her brow creased up. 'Hasn't Mona gone travelling?'

'That's right,' I said. 'She has gone travelling. Camping. She told me about Claire before she left. At least I think it was Claire. Maybe I misheard her.'

'Oh, I doubt it.' She drew so hard on the cigarette she reached its filter. She threw the stub on to the pavement. 'Mona has wanderlust where her brains should be. She's quite capable of calling Cathy Claire. Anyway, she's not here.' She laughed. 'Cathy, I mean. You want me to give her a message?'

'Thanks,' I said. 'But no thanks. I'll catch her later.'

'Right. Well.' She was concentrating on lighting up another cigarette. Her disposable lighter was up too high. Its flame erupted, missing the tobacco but almost hitting her cheek. 'Shit,' she muttered. She shoved the lighter in her pocket. Now she needed another source of fire. She looked at me, said, 'Enjoy the workshop,' stepped inside and closed the door.

In contrast to Homerton, Richmond was the kind of place where the sun loved shining. It was on full beam as I drew up outside the Ellises house.

I walked up the crazy paving and pressed the white bell. I waited while the chimes died away. Through the door's glass top half, I thought I saw a shadow shift. I kept on waiting.

Nothing happened. I pressed my face against the glass. It was thick and burglar proof, and it distorted vision, but I was sure I had seen something move. I lifted up the letter-box flap. 'Mrs Ellis?' I looked through the opening.

I could see her stockinged legs, pressed against the hallway wall.

'Frances?' I called. The legs moved, heading my way. I straightened up. She turned the catch and pulled sharply, opening the door. Then she stood there, staring at me.

I had come early so I would catch her alone, so I might get her talking, but if my intention had been to make her crack, I was too late. She seemed to have managed it all by herself. Unless of course she always looked like a crazy when she wasn't expecting visitors.

When I'd last visited her she had been perfectly coiffed. Now her blonde hair was all mussed up. There were loose strands of it splayed out on the shoulders of her black cardigan, too many for natural fall out. I wondered whether she could have been pulling it out.

I didn't have to wonder long. Her hand moved up to the crown of her head and plucked sharply at a single hair. She brought it down. 'Got it,' she said, turning her fingers, scrutinizing the hair. Her eyes were bloodshot. If I'd been able to smell any alcohol, I would have assumed I'd caught her in the middle of a heavy drinking bout.

'You can always tell the grey ones,' she said. 'They're so much coarser than the others.' She opened her fingers. We both stood watching as the hair floated through a ray of sunlight. When it was no longer visible, she produced a sharp titter that contained no joy. She glanced at me. 'I'm sure grey hairs don't cause you any sleepless nights,' she said. 'At least not yet.' She laughed again.

Her laughter made me shiver. She was staring at me, now, in a mixed-up kind of way, as if she were trying to work out who I was. I thought of introducing myself.

I didn't need to. 'But I'm forgetting my manners, Miss Baeier,' she said. 'Good of you to drop by.' She stepped back. 'Do, please, come on in.'

Chapter

twenty-eight

The house was as immaculate as it had been before. We went the same way as well, to the sitting room. I was struck again by its dull lifelessness. I looked out of the window. Such a contrast: in the glistening sunshine the massed banks of spring flowers looked almost psychedelic.

Frances's cough drew me back inside. She was standing awkwardly as if she didn't know what she was supposed to do. Seeing me looking at her, she opted for speech. 'You must think I'm a vain woman.'

She'd lost me. 'Vain?'

'Rattling on about grey hair. Silly, especially since I don't mind ageing. In truth, I despise women who spend their energy trying to stay young. It's so undignified, don't you think?'

I hunched my shoulder in a manner that could have meant either yes or no.

She didn't care which it was. 'I rather welcome old age,' she said. 'The end of struggling. The end of . . .' She couldn't manage the end of the sentence. She was too busy battling with her face. Her jaw muscles were drawn in, making of her mouth a thin line of control. Her upper lip was pulled down tight, ensuring a perfect seal. But the rest of her face betrayed her: it seemed to be crumpling in on itself. She looked as if she was going to cry. In fact I could have sworn that she was crying, except that she was swallowing down her tears as fast as they surfaced.

'I've come at a bad time,' I said.

'No.' She shook her head. 'Not at all.' She seemed literally to be drawing herself together. Her willpower was impressive. When next she spoke, she sounded positively chirpy. 'You have more questions for me?'

I nodded. 'A few.'

She looked at the sofa, but didn't go to it. She didn't do anything. My eyes were drawn back to the garden. I resisted its pull. It was too much of a contrast: all that vibrant life outside and the emptiness within. I turned instead and gazed at the mahogany sideboard, scanning the Ellis family photos. There was nothing there I hadn't seen before. My vision started flickering, my morning's hangover beginning to repeat on me.

'Heritage of the dead,' I heard. I turned and looked at her. Her gaze was focused on the sideboard. She spoke: 'Mementos of a life.' Her voice was as dry as parchment. 'Although the real moments are never captured on film, are they?'

I didn't know how much more of this elliptical nonsense I could take. 'Moments like what?'

In place of an answer, I got a vague medley of widely spaced words. Words like: 'Oh . . . you know . . . never meant to . . .' until she had faltered her way into silence.

I needed grounding. I cleared my throat. 'Why don't we sit down?'

'Good idea.' This time when her gaze touched the sofa her body followed through. She went over to it. 'Please,' she said, gesturing.

I settled down opposite her.

Her hands folded themselves neatly in her lap, changing her, momentarily, into a model interviewee. 'What did you want to know?'

'Just some background details I forgot to ask the other day.' I took a notebook I didn't need out of my bag. 'If you don't mind.'

'No. I don't mind.' She made a valiant attempt to rally her face into a smile. Only her mouth responded. The rest of her features – her eyes, her cheeks, her chin – were all deathly still. 'Go ahead,' she said, bravely, as if she were facing a firing squad.

I shot off my first salvo. 'Does Rodney bring his work home?'

She frowned. 'His paperwork?'

'Not exactly,' I said. 'What I meant was, does he ever discuss his work with you? Do you, for example, help him with problems with the men?'

'The men,' she echoed musingly, as if it were a new word to her.

I tried to coax her back on course. 'It must be quite a responsibility, having to manage such a big team.'

'Oh no.' She was all sparkling animation now. 'It's no problem for him. After all, he rose up through the ranks himself. The men respect him for that. And he sets such a wonderful example. He's a good friend, you know.'

I didn't know what that had to do with anything but I knew there was no point asking. She had phased out on me again. She turned her wrist and looked at a watch that wasn't there. Then her eyes started flitting zanily round the room, trying to find something safe to latch on to. They went full circle and ended up on me. 'Would you like a drink?'

I seemed to have caught her repetition compulsion. 'A drink?'

'Whisky. Gin. Wine. Beer. Anything?'

The back of my skull was pushing at the front. I wondered whether a drink would make it better. I thought I might give it a try: 'If you're having one . . .'

She shook her head. 'No. Not for me. I don't drink. Thanks anyway,' she said politely, as if she were the guest.

She was right: things were topsy-turvy enough without adding alcohol. 'Then not for me either,' I said.

She shot me another of her half-smiles. I revised my earlier impression. Her eyes weren't dead: they were unbearably sad. I looked down at my notebook.

'It's such a lovely day,' she said. 'Why don't we go outside?'

Great idea. I needed air. I looked up eagerly. 'Sure.' I stood, and so did she. But she didn't go where I'd expected, to the glass door that led to the garden. Instead she made her way to the sideboard. I saw why when she opened a small silver box and took out a key. I stepped to one side, giving her room.

Once again I had misjudged her movements. She picked up one of the silver-framed photographs. It was the wedding snap, the one of her and Rodney, standing smiling, their arms lovingly entwined. For a moment, as she stared at it, her eyes seemed to lose focus. That battle for control was on again. A muscle in her cheek jumped. She stilled it with a hand. She blinked and, eventually, spoke. 'Wasn't he handsome?'

I registered the use of the past tense.

She'd strayed off again into territory that excluded me. Her mouth etched out its boundaries. 'Poor Rodney. It wasn't his fault. He was a good husband. It's just that . . . that I . . .' The tears were brimming as she put the photo down.

I felt so sorry for her. I wanted to reach out.

She shivered and re-entered the present. 'Shall we?' she said brightly. She walked briskly past me and over to the door. 'There.' She unlocked it and pushed it open. 'That's better, isn't it?'

I stepped out, hoping it would be better. And, at least for the first five minutes, it was. Although she had told me the garden was Rodney's domain, she was very knowledgeable. She toured me round its borders, pointing out the special, the difficult, the new. I listened with only half a brain: the other half was busy working out how I was going to get her back on to the subject of her husband.

'What's this?' she muttered. We were by a particularly dazzling orange azalea. She bent down and reached her hand into its midst. When she straightened up again, she was holding a long hoe. 'Not like Rodney to leave it out here.' She frowned.

That was my cue. 'Perhaps he's particularly distracted at work,' I suggested.

I needn't have bothered. Her brief foray into reality was over. 'I hate anniversaries,' she said. And then: 'It's tomorrow, you know.'

No, I didn't know. 'Which is it?' I asked, trying to remember what she'd told me. 'The twenty-sixth? Twenty-seventh?'

She'd gone back to disconnected speech. 'That's right. Twenty ... yes ... I don't know ... no one counts.' Variations on the theme of ageing, I thought. She moved quickly on. 'Miss Baeier,' she said. 'Do you believe in fate?'

I shrugged, thinking that I was prepared to believe in anything as long as I could get some sense out of her.

She was a one-woman conversational black hole. She'd moved on to wildlife. 'Take this snail,' she said. Following her gaze, I saw an ordinary garden snail slithering past her foot. 'Look at it. The slimy thing, minding its own business, doing whatever it is that snails like to do. But now . . .' She placed the blade of the hoe down on its shell. A pause and then she dug down, slicing the snail in two. She pushed down again so that, by the time she had lifted the hoe, fragments of shell were mixed in amongst the glutinous remains.

I looked away.

'It's dead,' I heard her saying. And then, in an inquiring voice: 'Was that its fate, do you think?' Her voice compelled me to look back. She smiled. 'Was it pre-ordained that this particular snail would be trailing along at this particular moment in time, trying to sneak past you and me? And is that why it was necessary for you to drop by so as to fulfil the snail's destiny? Were you the catalyst it needed? Did you, in fact, make it happen?' She bent down suddenly and scooped up the mess. As she inspected its remains, lying in her palm, her face was grotesque in its anguish. She shook her head. 'No,' she said. 'That's all silly. It's not your fault. I did it.' The tears that she had so effectively kept at bay were now welling.

'It's only a snail,' I said as gently as I could.

'Yes.' She bit her lip. 'It was only a snail.' She flicked the mess out of her hand which she then used to wipe her face. When she eventually spoke, her voice was hard. 'I think you had better go.' A pause before she added, more quietly: 'I'm sorry.'

I was also sorry. Sorry that I'd come at such a bad time, and sorry because I had no idea what was troubling her or what I could do to help. 'Goodbye,' I said. It came out a neglected whisper. She gave no sign that she had heard me. 'I'll see myself out.' I walked slowly over the immaculate lawn, heading for the back door. As I went I told myself that yes, I was sorry. But I had to recognize that I was feeling something else more dominant: relief. Relief that, unlike Frances Ellis, I could get up and walk away.

Chapter
twenty-nine

I sat in my car, trying to wipe away the memory of the gloop in Frances Ellis's hand. Forget it, I told myself, it was only a snail. But since it wasn't the snail that was bothering me, that didn't really help.

My stomach hurt. I decided I was hungry.

The image of snail replayed itself.

I wasn't hungry. Which was just as well, since I also wasn't going anywhere. I was staying in my car until either Rodney came home from work or it was time to meet Carmen.

I didn't want to be too obvious. I drove a few doors down. I parked, switched off the engine, leaned back, put my feet up on the dashboard, adjusted the mirror and set myself to wait.

I was there for almost three hours. If I'd loitered in Camden Town that long, the whole world would have passed me. In Richmond things were different, the world lay snug behind its white lace curtains. There was some movement of course – a woman hurrying her small brown chow around the block, a child bouncing a ball, another woman paying a visit on a neighbour – but for the main, my only excitement was the sight of an occasional puff of cherry blossom floating down to earth.

Around six, things started hotting up. The menfolk, having laid their sharpened pencils down, sloped homewards. I watched cars drawing up, keys turning, young children launching themselves at trousered legs, doors closing. I thought of Frances Ellis alone with her ripening melancholy. I wondered how long she'd been struggling to keep it at bay.

By seven, the air was pungent with the smell of roasting meat. Snail or no snail, I was starving. I found a piece of chewing gum and tried to pretend it was a three-course meal.

At seven-thirty Rodney Ellis drew up. I junked the gum and scrambled out. I needn't have bothered hurrying. He was so methodical. He took a briefcase from the back seat, checked he hadn't left anything, clicked the car door closed, waited for the thunk of his central locking to sound and only then began walking towards his house, by which time I was within easy hailing distance. 'Chief Superintendent.'

His glance, which had started out as inquiring, changed to astonishment. 'Miss Baeier. What on earth are you doing here?'

I stood in front of him, blocking his forward motion. 'I want to talk to you.'

He was still bewildered. 'Couldn't you have come to the station?'

'Not my favourite place, I'm afraid.'

He was too distracted to register what that meant. His glance veered sideways to his house and then back to me. 'Did you . . .?' He couldn't manage the end of the sentence. I thought I knew why but I didn't know how to help him out. He found the courage somewhere. His eyes veered off again, their return journey punctuated by speech: 'Did you talk to my wife?'

I nodded. 'I tried to.'

'Was she . . . was she . . .?'

She was all of that. I nodded again.

He winced. His eyes were softened by grief, his face overtaken by the same, involuntary spasm of pain that I had witnessed the night of the fire.

'Has she been this way for long?' I asked.

'It comes,' he said. 'And . . .'

And goes is what he meant to say. He didn't. He caught my look of sympathy. He didn't like it. He went on the attack. If looks could kill, my blood would have already been smeared over the unspoiled pavement. 'Miss Baeier, there's a charge pending against you, is there not?'

As if he didn't know. 'Something like that.'

'Don't you understand that coming here can only make your situation worse?' Our conversation, his body language said, was terminated. He launched himself forwards.

My voice restrained him. 'What else am I supposed to do? Sit nicely in my flat waiting for your men to plant more drugs on me?'

I expected bluster, loud denials followed by threats. I got none of that. He stopped. He looked at me, his face blank. I thought maybe he hadn't understood.

He'd understood all right. 'That's quite an accusation.' His voice was softer than I had ever heard it. 'Why on earth would any of my officers do that?'

'Beats me,' I said. 'That's why I'm here. I thought you might know.'

That was all he needed. He went into hyperdrive, stepping up close. 'You've taken advantage of your position of trust as a journalist by coming here,' he said, taking advantage of his superior height. 'Making wild accusations.'

'I need to know what's going on,' I said.

He wasn't listening. His eyes had swivelled away from

me, drawn back to the house. I looked, too, and saw that his wife had emerged. She'd upped the melodrama, wringing her hands Lady Macbeth style. Her husband glared at me. 'Go. Now. Before you find yourself facing a further charge of obstructing the course of justice.' His face was inches from mine. 'Or something worse.'

Worse? I thought. Like being accused of Melville Adams's death? I didn't say it. Given the ferocity of Rodney Ellis's expression, I didn't think it would be wise.

'Go.' He was angry enough to be on the verge of getting physical.

Which is the last thing I wanted. I went.

I went in search of food. I ended up in a Greek restaurant whose meze was almost good enough to wipe out the sour taste left by witnessing the Ellis double act. It had continued without my help. After I'd reached my car, I'd watched the show in my rear-view mirror. Although I couldn't hear what they were saying, there was no missing the meaning of the exchange. He was using the anger I had provoked against her. He had his hand on her elbow and was pushing her forwards. She flailed about in protest, but it was pretty token. Having witnessed the set of her jaw before she offed the snail, I was sure she could have done better if she'd tried. I was also sure that she was a woman who had long ago given up trying.

Not my problem. I left. And satisfied my hunger with tiny parcels of wafer-wrapped goat's cheese, garlic-infused raita, aubergines in sour cream and bitter black olives. By the time I finished, the world looked benign again. Just right for a spot of breaking and entering, I thought as I called the waiter for my bill.

*

Carmen was in her battered old VW beetle, her eyes fixed on Valerie's front door. I opened the passenger door. 'You rang her?'

'Yup.'

I climbed in. 'What did you say?'

'That I was an heiress who was thinking of donating to the Crisis Centre. She was almost salivating. Said the council had just dumped them.' Carmen didn't take her eyes off the door. 'We're supposed to meet outside Highbury and Islington tube. At nine.'

I glanced at my watch. 'She's going to be late.'

'Unless she booked a taxi,' Carmen said.

'Don't be silly,' I said in my most patronizing voice. 'She never takes taxis.'

Carmen must have been keeping an eye on her mirror. A black cab passed slowly by, rolled to a halt and beeped its horn. Carmen didn't stop to gloat. 'Watch yourself.' She got out of the car.

I lowered myself down until I was on the floor. With my eyes peeping above the dashboard I watched Carmen walking over to Valerie's front door. Her timing was impeccable. As she raised her hand, keys visible, to the iron gate, Valerie opened it. Carmen smiled. She said something. Valerie smiled back. And kindly held the door for Carmen to pass through.

I lowered my head. I kept it low as I heard Valerie's footsteps coming closer. Her footsteps stopped: a door closed. The diesel engine went from ticking into shudder – the cab taking off. I counted to ten, then I was up and out of the car, walking swiftly to the door that Carmen held open. 'First floor,' I said, pulling the gate shut.

We were by Valerie's flat. Carmen held out one expectant hand. I slapped a credit card into it. She turned and bent to her work. It took her all of two minutes to slip the Yale. Valerie, who counselled women on how to avoid attack, should have known better. Not that I was complaining. We were in.

'How long do you think before she realizes no one's going to pitch up?' Carmen said.

'Twenty minutes?' I shrugged. 'Thirty at the outside?'

'Instructions?'

'Anything,' I said. 'Anything personal. Or odd. Or suspicious.'

There were two bedrooms in the flat. I chose the lived-in one, Carmen took the other. The room I was in was an undecorated concrete box. The bed was a mattress on the floor and the cupboard an exposed hanging rail supplemented by a chest of drawers. There was nothing on the rail except clothes. I went to the chest. I grabbed hold of the bottom drawer handle. And froze as I remembered the sight of a policeman thumbing through my underwear.

I heard something crashing in the next door room and Carmen's barely suppressed 'Damn'. I shook myself into motion. I was no policeman. And besides, Valerie had lied to me. I wrenched the drawer open, rifled quickly through and then moved on to the three above. I shouldn't have bothered. All I found were layers of neatly folded clean clothes. I shut the top drawer.

'Nothing in the other room,' Carmen said. She was standing in the doorway. 'Should I do the living room?'

I nodded and went to the only item I hadn't yet inspected: a huge old steamer trunk. I undid the latch and pushed up the metal lid.

Inside was a treasure trove of documents all meticulously stacked. There were old leaflets, filed in date order; posters, neatly folded; letters, bunched together by correspondent;

minutes of meetings for organizations long defunct; and a crowd of photo albums. There was no way I could get through even a fraction of this lot before Valerie gave up on her phantom heiress. I picked up one of the photo albums and started flitting through.

I had meant to only glance at it. I ended up entranced. I was looking at an album that dated back to sometime in the seventies, at a time when my and Valerie's circles had intersected. Page after page was packed with images of people that I had also once known. My eyes slowly scanned the collection. When I got to the end of the album, I was hooked: I picked up the next one in the sequence. This one was equally fascinating. I even found a photo of me amongst a group of earnest young things. I must have been in my early twenties then. I looked so very young. And angry. I wondered whether I still had that much anger left.

'Kate.' Carmen was back in the doorway, frowning mightily. 'We don't have much time left.'

She was right. I'd been looking at the albums longer than I knew. Our half-hour was almost up. I closed the album. 'Anything?'

Carmen shook her head. 'Bills on the desk, all current ones. Nothing else. Nothing personal. Not even an address book. She must carry it with her. Nothing in the kitchen. Definitely no drugs. And no –'

She stopped abruptly. I knew why. I'd heard it too. The sound of a taxi drawing up outside. I went over to the window and peered out. In time to see Valerie emerge. 'It's her.' I moved fast. I shoved the photo albums back into the trunk and closed the lid. 'Let's go.'

We ran towards the front door. But as Carmen reached it, I changed my mind and peeled off.

'Kate!'

'In a moment.' I was by the desk, sifting through the bills that Carmen had said were there. I heard her voice again, more urgent now: '*Kate.*' I found what I was looking for. I shoved it in my pocket. Then I ran through the living room and out of the door that Carmen was holding open.

Chapter
thirty

'. . . so I was checking to see that you're all right.'
Gavin said. 'Give me a ring if you have the time.' That was
it. Message over. Nothing else. Not even a goodbye. I
picked up the phone. I had the time. I dialled his number.
Nobody answered. Not that I minded: I didn't know what
there was to say. I hung up.

I went into the kitchen and plugged in the kettle. While
it was doing its thing, I unfolded the bill I'd stolen from
Valerie's front room. There were four sheets in all. Thank
God for modern communication systems. I scanned the
lists. They showed that Valerie certainly liked to chat.
There were so many numbers that if I tried to get hold of
all of them, I'd be trying for a very long time. I went down
carefully, picking out the ones she most frequently dialled.
Out of these, I chose the longest-lasting calls.

I ended up with three possibilities. No time like the
present: I dialled the first. A mere two rings and I'd made
connection. The voice on the other end was familiar: it
belonged to the woman I had met at the Rape Crisis
Centre. I knew she wasn't the one I wanted. 'Sorry. Wrong
number,' I said and hung up.

I dripped water over coffee grounds as I dialled the
second number. Wednesday at ten-fifteen was obviously

the time to contact Valerie's friends – this one also answered double quick. I asked to speak to Mona, she told me pleasantly that there was no Mona there.

'I'm sorry,' I said quickly. 'I meant Claire.'

When she said, 'Claire's in bed,' her voice was sharp enough to stop me asking whether Claire could possibly be disturbed. I asked whether I could get her in the morning. 'She'll be at school then,' the woman said, following through with a wary: 'Who is this?'

School? I did a double-take. 'I'm sorry to ring you so late,' I said. 'The name's Carmen. Carmen Thompson. I'm a casting agent who saw your daughter in a school play. I'm looking for a girl about her age for a TV serial. I thought she might fit the part. But first I need to know: exactly how old is she?'

'She's eight.' Her voice had reverted to its agreeable beginnings. 'She'll be nine in July. Is that the right age?'

I didn't think so. 'I'm afraid not,' I said. 'Sorry to bother you.' And hung up.

I crossed that number off my list. Only one more to go. I was on a roll. I punched the number in. This time, however, there was no instant gratification – the line was engaged. I put the receiver down. The coffee was ready: I transferred it to a cup. As I added milk I saw the *Standard*, the one that Gavin had given me, lying close. Thinking I hadn't read the article which had made me infamous, I started turning pages.

Before I found the piece on me, my glance was attracted by another. 'WPC LEFT FOR DEAD', was its headline. Since the police were rapidly becoming my obsession, I started reading through.

It was a small report, three paragraphs long. From the first it had me riveted: '*WPC Janet Morris is recovering in*

St Bartholomew's hospital after an attack by a group of young thugs', it said. I stared at the print telling myself it could have been a coincidence, another Janet Morris walking the Islington beat. Somehow I doubted it. I read on. What followed was a description of a knife attack which had left Janet bleeding in the gutter where her colleagues had eventually found her. The wounds were said to be extensive, although the hospital's carefully coded *'resting comfortably'* meant she was in no danger.

Poor Janet Morris: she didn't have much luck. And poor me. She wasn't my favourite interviewee but I knew I would have to go and see her, if only to satisfy my curiosity. Heavy day ahead – one funeral, one hospital visit – and I needed sleep. But first I needed completion. I hit the phone's redial button and made it do the work. Third time lucky. I heard another woman's voice. Since I'd found a Claire already, I asked for Mona.

'No, it's Mo –' She stopped.

She didn't need to go on. I knew which 'Mo' she was. 'Moira?' I asked.

'Yes?'

'My name's Kate Baeier.'

'Oh.' That's all she said. That one tiny 'Oh' which told me plenty.

'We've been playing tag with a key, you and I,' I said. 'You know the key I mean?'

A long silence and then an intensely quiet: 'Where did you get my number? Did . . . did . . .'

'No,' I said. 'Valerie didn't. She wouldn't. She's far too loyal – to some at least. She lied about you, which is why I'm ringing.'

The silence stretched on for so long, I thought she'd hung up. But no, I heard a man's voice shouting, *'Moira.'*

'Have you still got the key?' I asked.

'I can't talk about it.' She was whispering. 'Not now. I have to go.'

I heard it again: a peremptory 'Moira' followed by her nervously shouted 'I'll be with you in a moment, darling.' Then, whispering: 'I'm sorry, I have to go.'

'Course you do,' I said. I steeled myself and went for the low blow. 'Before your husband asks who's on the phone. Does he know you visit the Crisis Centre?' She didn't speak. I had to go on. 'I could tell him,' I said. More silence. I wasn't sure what I'd do if she called my bluff.

She didn't. She came up, finally, with a resigned: 'What do you want?'

'To meet you. To find out what happened.'

The man's 'What the fuck are you up to?' mixed with Moira's strangled 'I can't.'

'Yes, you can,' I said. 'You don't even have to leave the house. Give me your address and I'll drop by tomorrow morning.'

'No.' Her whisper was desperate. 'I can't. 'Please . . .' Her voice cracked.

I wondered for a moment what I was doing, bullying unhappily married women. Then I remembered the photograph of Melville Adams, rigid in death. I hardened my voice. 'If you don't agree to meet,' I said, 'I will keep on ringing you. And one of these days I'll get your husband. And when I get him . . .'

There was no need to finesse the threat. 'All right. All right. I'll meet you at ten-thirty. At Suttons, on the High Street.'

'The High Street?'

'In Southgate,' she said and slammed the phone down.

Progress at last. I looked at my watch. Ten minutes at

the outside, I told myself. Taking my coffee to the living room, I turned the answerphone back on. Then I sat, in the midst of the wreckage, waiting.

It was only seven minutes before the phone started ringing. I didn't bother picking up. I sat as the machine went through its motions. A click and then I heard her voice: 'Kate. It's Valerie.' I got up. 'What the hell do you think you're doing, scaring Moira like that?' I walked to the door. Valerie's voice pursued me, telling me what Moira's husband would do to her if he ever found out she'd gone to the Centre and ending with her fervent hope that I felt thoroughly guilty.

The hope was lost on me. I didn't feel guilty. She'd lied to me. I'd nailed the lie. Now all I wanted was sleep.

Valerie phoned again, three times in all: once in the middle of the night and twice in the morning. Each time her hysteria level had escalated. I didn't care. I brushed my teeth to the sound of her berating me, and left the flat to it as well. I got into my car.

I drove north and kept on driving. It took me about half an hour before I reached Southgate. The High Street was easy to find, a main road where squat buildings were continually interrupted by rows of shops. I drove slowly, reading off the names. By the third block I struck lucky. Between signs pointing to a toy shop and a haberdashery was an ornately written 'Suttons'. I pulled in.

It turned out to be one of those bakery come tea shops that litter north London. A bell tinkled, announcing my arrival. I went past the glass cage in which pastries lay oozing crimson jam and imitation cream, and into its dingy back room. The tables were narrow and Formica-covered while the seats were fused brown plastic of that kind that is impossible to budge. I chose one with a view out and squeezed my way in. When the waitress came, I ordered coffee. In reply to her urgings to try a pastry as well, I patted my stomach. That seemed to satisfy her. She went away, returning soon with one of those fused filter efforts which produce a brown liquid that may or may not have once been related to coffee.

I nursed it for about fifteen minutes. In that time women, any one of whom could have been the mysterious Moira, came and went. Few stayed longer than it took to buy a loaf of puffy white bread, or a selection of pastries. None as much as glanced in my direction. Every time the door opened, I half expected to see the avenging Valerie.

The bell tinkled again. I looked up. Another in a long line of neatly turned out suburban housewives entered. This one was taller than the others, but dressed to blend. I caught her eye. She looked away. I decided it wasn't her.

I was wrong. She came up to me. 'Miss Baeier?'

I said, 'Moira.' And then: 'Moira what?'

Her face showed she wasn't going to say. She slid into the seat opposite. She put her handbag on the table and laid her hand over its gold clasp. Her nails were cut so short I thought she must be a biter. She certainly had the teeth for it – big and white in a full mouth. Her other features – a broad forehead, a straight nose, two large deep-set eyes – were oversized to match. She was, I reckoned, in her mid thirties; I could have been wrong. She had that tired, worn-out look of someone who was ageing badly.

Her eyes wandered in every direction save mine. They landed on the waitress, who came over. Moira ordered tea and a chocolate éclair. While she was waiting for it, she kept busy. She opened the bag, took out a powder compact, checked her face, used a tissue to blot her lips, put both back and clicked the clasp shut.

Her tea arrived. She poured out a cup and lifted it. She didn't drink. She spoke. 'I don't have the key.'

I kept my mouth shut.

When she put her cup down, her eyes went with it. I had the feeling she was the kind of person who retreated in the face of speech. I held my tongue.

'I lost it,' she said.

'You *what?*' My voice was so loud it turned heads.

She waited for the interest to subside. When finally she spoke again, she was quiet enough for two. 'I'm sorry. I didn't want to get you into any trouble. I asked Valerie to lie for me. The fruiterer had told me that another woman looked in the envelope so we agreed Valerie would tell the police it must have been that stranger who took the key. I'm sorry. We didn't know it was you.'

I raised one sceptical eyebrow. 'You mean it's OK to throw the blame around as long as you don't know the name of the person you're implicating?'

She looked away.

'The key,' I prompted.

'I thought I put it in my bag but when I looked for it, it wasn't there. I'm sorry.' Tears welled, softening her hazel eyes.

I felt no sympathy. 'Did you use the key?'

'Yes.' She started fiddling with her handbag's clasp.

I put my hand down, roughly, on top of hers. 'Why don't we leave the face repair till later?' She jerked away, which suited me. 'You went inside?' She nodded. 'And found the corpse?'

'No,' she said. 'There was nothing.' I could barely hear her. 'Nothing unusual.' Her voice cracked. 'All I did was phone Valerie. She told me she was busy. I didn't stay. I left.' She looked at me. 'I locked the door when I left.'

Great, I thought. 'And then you went and lost the key.'

Her tears came spilling down. 'I know you don't believe me, but I did.' She was crying hard. 'I'm sorry. I couldn't go to the police. I can't. You see, my husband . . .'

She didn't say what he would do. She didn't have to. There was no missing the great purple bruises on the underside of her arm. I wondered why she stayed with the monster who had done this to her. Wasn't my idea of a love match. But then I wasn't her idea of a tea companion. She was on her feet.

I put my thoughts into words. 'Why don't you leave him?'

'He'd kill me.' She shivered. Her eyes filled with tears. 'I'm sorry. I didn't want to get you into trouble. But I don't know anything. I swear I don't.' She barged her way out of the plastic constraint. But stopped then, turned, reached over.

Her expression was so intense, I thought she was going to hit me.

She didn't. She grabbed her uneaten chocolate éclair and stuffed as much of it as she could into her mouth. And then, turning on her heels, she fled.

Chapter
thirty-one

I paid and went after her. She was too involved with her own misery, and too busy disposing of the éclair, to notice. Her throat was working overtime trying to pulp the pastry small enough to swallow. She managed it eventually, one great gulp and it was gone. There was fake cream smearing her top lip. She didn't seem to care.

Her walk was jerky, as if she had trained her legs to take smaller steps than were natural. She went to a mid-blue Fiesta. Keys were not her forte – she had them in her hand, ready to open up, but before she made contact they dropped into the gutter.

While she fumbled for them, I made it to my car. She was terribly slow. I had started up the engine, and got myself into a position to pull out, all before she was ready. She pulled out, so jerkily she almost hit the car in front. I watched until another car had inserted itself between us, then I got in the queue.

It was easy following her. She drove slowly, signalling her moves well before she made them. She went up the road a while and then turned left. The buffer car went too. So did I. But at the next turn, our procession was severed. While Moira went right, the car behind her continued on. The roads were too empty to follow her without camouflage.

I stopped and waited. By the time I reckoned she would have put enough distance between us, she was halfway up the road, inching forward. I rounded the corner and stopped again. Good move. I saw her indicator flashing.

She turned into a driveway. I waited some more. She got out of the car and walked to her house. I inched slowly along the road. The houses were all the same, semi-detached couples standing together in a sea of driveway and orderly gardens. They had gables up top, and leaded windows in the front – thirties mock Tudor stranded on a long flat road. Hers was no different from all the others. I drove past, seeing her car, and her door, firmly closed. I noted down the number and then I got going.

I went to St Bartholomew's Hospital. I parked my car, and saw, in the rear-view mirror, a Saab the same black as Gavin's rounding the corner. I swivelled round – too late. The car had gone. I sat for a moment, berating myself for the Pavlovian reaction. Black Saabs were such a frequent sight in London that if I kept reacting like that, I would soon have developed an ugly twitch.

It had been that way after Sam had died. I would catch myself thinking that the man three paces ahead, or there on a bridge, or disappearing round the corner was Sam. But this – this was even more ridiculous. I'd known Gavin for a tiny fraction of the time I'd been with Sam. And besides, Gavin wasn't dead.

He might as well be, he was so unreachable, went a small, bitter thought in the back of my head.

I got out of the car, fed the rapacious meter and walked towards the hospital. The porter's lodge was snuggled in the corner of its majestic gates. I asked for Janet Morris and was given cheerful, complicated instructions on how to get to her ward. The courtyard was crowded with bustling staff and limping patients and lined by grand red brick. I kept on going, up a ramp and into a cavernous hall. The place was sub-divided into clinics – a demonic vision of a health service in decay. The staff had sealed themselves in behind closed doors, while the patients were slumped on plastic chairs waiting for that magic moment when their names would be called. Behind them, paint was peeling off the walls, and I couldn't swear that the occasional brown-red stain wasn't dried blood.

I skipped the lift queue and went to the grand staircase. As I climbed progressively higher, the sour odour of over-cooked vegetables engulfed me. I went faster, arriving in Janet Morris's ward to find an orderly spooning the mush on to clean white plates. She didn't even look up as I went by. I prowled the corridor, checking out nameplates. Nobody came to ask me what I was doing.

Janet's name was typed below another's at the end of the corridor. I pushed the glass door open. The room, painted a dirty gloss cream, contained two beds, one of which was screened by faded floral curtains. As I came in, the middle-aged woman in the first bed looked up. Seeing me her anticipatory smile died; she went back to thumbing her way through her glossy magazine. Meanwhile I walked over to the curtained enclosure.

I found a gap and pushed through. There was a woman lying on the bed. 'Janet Morris?' My voice came out hospital soft. She was curled up on her side, her back to me. When she gave no sign that she had heard, I said her name again.

Still she didn't move. 'I don't want anything to eat,' she said.

'I don't blame you.' I laid my care package of assorted fruits on the tray which floated freestyle above her knees.

There was a plastic chair on the other side of the curtain. I pulled it closer and sat down.

She turned, slowly, as if each tiny movement hurt. Her chest was bandaged, so was her right arm and her skull. Her face was almost unrecognizable: her jaw was wired, one cheek was bloated, the other darkened by bruises, one eye was closed, a jagged line of aubergine-coloured cross-stitching etched in where its eyebrow had once been.

Someone had enjoyed what he'd done to her. My stomach dipped. I hoped desperately that my persistence in searching her out wasn't responsible.

Her one good eye was facing me. She didn't seem to recognize me, not at first. Her bloodshot pupil kept on looking.

'It's Kate Baeier,' I said. 'We met in Islington. Do you remember?'

She blinked, then spat out through cracked lips: 'You've got a nerve.'

She stretched out one heavily bandaged hand. I had a pretty good idea where it was heading. I was having a day of it, I had already emotionally savaged a battered woman. Now, pushing conscience away, I moved the bell out of Valerie's grasp. 'What happened?' I asked.

She grappled for it but after her hand kept clutching air, she lay back exhausted. '*You* happened. *You* came along. *You* did this.' She beat out a rhythm with each successive '*You*'.

Which is what I'd feared she'd say. But I couldn't let it stop me. I leaned forwards. 'The paper said you were attacked by thugs.'

Her good eye closed. 'Before they surrounded me, I called for urgent assistance,' she said. *Urgent assistance* was the police distress call that was always given priority. Not in her case though. 'Nobody came.' She opened her eye again, reliving the moment when she had been left alone and hurt. Her eye filled with tears.

She blinked and glared, one-eyed, at me: 'Because of you. After you accosted me in the street that rumour started up again. You spread it. You . . .' So much venom accompanied her words that she started coughing. Slowly at first, but then she gained momentum. She was lying flat, and couldn't get her breath. Great, silent, spasmodic gulps racked her body. She was choking. There was less pink now in her face and more blue. I stopped worrying about whether she would break if I touched her and started concentrating on the possibility of a full-scale cardiac arrest. I leaned over and hauled her upright. Her arms flailed out, hitting me in the face. But at least she was half sitting, taking in great lungfuls of air. I poured out some water and brought the glass up to her mouth. Her hand closed over mine as she pulled it closer. She started drinking, so fast I thought she was going to choke again. I tugged the glass away, waiting until her chest had stopped heaving, and then handed the glass back.

The blue tinge of her lips was remixing itself with pink. I sat down. She drank some more. When finally she spoke her voice was dull. 'I want you to go.'

I resisted the something inside of me which said that I'd done enough harm and I should do what she wanted. 'I will go,' I said, 'after you tell me what rumour.'

She made as if to turn. No longer so concerned about hurting her, I put my arms on hers, restraining her. She had no strength. She sighed. 'You told my new partner that I accused my colleagues in Hackney of rape.'

'I did *what*?' It came out involuntarily loud.

She was back to her rhythmic yous. 'You told him. You

must have.' Then she diversified. 'After I met you, that's when the rumours started. Nobody believed me. Not after it got round. That's why they didn't come when I was being attacked. Anybody who falsely accuses a brother officer of rape is fair game.'

I registered the *falsely*. 'But you phoned the Crisis Centre.'

'I did not.' It came out as a squeal, which escalated. 'I told you. I wasn't raped.'

As she shouted it out again, I heard footsteps and the swish of starch. The curtains parted. 'What's going on here?'

'I want her out.' Janet Morris was leaning forwards, yelling fit to bust. 'Now.' A hand touched on my shoulder. 'And take your fucking fruit.' Her bandaged hand shot out, knocking the bag I'd brought hard, sending grapes and kiwi fruit shooting all over the bed.

'Don't worry,' the nurse said. She lowered her voice. 'You should go now. But don't give up. Just give her time. She'll start allowing visitors in soon, I'm sure.' And then, as I got up, she sat down on the bed, took one of Janet's hands in hers and started making nice-nice in a soothing voice.

I walked towards the door. The occupant of the other bed had laid her magazine aside and was watching me, her curiosity undisguised. I took no notice. I was too busy reassembling my thoughts.

Janet blamed me for what had happened, perhaps with reason. I couldn't be sure. But one thing I did know, no matter what she thought, our positions weren't so different. We'd both been set up, and in the same way: poison through the phone. Someone had rung the Crisis Centre pretending to be a distressed Janet Morris, just like they had rung me, first as Janet, and then as the non-existent Claire. I was willing to bet that all three calls had been made with the intention of trapping Janet and me. What I didn't know was why.

Chapter
thirty-two

Despite Melville Adams's inexplicable presence in the Crisis Centre, Erica Cadogan had phoned to tell me that the police had decided there was no case to investigate. Nobody cared much about the death of a black junkie – not even enough to try and implicate me. Nobody, that is, except his family. Carmen had discovered that his body had been released for burial, and she had also found out where the service was to be held.

The church was a simple white building set off the road; standing between two low-rise office blocks, it was dwarfed by both. A banner above its door proclaimed how much Jesus loves us. The sound issuing from the open door showed how much the people inside believed it.

I was late. I hurried in.

The place was packed with people decked out in their Sunday best. As they swayed to the sound of a gospel choir, satins, artificial silks, and stiff-brimmed hats swayed with them. Their scent was of strong soap and sweet perfume.

I didn't have to stand for long. A man got up. 'Welcome, sister.' He handed me a prayer book and showed me to a pew.

A line of worshippers shuffled together to give me space. There was an air of celebration, not of grief. I sat and listened as the white-bibbed singers tried pulling heaven closer. Their voices soared, making the church seem much bigger than it was. And then, with one balletic wave of the conductor's hand, the sound ceased. As shouts of 'Amen' ricocheted around the church, a preacher slowly made his way to the dais.

I craned my neck, searching out Melville's brother, the one I'd seen at the police station. He was in the front pew. His legs, clad in expensive black linen trousers, stretched out into the aisle as if he were planning to trip up anyone with the temerity to walk past. There was a woman beside him who could only have been his mother. Her face had a bruised look about it, the kind that said the death of her son was only one in a long line of tragedies. While the preacher took his time preparing himself, her gaze roved blankly over the congregation. Her face was made impassive by grief and the patches beneath her eyes were almost black on that coffee-brown skin. When the preacher cleared his throat, she set herself back to staring straight ahead.

'Our brother, Melville Adams,' the preacher said, 'took a wrong turn. But that is over now. Now he can go to Jesus.' He had one of those voices that can possess a room. He played it to full effect, letting it rise and fall with his rhetoric. It didn't work entirely – at least not on me. As I heard him praising God, I could think only of the awkward tilt of Melville's head, and of the pool of vomit beside him.

The rest of the congregation filled the place with righteous agreement, especially when the preacher turned his attention to Melville's mother, Blanche Adams, and to the struggle that she had waged to bring her boys up properly in a world of sin. I watched while he was talking of her; she had lowered her head and covered her eyes with her hands, frozen in misery. He had quite a mouth on him, the preacher, he kept on going for half an hour. When he had finished the choir rose and sang to the glory of their God until it was time to go.

At the cemetery, we walked, single file, to the graveside. A substantial section of the congregation had stayed to see this final laying to earth of Melville Adams. I looked at his mother, Blanche. The way she held herself erect was a heartbreaker, as was the bleak acceptance in her eyes: I knew that the size of the crowd was a tribute to her.

The younger people present, the ones Melville's age, looked blankly ahead as if they couldn't quite comprehend what was happening. I wondered whether he would have called any of them his friends. I wondered whether the demands of heroin left any room for friendship.

I caught Blanche Adams's eye. She nodded politely before looking down. A hand, her son's hand, drew her aside. They went a little distance away and stood enduring a string of murmured condolences as the file of mourners shuffled past. Blanche Adams handled it all majestically, squeezing a shoulder here, a hand there, smiling at pleasantries, hugging the overcome. Her son Lloyd was less at ease. Towering above her, he wore a distant, angry look designed to scare off all but the most courageous of passers-by.

I counted myself amongst them. I had to be – that's why I was there. As the people in front of me moved forward, I stood, waiting. He looked everywhere but at me. I remembered his name: 'Lloyd?' He ignored that. I told him mine. Again with no result. 'I saw you at Parchment Road police station,' I said.

That got his attention. His head jerked downwards. 'What you talking about?' His gaze was quite ferocious.

'The night Melville was held,' I said. 'I was there. I saw you arguing with the desk sergeant. What's his name?'

'Reynolds,' Lloyd Adams said. 'Sergeant Gary Reynolds.'

'Know him well, do you?'

Lloyd's shrug told me nothing. He was interested enough, however, to put distance between himself and his mother; I followed. I wouldn't have described the way he was looking at me as friendly. 'What were you doing at the station?' His voice was harsh.

'I was looking for somebody, and I overheard what you told Reynolds. You mentioned the Richton estate.' His eyes were hard, boring into my face. 'What did you mean?' I asked.

He shrugged. 'I don't remember.'

I didn't believe him. 'You implied Reynolds was involved in some form of graft.'

'Yeah?' He yawned. Straight in my face. Deliberately. 'They're all on the make, aren't they?'

His jutting jaw told me that this line of questioning wasn't going to get me anywhere. I tried another: 'Any idea how your brother got into the Crisis Centre?'

He narrowed his eyes. 'How the fuck should I know? Must have broken in. That would be his style, stealing from penniless dykes. He always was a loser.'

I told myself that he had buried his brother, that I should have felt sorry for him. I didn't. I felt annoyed. 'You think the police might have anything to do with Melville's death?' I said.

'The police!' A short burst of contemptuous laughter. 'You crazy? Why would they do that?'

'Because he saw something – that night in the police station?'

'Saw something?' His head swooped down, moving in on my space. 'Like what?'

'Like something about the way James Shaw died.'

His face was so close to mine his eyes were bulging. 'James who?'

'The tramp,' I said.

'Oh.' I'd lost his interest. He shifted back. 'Him. Nah. Melville was so wrecked that night he wouldn't have even noticed if Charles had been shafting Camilla on his bunk.'

'He didn't say anything to you?' Lloyd didn't bother answering, he just looked at me. I tried another question. 'You know who his dealer was?'

That got a reaction. A 'What the fuck does that mean?' shouted out. Heads turned; he didn't care. He was shouting mad, closing in on me: 'What the fuck you trying to say? Who the fuck are you anyway? You drugs squad?' His finger was out, prodding my chest.

I backed away. 'I'm not drugs squad.'

The finger was glistening as it came again. 'Who the fuck are you? Hey? Tell me that.' This time the manicured finger headed for my throat. I stepped back. I suspected I was perilously close to Melville Adams's open grave. With Lloyd still bearing down on me, I decided not to check. 'You think because you have a white skin you can come here asking questions. You think –' He never finished telling me what I thought. When a hand landed on his shoulder, he whirled round, fists raised. To find himself facing the preacher.

'Come, Lloyd, your mother needs you,' the preacher said.

I turned. My apprehension was well founded: I was six inches from Melville's grave. I circumvented it, putting distance between myself and Lloyd. I needn't have bothered. He went meekly where the preacher led him. I looked beyond the grave. Eyes which had been fixed on me were rapidly dropped as conversation started up again.

I'd done enough for one funeral. I began walking to my car. Halfway there I heard the sound of heavy footsteps. I looked back to find Blanche Adams coming after me. I stopped and waited for her.

She took a moment, after she had reached me, to catch her breath. Then she said, 'I wanted to thank you for paying your respects to Melville.'

I nodded. 'I'm sorry about his death.'

She gave no sign she'd even heard the platitude. 'I also wanted to apologize for Lloyd's behaviour. Life is hard for the youth. They have hatred in their hearts.' Her face was full of pain. 'Melville was possessed by hatred,' she said. She swallowed. 'But Melville turned it inwards.'

She didn't say what form Lloyd's hatred took. She didn't need to. I looked at her and thought again what had occurred to me in the church, that she had known much grief. If she saw me looking she didn't make a sign. She was too caught up in something she had to say. 'When Melville first started with drugs, I tried to understand. But when he began stealing from me, his mother, I was filled with anger. I told him I would not tolerate his behaviour. I turned my back on him. And now he's gone.' She said it in a matter-of-fact way as if she'd been practising it. 'What do you think?' She seemed genuinely to be asking me. 'Do you think we learn from loss and grief?'

I didn't know whether I had. I held my tongue.

'I've learnt something,' she said. 'I've learnt that, no matter what our loved ones do, we must keep our hearts open. We must give them a second chance, and another chance after that.' Her hand reached out and touched me, briefly, on the cheek. 'Because if we don't,' she said, 'they die alone.'

She turned then, and started walking back. I didn't try to stop her. I watched her going, wondering why she'd chosen to unburden herself to me. I couldn't find an answer. All I knew was that she had touched me.

Chapter
thirty-three

It was raining hard. The windscreen wipers were beating rhythmically, clearing the glass long enough to show me that the traffic jam ahead showed no signs of lifting. I sat, staring straight ahead. Faces came floating in and out of my mind, men's faces: Gavin's, James Shaw's, Melville Adams's. And a voice: Blanche Adams's voice, repeating what she had said.

I didn't want to be sitting there, waiting for the car in front to move. There was a pub on the left. Pulling in, I ran through the rain and into its premises. I ordered a double whisky. I was going for effect, I didn't care which kind it was. I got a Bells. I lifted it up.

But I didn't really want it. I put the glass down, got off the stool, went to my car and drove west, to where my father was staying.

There was no-one waiting on the fifth floor. I rang the bell. The door was opened by one of my father's henchmen. He was wearing dark glasses and having trouble with his expression. He stood to one side as I entered. He took me to my father's room, rapped briefly on the door and, without waiting for an answer, opened up and waved me in.

I walked in on a meeting. There was a set of high-backed

winged armchairs arranged in a circle, each with a man ensconced. They hadn't been expecting me. Five pasty faces turned to glare; five pairs of flabby lips grimaced.

The sixth man in the circle was my father. He looked up, sharply. Fury darkened his face, a familiar kind of fury that brought old memories hurtling back. In that moment I wondered what the hell I was doing there, but I was wrong. Suddenly he wasn't angry, he was smiling. 'Kate! What a wonderful surprise.' He pushed himself up, leaned on his stick and started making his way to me, tossing over his shoulder an explanatory '*Minha filha*', which set his companions off into understanding nods.

'Kate.' He kissed me, briefly, on each cheek. 'You should have told me you were planning to visit. I would have put off my meeting.'

I felt like a gatecrasher at a party that I had never even wanted to attend. I wanted out. 'I can come back,' I said.

He wasn't having that. He linked his arm to mine. 'Please, wait for me. We will be finished in no time.' Throwing a holding message over his shoulder, he steered me out of the room and into a small adjoining chamber. 'I will send in refreshments,' he said.

He left, closing the door behind him, and I sat down on the small white sofa which was one of the room's few pieces of furniture. I picked up a magazine which lay on an elegant glass side table, but I couldn't concentrate on it. I was too disturbed by the murmuring of men's voices which filtered through the walls.

I couldn't hear what they were saying. But I didn't need to know the details, the generalities were too familiar. It had been just like this throughout my childhood – me trying to go about my business while in the background powerful men plotted things I didn't like. Decades later nothing had changed, my father was the same. I threw the magazine down and watched it sliding over the glass and on to the white carpet.

At which point, the door was opened. Not refreshments but Zetu, accompanied by a silver-haired, bow-tied Englishman. I stood up. I could smell the acrid tang of stale tobacco as Zetu hugged me. 'I'm so pleased you came.' He introduced the other man as my father's doctor, Dr Abrahams.

Abrahams was all teeth and smiles and sloppy handshakes – the kind that said his bedside manner cost plenty. He dealt with me as an intimate. 'Just a routine check-up today,' he said. 'Your father's doing very well. Although' – his voice grew sombre – 'as I'm sure you know, he is a very sick man.'

I nodded, and at the same time berated myself for ever having doubted it. And I thought that Blanche Adams was right: after death there were no second chances. That small, suspicious voice, the one that I'd carried from my childhood right up to the present day, was momentarily stilled.

I heard raised voices and the traffic of moving doors: meeting over. My father entered, apologizing for having kept me waiting. His doctor cleared his throat. I could see my father's eyes moving from him back to me, not wanting to put me off again, but I didn't want to stay. Not any longer. I didn't need to. 'I have to go anyway,' I said. 'I only came to tell you that I am prepared to give my consent to the sale.'

Out of the corner of my eyes, I saw Zetu beaming. My father's response was much more restrained: he simply nodded. Which is all I had expected. My father never overplayed his hand. Part of me felt grateful that at least this hadn't changed.

'Stay,' he said. 'The doctor won't be long. We can share a meal together afterwards.'

What I had done had been radical enough for one day. I shook my head and told him I had another date. Then I got out and waited for the lift, shivering. It's only hunger, I told myself. I hadn't eaten all day. But I knew that was wrong. I was shaken by an undercurrent of something deeper – by the knowledge of the risk I was taking by trusting my father again.

The lift arrived. I thought of Melville's mother, and tried to push the fear aside.

I ate in a Japanese restaurant, a huge plate of tekka and kapa maki accompanied by cold Udon noodles. Maybe it had been hunger: by the time I'd polished that lot off, the shakes had gone. I drove back to my flat.

It was as it had been when I had left it, clean save for the living room. I ignored the blinking answerphone light and started clearing up the room, but not for long. It had been a long day. I went to bed.

I surfaced to the sound of a ringing phone. I reached out for it. The light filtering through the curtains told me it was already morning. My mouth was dry, my forehead bathed in sweat. I was grateful to whoever it was on the other end who had wrenched me from my uneasy sleep.

It was Charles, as blunt as ever. 'Kate? She topped herself.'

'She?' I licked my lips

'Frances,' he said. 'Frances Ellis.'

'What?' I sat up.

'Pills,' he said. 'Came over the wire yesterday. Left you a message. There's so much press interest, the coroner's

224

sitting this morning. He'll adjourn, of course, to give them time to do the business, but be a love and pop over there and check it out, will you? I'll fax the details. Hope we don't have to spike the article. Ring me later.' He didn't wait for me to say anything, he hung up.

I put the receiver down. I saw Frances as she had been when I had left her: standing stranded in the precise beauty of her husband's garden, her hand despoiled by another death. I was stunned. Not that she had killed herself – she had certainly been depressed enough for that – but that she had done it the day after I had gone to see her.

I was waiting amongst a scrum of newspapermen when Rodney Ellis pitched up. He acted like no one else existed. He got out of the car and walked up the steps, his concentration taken up entirely putting one foot down in front of the other. His face was pale and stiff. I wondered whether he had found her. I thought he must have, for I had the sense that Frances had precious few visitors. I couldn't imagine how that must feel: coming across the corpse of a wife who was so unhappy she had killed herself.

I didn't want to think of it. My eyes moved to the squarely built young man by Rodney's side. Their son, I assumed, who was swallowing compulsively, as if that way he could make unpalatable reality disappear. He was accompanied by a frightened woman who had to be his wife. As a camera bulb flashed, she put her hand on his arm and then quickly took it off as if she'd committed some awful social gaffe.

They went inside. I went in after them, to see a knot of people gathered round Rodney. I recognized several of them, including my least favourite of the Parchment Road boys in blue – Brian Turner – as well as Sergeant Harrison, the policeman who had allowed me a phone call the night I'd been arrested.

Just my luck – Brian Turner spotted me. He scowled and pushed his way to Rodney Ellis. They shifted to the side and when Turner whispered something into Ellis's ear, I thought I must have been the subject.

But maybe not. Rodney Ellis didn't even look my way. He shook his head instead and said something back; by the way his brows were knitted together, it wasn't something nice. Ellis suddenly turned away and went over to his son. It was time. The group of intimates moved through the ornate wooden doors. I stood and watched them go. I didn't follow. I knew that what went on inside would be mere first-round formalities. So I hung about. A standard journalistic ploy – some of my best scoops happened when I'd had time to hang round, trawling for nothing in particular.

This time, too. I landed not a big fish, but the one I wanted – Rodney Ellis's daughter-in-law. She slipped out guiltily and made for the front door. By the grey tinge to her skin, I thought I knew what she was after.

I was right. I found her at the bottom of the steps, lighting up. I let her get in one deep drag before calling out: 'Mrs Ellis?'

Caught. The cigarette was shoved behind her.

'Coroner's courts make me want to smoke as well,' I said.

She relaxed, brought out the cigarette and pulled on it. It was invitation enough; I went to join her. I told her my name. I also told her that I had done some work for Rodney. She didn't ask what kind of work. I told her I had spent some time with Frances. Which prompted her to offer me a fag.

I wanted to get to know her. I took the cigarette. 'A terrible thing,' I said as she lit it for me.

'Yes.' Her face was sombre. 'Mark was devastated.'

'Mark?'

She looked suspiciously my way. 'My husband,' she said. 'Mark Ellis.'

My quick smile pushed away a niggling memory. 'Of course,' I said. 'Mark. I realize now that Frances always referred to him as "my son".'

The mention of the recently deceased made Mrs Ellis junior stub out her cigarette, which meant I could follow suit. For a moment we stood in silent contemplation of the pavement.

'Well.' She glanced awkwardly at me. She had few social graces — cocktail parties must have been a torture. 'I should go.'

I nodded to show her she probably should, but I delayed her with words: 'This can't be easy on you.'

Her eyes filled with grateful tears. 'It isn't.' But she wasn't used to being the centre of attraction: blinking, she substituted self-sacrifice for pain. 'Not as hard as it is for Mark,' she said. 'Or Rodney, of course.'

'Awful that Frances felt she had to kill herself on their anniversary,' I said.

'Anniversary?' Confusion clouded her wan face. 'You don't mean their wedding anniversary?'

I thought I did. I nodded.

'But that was months ago,' she said. 'In January. Their silver. We gave them a big party. Frances seemed happy then. Or at least as happy as Frances could get.'

I thought rapidly about other anniversaries. I could only come up with one. 'Was it Mark's birthday?'

She was appalled. 'Of course not. Frances would never

have killed herself on his birthday.' Suspicion worked its way across her face. 'You didn't know her very well, did you?'

'Not really.'

Her eyes half closed in calculation.

I jumped in quick. 'As a matter of fact,' I said, 'I need to know lots more. I'm going to write the obituary, you see.'

She was gullible, this one. She didn't ask what obituary. Instead, she looked quickly at her watch. Panic flitted across her face. 'I told Mark five minutes. He'll be worrying about me. I'm sorry.' She took the cigarettes out of her pocket and buried them in her bag. She saw me watching her. 'He thinks I've given up,' she said, twitching her nose upwards, in a gesture Mark probably found adorable. She hoisted her bag on to her shoulder. 'I tell you what,' she said. 'Take down my number. In case you need to know more.'

I thanked her and took it down.

'Sorry,' she said. 'Must dash.' And then, without another word, she went.

Chapter
thirty-four

I went in the opposite direction, making for my car. I was thinking about the new lead I had to chase and how I would go about it when a heavy hand landed on my shoulder. I turned abruptly. Sergeant Tom Harrison was standing close behind me. Mark Ellis's wife must have sent him after me, I thought. I took a step backwards.

He was a big man in his mid-fifties, tall with the broad shoulders and flat stomach of somebody who had worked out all his life. Seeing me looking him up and down, he smiled. A confident man as well, I thought, one who was used to getting his own way. I glowered at the memory of the imprint of his hand.

His smile hardened, the skin around his eyes crinkling upwards. 'I'm sorry,' he said, 'I didn't mean to frighten you. I did call you.'

Under the pressure of my silence, his smile stretched thin. But he didn't lose it altogether: he was still trying to be nice. I stood, remembering my first impressions of him as a benevolent father, someone who could be trusted. Not that I was an expert on fathers, of course. Still . . . I raised an eyebrow and broke the quiet. 'Something you wanted to say?'

His bull neck moved, swivelling round so he could look

in the direction of the coroner's court. Nothing there. He looked back at me. 'I came to warn you,' he said. 'You're treading on dangerous ground. You might get hurt.'

His soft voice and his omnipresent smile both said that the warning was given in friendship. But I wasn't about to trust a policeman – any policeman – after what had happened to me. I stilled my tongue and looked at him, waiting for more.

He gave me some. 'I know you're no dealer,' he said.

I nodded.

'It's all a misunderstanding,' he continued.

'Sure.' My laughter was short lived and devoid of humour. 'The kind of misunderstanding that will buy me ten years in jail.'

His brown eyes were sympathetic. 'I know you must be scared, but don't worry. It will all be sorted,' he said, his voice full of the kind of confidence I wanted to believe. 'I'm on your side, if you ever need help.' He looked rapidly around again, checking if it was safe. It seemed to be. He reached into his pocket and pulled out a card. 'My pager number. It'll get me any time.'

I took the card, stowing it away in my bag.

'Be careful,' he said. He made as if to walk away.

It was my turn to use restraining hand action. I touched his sleeve. 'Have you known Rodney Ellis long?'

'Long?' He looked surprised. 'Yes.' It came out more a question than a confirmation.

I ignored that in favour of a question of my own: 'Was the day Frances killed herself some kind of anniversary?' I could have sworn that, behind his negative shake of his head, was a flash of startled recognition. I tried to push it out of him. 'Something in Rodney's past? Or in Frances's?'

I'd lost him. In one of his circular searching sweeps he'd

spotted what I could now see: the Ellis party spilling out from the court. Rodney, flanked on either side by son and daughter-in-law, was already halfway to a waiting car. But what concerned Tom Harrison was not his boss. It was another man – Sergeant Brian Turner – who was standing on the stairs, staring straight at us. Tom Harrison was already on the move, muttering, 'Ring me if you need me,' in a barely audible aside.

I let him go, watching as his powerful legs carried him away. I wasn't the only one watching. Brian Turner's eyes were half closed as he concentrated on each of Tom Harrison's extended strides. But when Tom Harrison veered away, heading for the car park behind the court, Brian Turner chose another target: me. His head went up. He stared at me, with a vehemence that bridged the gap between us. I could almost feel his hatred. The fact that I didn't understand why it was directed at me only made the feeling worse.

He kept on looking. He was playing chicken. I played, too, trying to show him I wasn't scared. It didn't work. His look was so intense I couldn't help myself, I looked away. Only for a second but it was long enough to give him the victory he craved. I looked back in time to see a smug smile cross his face, and then he began walking down the steps towards a waiting police car.

I had played his game and lost. I turned away and moved slowly to my car. The motion helped the strength return to my muscles. As I got into the car a flash – Brian Turner's eyes locking with mine – hit me again. I shook the image away. I couldn't afford to let myself dwell on it, not any more. Despite Tom Harrison's reassuring words, I couldn't stop now. I had something else I had to do.

I was convinced that what had happened to Janet Morris

and to me, to Melville Adams and perhaps even James Shaw, was somehow connected to Frances Ellis's distress. The only way I could unravel the whole was to start at one end and move forwards, which meant I needed to track down what anniversary it was that had driven Frances so deep into despair.

It didn't take me long to find the notes I'd made when I'd first interviewed Rodney Ellis. I remembered that meeting clearly. It had been an awkward half an hour's worth of questioning a man who was either too shy or too taciturn to reply with much more than the occasional monosyllabic grunt. Not the stuff of riveting profiles, which is why I had tried to unbend him by taking him through his entire career. I've had more luck mellowing fake camembert, but I had at least managed to find out where each of his posts had been. Precisely what I needed now.

I flicked through the pages of my notebook, going backwards until I got to the start of his career. Frances had talked about the anniversary being twenty-something. I looked at what Rodney had told me. I took the five years, 1970 to 1975. If that didn't work, I knew I'd have to take the five years before that. In the meantime, however, I was relieved to see that in the first half of the seventies, Rodney Ellis had been based at two adjoining police stations in Croydon, first as a sergeant and then as an inspector. Which meant I had to hit the Croydon libraries.

It was my week for suburbia. I worked my way through south-east London, down the Blackwall Tunnel, heading towards Gatwick airport. Before I got there, I hit Croydon. The place was all squares and right angles. I drove past rows and rows of red-brick houses where even the flowers stood up to attention, through a huge square office complex made of sixties concrete and finally to the local library.

It was calm and quiet inside. A librarian, relaxed in a way that she would never be in inner London, set me up with a microfiche machine and spools of ancient *Croydon Chronicle*.

Twenty-something, Frances had said. I started with the spool for 1975, threading it on and winding through. Black and white print pulsated by in one blurred mass. Every now and then I slowed it down and checked the date. When I got to May I went much more slowly, finding the date twenty years ago which Frances had commemorated by killing herself. I didn't know what I was looking for, so I had to read the lot.

I started with a less than riveting front page lead about Mrs Betty Braithwaite, a 'plucky' pensioner looking for her long-lost beau, and graduated from that to an advert for Croydon's best-baby competition. Between those two items was all human variety – burglaries, births, marriages, school fêtes, convictions – the stuff of life that turns a keen cub reporter into an ace cynic. No mention of Rodney or Frances Ellis or of any of their associates, however.

Since I know how long it takes to put a local rag to bed, I scrolled on to the next week and to the week after that. All I learnt was that Betty Braithwaite had been contacted by four friends she hadn't seen in years and that Sally Murphy aged six months was named best baby, the prize accepted by a beaming mother who couldn't stop saying what a healthy eater darling Sally was.

Resisting the impulse to keep on reading until I got completion on the Braithwaite story, I changed the spool to 1974. Twenty-one years ago, a Sally lookalike won the best baby competition, while one mother complained of her teenager's obsession with that Gary Glitter.

Another change of spools, another three weeks in May. And another, without a single worthwhile clue. By the time I'd done 1970, my vision was phasing in and out while the microfiche machine was buzzing loudly. I reran the last spool and put it back in its case. My hand stretched out to turn the machine off.

There was another spool lying beside the switch. I picked it up. The librarian, I saw, had been over zealous: its label read, *Croydon Chronicle 1969*. Five years of local gossip had done my brain in – I couldn't even remember whether Rodney Ellis had been here in 1969. I could have checked my notes, but that would have required the kind of initiative I no longer possessed. So I did what I'd been doing before: I threaded the spool and tried to keep my eyesight on line as I ran through to May.

On the front page was a story which made me long for Betty Braithwaite: the recounting with every gory detail of the hit-and-run accident which had killed seven-year-old Steven Parker.

Steven.

A string of words jumped into my mind. *What if it were Steven.* I heard Rodney Ellis's voice. That's what he had said before he'd run back into the burning house. I had assumed then that he had been talking about his son. No wonder the name Mark had come as a surprise.

But surely it must be a coincidence. Steven was such a common name. Except the accident had occurred on the same day that, twenty-six years later, Frances Ellis had swallowed her way into death.

I read the article. Even after twenty-six years, it was enough to pull the heart strings. Steven Parker, pictured

234

smiling through gap teeth, was two days past his seventh birthday, riding his new bike outside his home, when a fast-moving car had, for no apparent reason, mounted the pavement. Steven never stood a chance. He was hit so hard he somersaulted through the air. By the time his mother Susan had run out to see what the noise was, he was lying on the pavement, bleeding profusely. A neighbour called an ambulance, which arrived within ten minutes. Too late: Steven was already dead. The police came fast as well, but there was nothing much for them to do either. The car had never stopped.

The report dwelt on each of the incident's separate details, adding a few maudlin comments from the Parkers' neighbours. It ended with a police vow that they would catch the driver of the car. They would be interviewing all the inhabitants of the road, a spokesman said, trying to find out the identity of the driver. And that was it.

It wasn't much to go with – one name, and a common one at that, and a coincidence of dates. But it was more than anything else I had. I didn't bother trawling through the rest of the paper. I fast forwarded searching out the issue that followed.

A series of previous hit-and-run accidents ensured that Steven Parker's funeral was front-page news. The *Chronicle* was on a crusade: they layered photographs of the huge crowd watching Steven's devastated parents walk behind the small coffin with calls for stiffer penalties for drunken drivers. Not that they knew Steven's killer was drunk. The police were still, that week at least, following various leads.

The week after, the story had been demoted to page four. A trust in Steven Parker's name had raised £349 and Steven's mother, Susan, was quoted as giving grateful thanks to all who had donated. The police were interviewed as well; they were looking, they said, for a woman who had been driving a red Cortina.

I kept on reading. All I learnt was that they never found the woman. There were two separate police requests for witnesses to come forward with her identity – she had, according to the police, been wearing a blue dress – but without result. A couple of months later, the story had gone dead.

Chapter
thirty-five

Twenty-six years after their son's death, the Parkers were still in the same house in Croydon. The sky was grey, hanging low, as I walked up a small path which led to a semi-detached red-brick house identical to its neighbours. Identical, that is, except for tell-tale signs of disrepair: a brown door which badly need repainting; a front garden where sickly shrubs made only a half-hearted attempt at ground cover; and a set of net curtains which were yellowing with age.

I pushed the bell. Nothing happened. I picked up the tarnished brass horseshoe that served as a knocker, but before I had a chance to drop it against the wood, the door was opened.

The woman standing on a tattered door mat was unmistakably Susan Parker. The same sad features, the same drooping mouth, the same dank hair, now almost entirely grey, looked out at me. I said her name: 'Mrs Parker?'

She nodded.

'My name's Kate Baeier,' I said. 'I'm sorry to disturb you, but I need to talk to you about your son's death.'

She blinked. 'About Steven?' Her voice was hushed.

It was my turn to nod.

'I don't . . .' She turned to look down the narrow hallway.

As if on cue a querulous voice called out, 'Who is it, Susan?' and then immediately again, as if he was used to repeating himself: 'Who is it?'

'You'd better come in.' She was already walking dispiritedly down the narrow hallway. I followed after her. She led me to a room whose general shabbiness mirrored the neglect in the front garden. It was clean enough, but only partially furnished. One frayed armchair stood on a shabby carpet facing a huge-screen television. There was an arch midway, leading to another room. I could see a single bed, and beside it a small, hospital-shaped side table.

Steven's father, Harry, was sitting hunched up in the armchair, facing the TV. Counting back, I reckoned he couldn't have been much more than fifty. With his grey hair and skin the kind of ashen colour that said he never went out, he looked at least ten years older. He didn't seem to register my presence; he kept staring straight ahead.

Following his gaze, my eyes were drawn to the screen. The television, although on, was mute. Someone had messed with the colour balance: I saw a garish orange cartoon duck wiggling its way into a large maroon pond.

'Who is it?' His voice drew me back. He was leaning forwards, staring at me. His fists were clenched in his lap as if he was stopping himself from hitting out.

'My name's Kate Baeier,' I said. 'I've come –'

Susan Parker cut in. 'It's the woman from the charity shop,' she said. 'You know, I told you. She offered to pick up those suits you didn't want.'

'Not didn't want,' he said. 'Can't use.' I saw that it wasn't that his fists were clenched but that arthritis had twisted his fingers on to his palms. He caught me looking. Defiantly he reached over and used the knuckles of both hands to pick the remote control up off the floor. He brought the box up and, still holding it between his crimped fingers, used his chin to jab at the colour controls.

He was going the wrong way: the duck turned brown. Tears of hopelessness filled his weak blue eyes. I wanted to reach out and help him. I wanted to tell him it would be all right. I went one step closer.

He looked at me so savagely that I stopped.

'Come,' his wife said. 'I'll show you the clothes.'

The fury in Harry Parker's face told me there was nothing else I could do.

Susan Parker closed the door behind me. 'He's always worse when the anniversary comes round,' she said softly. She took me upstairs. There were framed pictures of boats planted equidistant all the way up. Every one of them was crooked. Susan Parker didn't seem to notice. She rounded the corner and began walking down the hall.

I followed, looking, on the way, into a double bedroom whose two single beds were covered with brown candlewick. Above one was the framed photograph of a laughing seven-year-old. She didn't ask what I was looking at. Instead: 'That's Steven,' she said. I nodded and went after her.

She took me to another bedroom. It was unlike anything else in the house. Not that it was modern; on the contrary, it was furnished with the kind of pieces that were all the rage in 1969: early MFI, a bed with drawers built in below it, an assemble-it-yourself pine desk, an anglepoise lamp, a set of bookshelves stuck on red brackets. But what made this room different was how lovingly it had been preserved. The carpet, a mottled green, looked new, and the walls, a light beige, were freshly painted.

Despite the work that had been done on it, I knew that

the room was as it had been when Steven had gone out on his last fatal bike ride. On a freshly laundered pillow that would never again hold a childish head sat a small stuffed rabbit. On the desk, a meccano construction waited for small hands to come and finish it. In the round metal bin lay a screwed up piece of paper, yellowed with age.

Sitting on the bed, Susan Parker picked up the rabbit and began to stroke it. 'We can't talk in front of my husband,' she said. 'He took Steven's death so badly.'

I looked at her hands, fondling the rabbit's baby-pink ears, and I wondered how she would describe her own reaction to her son's death.

'You can sit on his chair,' she said.

I went over to the desk. I pulled out a low swivel chair but before I sat down my eye was caught by a small object. I couldn't resist. I lifted it up and held it to the light.

It was the inner workings of a clock, each tiny piece shining and fitted together, each minuscule cog so thin that they were almost transparent as they moved slowly round. I gaped in admiration.

'My husband made it for Steven,' Susan Parker said.

I put the clock down. 'It's beautiful.'

'Harry was a jeweller,' she said. 'A craftsman. Before the arthritis took his control away. After Steven died.'

She said it in a matter-of-fact way that let me know this was how she dated all of life: pre and post Steven's death. I sat down on his chair. 'I'm sorry I have to bring it all up again,' I said.

Her shrug told me that she lived his death every waking minute of her life, and that she would continue living it until the day she died. 'What do you want to know?'

'Did they ever find out who was driving the car?'

Her face was impassive. 'No. Never.' She laid the rabbit

carefully down on to the pillow. 'They tried so hard, the police did. They talked to everybody.'

'Can you remember any of the policemen's names?' I asked.

She shook her head, not once but three times, very slowly.

'Can you remember the name Rodney Ellis?'

'Ellis?' Her forehead was creased in concentration. 'No, not Ellis.' She was dredging through old memory banks. 'There was one, I remember. A lovely man. So kind. He kept us informed on how the investigation was going. But not Ellis.' Her head moved from side to side again. 'No, I'm sure it wasn't. Let's see. His name was Harry – no, that's my husband. Harvey. No, that's not right either . . .'

'Harrison?'

Her face relaxed. 'Of course. Harrison. Sergeant Tom Harrison.'

Tom Harrison, who twenty-six years ago must have walked the same beat as Rodney Ellis.

Susan Parker's voice cut across the impact of her revelation. 'A lovely man. He knew what we were feeling. He had children of his own, you see. He told us that he wouldn't rest until he had found the woman who did this to our son.' The energy drained from her face. 'He never did.' She shrugged. 'Not his fault. And not that it would have made any difference I suppose. Once Steven was –'

Her husband's voice, louder than I would have thought possible, sounded out. 'Why hasn't she gone?'

Susan Parker jumped to her feet. 'He mustn't find us here. I'm sorry, you'll have to go.' I got up. 'Hurry,' she said. 'You'll have to take the suits.' After she had hustled me out into the hallway, she darted into her bedroom.

When she came out she was carrying a bulky bin liner. 'Here.' She pushed it at me.

I took it from her. Keeping my voice low, I said, 'The *Chronicle* says there were some eyewitnesses to the accident. Do you know who they were?'

Downstairs a chair scraped, a male voice cursed.

'Please. He doesn't like to talk about it. It will make him worse.' There was panic in her eyes.

'I'm sorry,' I said. 'But I need to know.'

His voice was like thunder. '*Susan!*'

I looked down the stairwell. I could see one of the damaged hands pushing against the side of the door, opening it slowly. I looked back at her. 'I need it.'

'Mrs Martin.' Her voice was barely audible. 'Number 37. Now, please' – she pushed me roughly – '*go*.'

I went. Down the stairs, carrying my plastic bag. Harry Parker watched me coming. 'Thanks for the suits,' I said as I passed him by. He didn't say anything.

I found myself walking unnaturally fast. I opened the door. While I'd been inside, rain, that kind of cold, steady drizzle that is an English spring speciality, had started up. 'Thanks again,' I said. I looked behind me. Susan Parker was standing at the top of the stairs, making frantic dismissal motions with her hand.

I walked down the driveway, my head bent against the double onslaught of the dripping sky and the memory of the Parkers' pain. I pushed the gate open. It was hanging awkwardly from its hinge and it needed oiling. I went through and closed it carefully behind me, feeling the relief that I was out of that house of death. My eyes were drawn up.

I saw Susan Parker standing by her son's window. She was staring out, her gaze fixed on something inanimate.

When our eyes met, she kept on staring. It was I who looked away. I walked to my car and put the suits carefully into the boot. I glanced back and up again. She was still there. I realized then that she was so caught up in that fatal day that she hadn't even asked me why I was investigating it.

I looked down the road. Number 37 was in easy walking distance. Nevertheless, I got into my car. I started up the engine. Before I pulled out, my eyes were pulled back to the upstairs window.

She was no longer visible. I could guess where she had gone: back to his bed, again, sitting in the hollow the passing years had made, petting a rabbit that had once been a favoured toy. I thought about the Parkers, husband and wife, living with a death they couldn't bear. It made me think about me and Sam. And about my mother, whose death had haunted me for so long.

Chapter
thirty-six

Mrs Ramona Martin was a tiny and gnarled white-haired woman who must have had a good thirty years on Susan Parker. She also had twice the animation. When I told her what I was after, she said she wouldn't dream of answering questions while I got wet on her doorstep. She showed me into the front room. She couldn't answer my questions there either, not until she'd fetched the tea.

I sat down in a two-seater sofa that was covered with brightly coloured tasselled scarves. Ramona – as she had insisted I call her – seemed to be heavily into tassels. They hung off the embroidered tablecloth, the fabric which had been laid over the mantelpiece, the cord that tied her curtains to the side walls, even the bottom of the chair covers. The net effect was multi-coloured disorder, a far cry from the bleakness that seemed to have enveloped the Parker household.

'She never got over his death, you know.' Ramona was back and burdened with a heavy silver tray on which were laid a silver teapot, two china cups and a huge plateful of giant shortbread biscuits. She put the tray down on the table and poured out two cups of tea. She handed one to me. 'Biscuit?'

By the way she thrust the plate at me, I reckoned refusal was not a viable option. I took two.

'Go on,' she urged. 'Have another.' I took another. She continued, then, as if the tea manoeuvre hadn't interrupted her speech. 'Susan Parker, that is,' she said. 'Never got over it. Neither did her husband. But Harry always was a strange one – so uncommunicative you ended up crossing the street to avoid having to talk to him. Steven was the only person who seemed able to bring him out of himself. And when he died . . .' She took a dainty sip of tea and shrugged. 'A terrible thing, Steven's death. He was a lovely boy.'

'You saw the accident?'

She nodded sombrely. 'I was outside, weeding.' She put her cup down. 'Steven was playing on his bike. A lovely boy, he was. The kind of child that makes me wonder whether scientists know what they're talking about when they go on about inheritance. Steven was nothing like his parents. He was so friendly, so full of life.' Her eyes went dreamy and distant, almost as if she could see him, her lovely boy, playing down the road. A long pause – I thought I had lost her – but she refocused. 'Oh well. If he had lived he would probably have turned into a sad sack like Harry.' She smiled.

I took a bite out of a biscuit. It tasted overripe, as if too much vanilla had been mixed into the batter. I swallowed, trying to keep my face straight.

'They're awful, aren't they?' she said. 'My daughter makes them. I chucked the last batch into the dustbin but she found them and threw a fit. She's over forty, with three children, would you believe, but she still worries that I love her brother more than her. She's got me on the run – I even end up palming her baking on to unsuspecting strangers.' She grinned.

I put the half-eaten biscuit down. 'The accident,' I said.

'Of course. I'm a silly old woman, aren't I?' Her tone told me she didn't believe that for one minute. 'I was out weeding. Steven Parker was playing on his bike. I thought it was strange that Susan wasn't watching him – she was an over-anxious mother who wouldn't normally have let him on the pavement alone. Of course, we learned later she had stopped to wash the dishes. She was on her way out when it happened. I saw the car – red, it was – coming fast, weaving from one side of the road to the other. I remembered thinking that the driver must be really drunk. Then the car mounted the pavement, close to Steven. I shouted out.'

She stopped and used a handkerchief to mop at the tears that had started welling as soon as she began her story. When eventually she managed to speak again, she sounded, for the first time, old. 'I was too late, of course. He didn't stand a chance. I don't think he ever knew what hit him, poor lamb. It hurts the worst of all, you know, the death of a youngster.' She looked at me. 'I'm going on as usual, aren't I? What my son calls my urge to witter. You're busy, I'm sure. So tell me, what do you want to know?'

'Did the police interview you?'

'Yes. More than once. A nice man came – a sergeant. Big, comfortable man. Name of Harrison. He took down everything I said. Not that it did any good, of course.'

'Because they never found the driver?'

She nodded. 'That also. But mainly because I got it wrong. It happened so fast you see. I thought a man was driving the car. But it was a woman – that's what all the other witnesses said. So what I had to say was no help.'

'Did you meet the other witnesses?'

She shook her head. Only one of the neighbours who was also outside. Not somebody I knew well. A man who'd

246

spent the best years of his life in the colonies and never quite recovered from it. An officious, awful man – we used to call him Colonel Blimp. He moved away years ago. What was his name? Jones? Smith?'

If it was either of those two, I didn't stand a chance of finding him.

'I know,' she said brightly. 'Hold on a minute.' She got up and bustled out of the room. She had only one telephone in the house and it was kept in the hallway. Through the half-closed door I could hear her finger turning on one of those old fashioned dials. When her call was answered, I heard her identifying herself. Given how freely she'd spoken to me, I reckoned she was going to be a long time. I got up and went over to the window. I looked out on to rows of red brick. I thought about the Parkers, trapped for twenty-six years in a misery that would never end, and I wondered what other tragedies lurked behind all those endlessly curtained windows.

'Jacks,' I heard.

I turned. Ramona Martin was standing in the doorway, a carrier bag in her hand. 'Ian Jacks,' she said. 'That's his name. I got his number for you.' She had it on a piece of paper.

I walked over to her and took it. 'Thanks.'

'Any time,' she said. 'I like visitors.' She got out of the way so I could pass. I walked down the hallway, hearing her coming after me. I opened the door. Ramona Martin was directly behind me. 'I think about her often,' she said.

I turned. 'About Susan Parker?'

'Her as well, of course. But what I meant was the woman who did it. I think about how she must have felt. Afterwards. She must have known what she'd done. Even if she was blind drunk, there was someone else in the car with her. He must have told her. And it was all over the local rag.'

I thought about Frances Ellis. I thought about the way, when I had last seen her, she had told me she didn't drink. I was certain that I knew when she had stopped. Twenty-six years ago   after she had accidentally killed a little boy.

'I wonder how she lives with herself,' Ramona said. 'I know I couldn't.'

Neither could Frances.

'Do me a favour,' I heard Ramona saying.

I looked back and saw her holding out the plastic bag. 'It's the biscuits. No need to eat them. But please, don't throw them out close by.'

'Sure.' I smiled and took the bag from her. 'And thanks for everything.'

'Any time,' she said, and then, having sent one cheery wave my way, she closed the door.

Chapter
thirty-seven

It was raining steadily. I drove to Camden, stopping only to deposit Harry Parker's suits in an Oxfam shop and Ramona Martin's biscuits in a skip. Then I went home.

The mess in the living room was beginning to look familiar. If I stuck around long enough, I thought, I might even grow to like it. I could patent it as a new style: interior design by police raid. Have to get rid of the answerphone though, it was too reliable. Every time I turned round it seemed to be blinking crazily. I listened with half an ear – there was a work message or two that I could afford to ignore, one from Erica naming my trial date and confirming the police seemed to have forgotten Meville Adams, and several from an increasingly irate Valerie. 'Ring me,' she said on the last of these. It sounded more like a threat than a request.

I picked up the phone. I didn't ring Valerie. I dug into my bag, took out the two slips of paper I'd collected that day and dialled the number on the second.

It was answered fast by a woman who spoke the kind of confident rounded English that is these days mostly restricted to royal circles. A perfect companion for Colonel Blimp, I thought, imagining her stout and hearty, striding through the bush. When I asked for her husband, she told me he was out of town but was expected back the following day. 'I will certainly give him a message,' she said.

I told her my name and phone number and asked him to ring me back asap.

'Concerning?'

I told her it was concerning Steven Parker.

'At long last,' she said. Before I could ask what that meant, she added: 'I will inform him,' and hung up.

I got the dialling tone again. I hit the redial button. Without success: Mrs Jacks was now engaged. I put the phone down.

It rang. She must be calling me back, I thought. I picked it up. 'Hello? Mrs Jacks?'

'Jacks, Jones . . . I guess it's all the same to you honkies.' Carmen followed that up with an irate: 'Where have you been?'

It was good to have Carmen hectoring me again. I smiled. 'If my mother had ever been sober enough to worry about my movements,' I said, 'I could have said you sound just like her. In the absence of that . . .'

'You could say I'm dead beat. This Lloyd Adams is a bad boy with the stamina of an overactive camel.'

'Trying to tell me he humps a lot?'

'That and everything else,' Carmen said. 'Here I am in my beat-up VW following The Man with the blonde bimbette and the six-cylinder BMW and – '

I froze. 'The what?'

'Haven't you heard? Only the ones with six cylinders have any street cred these days.'

'No. I mean the car. It's a BMW?'

'What else would you expect a bona fide homeboy to drive?'

My fingers were scrabbling through the pile of papers on the table. 'Got its license number?'

'Course I have.'

I found the notebook I'd used. I flicked it open.

'It's parked conveniently opposite,' Carmen said, and began reeling off its number plate. 'L31 . . .'

'. . . 6 RCW.' Our voices blended.

She sounded annoyed. 'You knew it?'

'I've seen it once before,' I said. Driven by Melville Adams's dealer, I thought. His dealer – his brother – who had waited for a swish blonde to sashay her way over to him. I wondered what it meant.

Carmen had no time to hear my wonderings. 'Shit' – she was almost shouting – 'I don't believe it. He's on the move again. Look, stay by the phone. By the way Lloyd's twitch to stride ratio has increased, I reckon something big is going down tonight. I'll call you when I can.'

The line went dead. I kept hold of the phone. I couldn't move – not yet. I was too busy trying to jam the pieces of a crazy puzzle together.

Lloyd's was the BMW I'd seen out of Melville's window. Which meant that Lloyd was Melville's dealer. Had he also delivered Melville's final fix?

I dropped the receiver down thinking that, having been on the receiving end of Lloyd's rage, I couldn't rule out the possibility that he had deliberately killed his brother. And yet the clue to Melville's murderer must lie in the placing of his body in the Crisis Centre. Why would Lloyd have bothered to do that and how could he possibly have got hold of the key that Moira had lost and that I was supposed to have stolen?

I thought about what had happened. I had so many fragments: Rodney and Frances Ellis, Frances's suicide on the anniversary of another death, the corpse of a tramp lying in a police station, a rape that wasn't, a wife too scared to leave her husband – all of that and more. There had to be a connection somewhere, some central thread. There had to be.

I had no idea what it was.

I wandered over to the window thinking that if I was going to clear myself of the drugs charge, I would have to work out what the hell had been going on.

Gusts of wind drove the rain, making it look like sleet. People scurried past, their umbrellas held at awkward angles to stop the wet from getting in, their feet hugging the far edge of the pavement in a vain attempt to avoid their ankles being splashed by passing cars.

My mind went back to Lloyd and his BMW. Was it likely that Lloyd had offed his brother? It was easily accomplished: the heroin Melville was accustomed to taking would be cut by other, diluting, substances. All anybody intent on murdering Melville needed to do was to present him with a small quantity of undiluted heroin. One shot through the veins and Melville's body would short circuit.

But wait a minute. When I'd been in Melville's room, I'd heard the blonde telling him that what she had brought was to be his last. So? Lloyd could have changed his mind and given Melville one last, free trip to paradise. He must have. It had to be Lloyd – the BMW said it.

I looked down at the street. I had cars on the mind. I saw a black Saab. Gavin's Saab, I thought. But of course it couldn't be: it was just one of the production line, the twin of the one I'd seen when I had been visiting Janet Morris.

The car door opened. Gavin got out.

I didn't think. I acted: going back a few steps, making sure he couldn't see me. But that way I couldn't see him either. I moved towards the window again, expecting to find him walking across the road. The road was empty. I

252

pressed my face against the glass, looking through the blur of rain, at the car. I saw that Gavin had mirrored my action; he'd also gone back. I could just make out his outline. He was sitting in the driver's seat.

I didn't stop to think. I ran out of the room, down the stairs, and across the road, straight to the car. I opened the passenger door. He was still there, sitting, doing nothing. 'Looking for me?' I said.

He hadn't noticed me coming, I was sure of it, but he showed no surprise. All he did was send a half-smile my way. I got into the car and closed the door. For a moment I sat there, looking at him. He seemed so familiar and yet startling as well. He looked tired, as if he had been up all night and hadn't had time to eat or shave.

He reached out and touched me on the cheek. 'You're wet.'

I nodded. 'Rain.' I found myself wishing he'd touch me again. I didn't know what to say.

He spoke. 'I shouldn't have come.' He grimaced, self-deprecating. 'But I couldn't stop myself.'

I didn't reply. I couldn't. I was too busy thinking that this man had such good control he could stop himself from doing anything.

'That's not true either,' he said. 'I wanted to see you.'

I felt myself relax.

His voice was soft. 'How are you doing?'

I shrugged. 'I'm surviving.' I said. 'Although my lawyer is a class act whose elegant daily letters suggest that if I don't get myself out of this one, she'll be writing to me in jail for a long time to come.'

His eyes were fixed on my face. 'I've been worried about you,' he said. 'Has anything else happened?'

He looked so interested, and I needed to talk. I opened

253

my mouth, ready to spill it all, to tell him how twenty-six years ago a chief superintendent's wife had mashed a seven-year-old to death and how sometime during the last week a man called Lloyd Adams had shot enough heroin into his brother's bloodstream to make sure he never woke up.

'A lot has –' I began. I stopped in mid sentence, for Gavin was staring at me, concentrated, willing me to continue. I was momentarily filled with suspicion. Was he too interested?

'Maybe I can help,' he said.

His voice was gentle. He wouldn't do me any harm, I knew that. I should tell him. 'A lot has happened,' I said. His expression was calm, quiet, expectant. 'Not much of it relevant.'

He knew I was holding back. His eyes clouded.

'I'm glad you came round,' I said. I had to do something. I leaned over and kissed him. I had meant to do it lightly. But Gavin pulled me to him, his lips pressing against mine, his tongue pushing hungrily into my mouth. I didn't need much persuading. I kissed him back, feeling the desire that had been there always, from the first moment that I had seen him. I put suspicion and despair on hold.

His arm moved round my back. I moved forward, straight into the gearstick. I grimaced and moved away.

As Gavin shifted back into his seat, we separated. 'Snogging in the car always was dangerous,' he said.

'I never tried it,' I said.

'Not even as a teenager?'

'Especially not then. I only had to step into a car with a boy and one of my father's spies would be hanging on the windscreen.'

'And you didn't want your father to know?'

'On the contrary,' I said. 'I would have loved that. But

the bloody boys were all too scared.' I laughed at the memory.

While Gavin waited out my laughter, his expression moved from wryly amused to serious. 'Scared like me,' he said eventually. 'Nothing changes, hey?'

'Oh, I don't know.' It was my turn to reach over and touch his face. 'At least *you* don't have acne.'

I couldn't raise a smile. He was staring ahead now at the windscreen and the rain flowing relentlessly down. 'I'm sorry about the other day,' he said. 'I hope you understand. If I were seen with you . . .'

I put one finger lightly on his lips, silencing him. 'I know,' I said. 'But thanks anyway. Thanks for coming round.' He turned to face me. I was relieved to see he was finally smiling. 'I think I'll go now, while we're winning.' He nodded, and I opened the door. 'See you.' I got another nod. I closed the door. He started up the engine. I stood in the rain, watching while he drove off.

Chapter
thirty-eight

I knew two things: I wasn't going to see Gavin's car driving up again – not that evening at least – and I couldn't keep staring out of the window. I edged away from it, going to the phone. Because of what Carmen had said, I couldn't leave the house. I was agitated, itching to do something. I saw two scraps of paper lying by my bag. One I'd already half dealt with. I picked up the other.

Mark Ellis's wife. I wondered if she could help. Worth a try. I punched in her number. She answered, breathlessly, with the set of digits I'd just dialled. I told her who I was.

'Hold on,' she said. There was a series of clicks – her moving phone – then her voice came back on tap, soft and confiding. 'I didn't want to talk in front of Mark. He's rather upset.'

It seemed a reasonable response to your mother's suicide.

She'd moved briskly on. 'How can I help you?'

'About the obituary,' I said.

Her voice lifted. 'Oh yes?'

'It would help if I could speak with some of her closest friends. You couldn't tell me who they were, could you?'

'Well . . .' She sounded doubtful. 'Frances didn't have that many friends. Not,' she said quickly, 'that she was unfriendly. Not at all. Liked to keep herself to herself, you know.'

More likely liked to keep herself to her snails, I thought.

Mrs Ellis, junior was an emotional yo-yo. She'd gone all bright again. 'There's Jean. She's a distant cousin. Yes, she would be good. Hold on, I'll fetch my address book.' I heard her footsteps retreating. Not for long. 'Here it is.' She read out the number so slowly that, if I had been writing it down, there was no way I could have got it wrong.

I was not, however, writing it down. 'Great,' I said. 'That's very useful. I can get the family angle from her. But I'm also interested in the work-related aspect.'

'Oh, but Frances never worked.'

'I know,' I said. 'But Rodney is such a prominent public figure, the reader will be interested in how his work impinged on her life. You know -- the woman through the man. It's awful, isn't it?'

'I suppose it is,' she said, chuckling to show she didn't really think there was anything awful about it.

I gave her amusement its head. When eventually it had worked its way out, I moved on: 'If there was anybody who worked with Rodney who might also have known Frances?'

'I don't know . . .' She was a trier, was Mark's wife. I could almost hear the cogs turning.

I gave her a hand. 'How about a policeman called Tom Harrison?'

'Of course.' Relief made her voice louder. 'Tom. Yes . . . they go way back, Rodney and Frances and Tom Harrison. I remember Mark telling me, when we first met, that Tom had been almost as familiar to him as his father when he was younger. Tom was happy being a sergeant, you see – he was never interested in climbing higher – so he had more time than Rodney. And after Tom got his divorce, he

257

was lonely. Always at their house. Wait a minute . . . yes of course, I remember the picture on their sideboard – the three of them – they went on holiday together, didn't they?'

'Recently?'

A pause. 'No, not recently. In fact, I remember thinking that Mark's parents didn't seem to see as much of Tom these days. I expect it was difficult – Rodney being the boss, and Tom a sergeant posted to the same station. Given the disparity I thought Rodney was loyal to have stuck with Tom so long. I wouldn't like it, would you?'

'No,' I said. 'I suppose I wouldn't.'

'But Tom Harrison. Yes. That would be good. Rodney and Tom actually trained together so Tom could probably tell you a lot about what Frances was like when she was younger. You want me to ask Mark for Tom's number?'

'No. Thanks. I've got it. I just wanted to make sure he was the right person before I phoned him. Thanks again. Would you mind one more question?'

'No.' We were best buddies. 'Of course not.'

I said it straight. 'What car did Frances drive?'

'What car?' She sounded taken aback.

'I know it seems silly,' I said. 'But in obituaries, it's the little details that help give a portrait of a person's life.'

'But Frances didn't drive.' There was a whiny quality to her tone that came from not being the star pupil, equipped with the right answer. 'She refused to. I never understood it. I mean, of course I prefer Mark to do the driving but in an emergency, I would manage. I don't think Frances would have.'

I thought I knew why. I also knew when Frances had stopped driving. I pushed a smile into my voice, said: 'Oh well, just an idea. Thanks.' I listened to her telling me that

I could ring her any time and she looked forward to the obituary, then I hung up.

After I had put the phone down, I stayed by it, thinking about the fact that Tom Harrison and Rodney Ellis had trained together. And walked the beat together as equals for a while, until Rodney had been promoted. Worked together and played together and cuddled each other's kids – the bonds of loyalty must have stretched tight between them. Tight enough for Tom Harrison to conceal the fact that Frances Ellis had inadvertently killed a child?

Another thread. Although I couldn't see the whole embroidery, I knew it was coming together. Newly galvanized, I picked up the phone and dialled Mrs Jacks again. It got me nowhere: she wasn't there, nobody was. I put the phone down.

The spurt of energy was short-lived; the window drew me back. The rain had lifted, but the sky, still grey and overcast, made dusk seem more like dark. The parking space that Gavin had vacated was now occupied by a motorbike, its leather-clad driver walking off down the road. I wondered when I would ever see Gavin again.

I moved away. I wasn't going to dwell on that. I had other things to do. Not least of which was to find something to eat. I located eggs, the rind of a chunk of Parmesan cheese and a few limp spring onions. Perfect. I made myself a Parmesan and spring onion omelette which I ate along with a chickpea salad. That finished, I went into the living room and switched on the television. It had been quite a day: I watched one feeble sitcom and then another without even registering what they were about. When I saw the credits of the second rolling past, I switched off.

It was past nine and still no word from Carmen. I ran a bath, stretched the phone cord as close as it could get, and immersed myself. I had the shampoo worked up into a healthy lather when it rang. I was half expecting it. In one movement, I was out the bath and picking up.

Carmen dispensed with greetings. 'I was right,' she said. 'Something is going down. Get over here. Now. The Richton estate, south entrance. My car's parked opposite the gate.' She hung up.

I rinsed off my hair and dressed. I didn't do a great job of either but, within ten minutes, I was out of the house and driving ferociously.

The Richton estate was the kind of place most people try and avoid, even during daylight hours. A set of high-rise towers stranded between two busy roads and a once-designated green area that had been turned brown by neglect, it was a no-go area at night for police, social workers, most people on foot and any strangers. What had once been a dream of cheap housing for the general populace had turned into a nightmare for the underclass. A car park made to fill the sixties dream of universal car ownership was now a graveyard for burnt and battered vehicles. Jagged barbed wire cut one area off from the other, combining with the council's other attempt at safety measures – high, bright lights – to make the place look like a maximum-security prison.

I rolled up at the south entrance and turned my lights off. I saw Carmen's car parked just ahead. I got out, locked up carefully, and went to join her.

'Good timing,' she said, pointing to the gate just beyond the entrance.

Lloyd Adams's BMW was parked inside the gate. Although its lights were off, I could just make out the figure of a man in its driver's seat.

'Lloyd?'

Carmen nodded. 'He's been coming and going all day. Now he's waiting, and has been for the last half-hour. He's the kind who goes around shooting his mouth off that he waits for no man, so this has got to be good.'

'He's on his own?'

She shook her head – no – and then tilted it first to the right and then to the left.

My eyes were more accustomed to the dark now. I followed the motion and saw the outline of a man on either side of Lloyd's car. Each of them was skulking behind another car, but casually, as if they didn't care whether they were seen. When the man on the right transferred his weight to one side, I thought I knew why. I took an involuntary breath in. 'Is that a gun?'

Carmen was staring straight ahead. 'Sure is.' Without taking her eyes off the BMW, she took a plastic cup out of the glove compartment, and poured into it from the thermos flask lying on her lap. 'Coffee?' When I said yes, she handed the cup to me. 'Sugar in the side pocket.'

I was holding the cup in one hand and tearing the sugar sachet open using a combination of teeth and the other hand when a car passed by. A normal enough occurrence you would think, except this car had its headlights out. I acted instinctively. Shoving the cup on to the floor, I shuffled down, hiding myself from view. Carmen did the same.

'That's its second time round,' Carmen said softly.

I edged my hand up and slowly undid the window. I waited a moment. No sound. My hand went out, adjusting the side mirror so I could see across the road.

Although the car had stopped, I could hear its engine ticking over. I shifted the mirror again. Just in time to catch the reflection of the BMW's headlights, flicking on once and then quickly off again.

'This is it,' Carmen said.

I lifted myself gingerly up so that I was looking out of the bottom of the window. I saw both doors of the visiting car open simultaneously. Two men got out. They were turned away from me: I couldn't see their faces. The one nearest to me went over to the boot and opened it. There was a light inside which came on as he opened up. His face was obscured by the boot's metal lid, but I could see his hand reaching inside.

When the hand withdrew it was attached to a small suitcase. The other hand went up, intent on closing the boot. There was one moment when I saw his face, the moment he had stepped back and before his hand slammed down. Just a brief glimpse was all I got. It was all I needed. I knew that face. It belonged to Brian Turner. Sergeant Brian Turner.

Chapter
thirty-nine

When Lloyd got out of his car he was holding a package wrapped in newspaper. Responding to some invisible signal, his bodyguard emerged from the shadows. Brian Turner's companion – another policeman, the one I'd privately named Action Man – loped over to his side. The two groups faced each other. A pause – time for the spaghetti western music to play in all our heads.

They started walking. They were the law round there, they had no need to hide. They did the exchange in the full glare of the council's security spotlight. Lloyd put the package in Brian Turner's hand; he got the suitcase in return.

'So now we know where Lloyd-boy gets his supplies,' Carmen whispered.

Neither party bothered checking the contents of what they had been given. They didn't need to: the fluidity of the handover showed that they'd done this many times before.

They separated, Brian Turner wheeling round and walking towards his car.

'You take Lloyd,' I said. Carmen nodded.

We didn't move, we couldn't, not until the men had gone.

Brian Turner's car left first, moving as slowly as it had come, its lights still out. Lloyd's exit was much flashier: the BMW's headlights clicked on, catching us in its glare. For a moment I thought he'd seen us, but he was just making waves. His engine roared and then he steered the car through the gates, speeding off in the opposite direction to his police associates.

I was out and running, fumbling for my key, cursing my security conscious reflexes. I heard Carmen starting up. She waited for Lloyd to round the corner. By that time, I'd breached my car's defences and was on the move.

We passed each other. I looked in my rear-view mirror and saw her taillights growing distant. Since I didn't know when Brian Turner and his companion would start deciding to obey the highway code, I drove more slowly. I went to the end of the road, to the limit of the estate, and turned the corner.

For a moment I thought that I had lost them. But then I caught a distant whiff, their grey-blue car turning right. Its lights were still out. I slowed down, counting to ten before I followed in its wake.

By the time I had turned into the main road, they were driving lights on and fast enough to keep up with the flow of traffic. Probably felt that there was safety in numbers; thinking very much the same, I put a buffer of a couple of cars between us.

I knew my cover was far from perfect. It's impossible to do a one-person tail, especially when the occupants of the front car are policemen used to surveying the territory and made doubly nervous by the existence of a large stash of dope money in their car. I spent a moment berating myself for sending Carmen after Lloyd. I was pretty sure Turner and his hit man were the ones who had set me up. Somehow they'd got hold of Valerie's spare key, left the door open and then arranged for somebody impersonating a non-existent Claire to decoy me over to the Centre. That's all they had to do — apart from sitting back while I smeared my fingerprints all over the place.

I put an abrupt end to my self-criticism session when the cars in front turned left. They had to: ahead was a narrow one-way street, two no-entry signs showing that access from this direction was barred. To everyone, apparently, except policemen: Brian Turner had gone straight down it.

I went the other way, driving on my horn, pushing down until the car in front of me got the message and moved out of my way. I saw a blur, one finger raised in anger, as I passed by. I kept on going, round the one-way system, hanging a right and then right again, driving like a demon. I went full circle, my sense of direction made uncannily acute by the force of my determination not to lose them.

But lose them I had. Or at least I thought I had.

At the end of the street they'd used was a crossroads, giving three choices of route. I stopped and looked down each in turn. I could see nothing remotely blue-grey in any direction. I heard angry beeping and I pulled in. The tension of the chase had squeezed my neck muscles uncomfortably tight. I got out of the car, meaning to stretch. I never did.

I heard women laughing raucously. Turning my head, I saw a group teetering on high heels in the middle of the one-way street. One of them said something which set them off again, screeching out their mirth. It was an infectious sound; it even got me smiling. I watched as they walked to the pavement and up to a door. One of them rapped on it.

There was a small window in the door. As it was opened, a shaft of light streamed into the street. There was an exchange of greetings and then the whole door was opened. I could hear faint music as the laughing gang teetered in. The door closed.

Perhaps, I thought. I walked slowly down the road.

There was no perhaps about it. Their car was there, facing the wrong direction. It was empty. No men. No newspaper wrapping either. They must have gone the way of the women – into what could only be some kind of private club. Which was where I would also have to go.

I was hardly in high heels and sparkling dress and I didn't have time to go home and change. If I wasn't dressed for fashion, I decided, maybe I could go for sleaze. I went back to my car and rooted through the boot. What I found was hardly promising – a couple of paper clips, a piece of string and an old pair of sandals I'd meant to have fixed, but they would have to do. I set to work on my hair, tying it up bouffant-style with the string and one of the paper clips. The other one I used to prick my finger. When blood oozed out, I smeared some on my cheeks and some on my lips. Glancing at myself in the mirror, I saw I was a frazzled Russian doll lookalike. Oh well, at least I'd made an effort. I sucked my finger, stopping the blood.

Even broken, the sandals were a better prospect than my off-white sneakers. I swapped the two, and experimented for a while, discovering that I could keep the sandal on my right foot only if I also kept my big toe permanently rigid.

I needed something to distract suspicion from the rest of my outfit. There was only one candidate – my T-shirt. I got into the car and took it and the sweat shirt off. Amazing what you can do with a paper clip – I used it to tear at the T-shirt's neckline. I was going for the scooped effect but over-did it: after I had stuffed some newspaper into the bottom of my bra and put the T-shirt back, my neck line had become a chest line, large portions of my breasts swelling out.

I walked back down the street. I knocked on the door and when the small metal window was opened by a bullish man, I sent a ghastly smile his way. I needn't have bothered, he wasn't looking at my face.

The cleavage was apparently acceptable. He opened the door; I stepped over the threshold. Because of the way he had positioned himself, I couldn't help brushing up against him. His hoarse voice sounded in my ear: 'Stick with me, babe.' He squeezed my bottom, leering suggestively. 'I could show you something.'

My eyes went down to his crotch and then came, dismissively, up. 'Yeah.' I filled my voice with scorn. 'I bet you could.' Concentrating on keeping my sandal on, I raised my knee, my own version of a suggestion.

He hadn't really been serious. He threw a half-hearted 'Cockteaser' my way before shifting to one side, and giving me room to pass. I walked towards a second door, which opened before I reached it. A thick smog of cigarette smoke, a loud cacophony of voices, music and a drunken man blasted out at me. I side-stepped the man and walked into the cavernous room.

It was a drinking club to match my cleavage, the walls purple brocade, the seats dark red velveteen, the lighting so low it almost wasn't there. Monotonous dance music blasted out of a juke box. By the long bar a crowd of lunging patrons were trying to attract the sweating bartender's attention. Everywhere I looked, I saw the kind of deep flirtation that was bound to end in bed – the smell of cheap perfume and rising testosterone was almost strong enough to cover up the stench of stale tobacco.

I plunged into the mêlée. I found a half-pint glass with a

slurp of beer inside, picked it up for camouflage, and kept on going, doing the rounds of the place. I got a lot of indecent proposals and a few suggestive looks but nothing else. No sight of Brian Turner, nor his sidekick.

My second time round, I noticed some extra traffic to one side of the bar. I stood watching. I saw that hidden in the brocade was a door. There was no visible handle, or other way of opening it, but every now and then it would swing ajar and someone would slip out.

I took myself and my drink close by. I leaned against the wall, watching. I didn't have to watch for long. A man tottered out, gasping for air, I slipped my foot into the doorway. I waited until he had walked away, and then I went inside.

My ears were enveloped by sound. Not music, but a heaving panting. It didn't take me long to find out why.

There was a screen on one wall. On it, rolling bodies, skin slick with sweat, mouths open, tongues lapping, fingers stretched out wide, nipples erect. The camera pulled back. There were three of them entwined – two men and one woman – caught up in a process that had absolutely nothing to do with making love. The woman groaned. The men moved in. I looked away.

There were rows of chairs facing the screen, occupied by lone men, staring straight ahead. I could see sporadic hands pumping up and down, tongues lolling as the woman moaned again. Either she was a bad actor or she was supposed to be expressing pain. I tried not to look. Instead, I peered through the darkness at a set of tables by a wall.

I saw Brian Turner. He was sitting with his back to the screen, deep in conversation with another man, their heads so close together I couldn't see who it was.

268

The woman groaned. My eyes were drawn back to the screen. One of the men was climbing on top of the woman as the other got ready to push his erect penis into her mouth.

I looked away. Brian Turner had shifted to one side, far enough to expose his companion's face. I recognized him immediately: it was the man who had told me his name was Superintendent David Newlands.

The woman screamed. This time, I didn't look.

Which was lucky really. Because if I had, I would have missed Brian Turner's head whipping round. He looked at me, straight at me, those same eyes that had chilled me in the courthouse boring into my face.

I didn't stop to think. As on the screen the woman reached her terrible climax, I turned and ran.

Chapter
forty

Pushing through the door and out in the bar area, I kept on going. When my right sandal fell off, I let the left one join it. Curses and occasional overspill of beer followed me through a knot of heavy drinkers. Nobody tried to hold me back. I dashed into the entrance lobby.

'What's the matter?' the bouncer said, but I was out of the door, hearing his 'Too ugly to score?' flung after me. I was running hard, my feet slapping against the pavement. There were some advantages to going barefoot: at least I'd hear if anybody was behind me. There was nobody. I got into my car and drove off, my eyes flicking continually between road and rear-view mirror.

I saw nothing to worry me as I drove home. But after I parked, I realized why. They didn't need to follow me. They knew exactly where I lived. The adrenaline which had driven me from the nightclub had evaporated. I was tired. Dead tired. I didn't have the energy to find somewhere else to stay.

I went upstairs and bolted myself in. There was a message from Carmen saying that Lloyd had gone back home and that she was going to do the same. I reckoned she must be asleep by now. Good idea, I thought, and dragged myself to bed.

Sleep refused to come. I lay in the dark thinking about a drug-dealing policeman's ring that involved Brian Turner, Action Man, and the one who had called himself David Newlands. I knew now for sure that the planting of drugs in my flat had been their doing. What I didn't understand was why.

I thought back to the beginning, to the body of James Shaw lying in a police cell. Was this what had set them on to me – a fear perhaps that I, who had been wandering unsupervised through the police station, might have seen how James had died?

I had another thought. Melville had been a target and Melville had also been in the station that night. Had he seen something? Had he been killed for what he saw?

My mind lurched away from that, turning to another imponderable – the Hackney Crisis Centre and the placing of Melville's body there. It made no sense.

I closed my eyes. And had one last thought – that a couple of policemen who were dealing drugs had seen me following them.

Somebody was thundering on my door. I sat up. It came again, a blast of noise, angry fists against hard wood. I looked at my watch. At least they'd waited for the morning: it was five past seven. The pounding started up again.

If they wanted to get in, they would. I pulled on my dressing gown and wrapped it tightly round me. The banging came again, duller now as if the fist that was hitting out was getting tired. I wondered why they didn't change places.

I found out when I opened the door. There was no they, only Valerie. 'About time too,' she said, pushing in.

I closed the door.

She was standing, hands on hips, glaring. 'How dare you?'

I yawned. 'Coffee?'

'I don't want coffee. I want to know . . .'

I went into the bathroom.

Her voice came through, muffled by wood. 'Kate. Get out of there.'

I ran the water in the basin. I didn't know exactly what I was going to do if she tried to come in after me. I put toothpaste on my toothbrush.

I heard her cursing. I gave my teeth the kind of thorough workover that would have left my dentist beaming. That done, I washed my face, brushed my hair and smeared all kinds of creams in all kinds of different places. There, I was ready.

When I opened the door, Valerie made straight for me.

I shifted to one side. 'Coffee?' I said again, brightly.

She shadowed my movements, standing in my way. 'What the hell did you think you were doing terrorizing poor Moira like that?'

Poor Moira. I smiled.

She was spluttering with rage. 'It isn't funny.'

I shrugged and, keeping my mouth firmly closed, I walked forwards. Despite her bluster, Valerie moved out of my way. I went to the kitchen, plugged the kettle in, ground some fresh Colombian and measured it into the filter. Valerie couldn't bear doing nothing. She humped two mugs down on to the counter and fetched the milk – so roughly that some slopped on to the floor. I took a cloth from the sink and handed it to her.

She did such a thorough job of wiping that by the time she'd finished I was at the counter, sipping coffee. I pushed a cupful her way. She took a reluctant slug.

'Now,' I said. 'What's all this about poor Moira?'

The name re-energized Valerie. 'How could you?' Her cup banged down. 'How could you put her at risk like that?'

'Put *her* at risk?' It came out as a yell. 'What do you think your precious Moira's lies did to me?'

'What lies?'

'About the keys.' I couldn't stop shouting. 'Or have you forgotten?'

When she flushed a bright shade of puce I knew she had forgotten. My mouth opened in amazement at the selectiveness of her memory. I didn't know what to say.

She filled the silence. 'Do you know what her husband would do to her if he found out she'd been coming to the Centre?' She directed big, soft, pleading eyes my way.

I glared at her. 'Oh come, on,' I said. 'She could easily have told the police the truth – that she'd had and lost the keys – thus letting me off the hook – without her husband ever finding out. Unless . . .' I hesitated. 'Unless . . .' The horror in Valerie's face told me that the leap I had just made was correct. 'Her husband's a policeman, isn't he?' I said.

Valerie didn't answer.

I didn't need her to. I knew that I'd slotted another piece into place. Moira's brutish husband must be one of Rodney Ellis's officers. Now the only mystery was which one. 'What's his name?'

Valerie's mouth closed tight.

I stretched across the counter, got hold of the right telephone directory, opened it at the Ts, and flicked through until I reached Turner. There were about fifty of them with a B as first initial. That didn't bother me. I knew Moira's address. I looked down the list, searching it out.

I found a Turner, B. J. L. He lived in Southgate, in the same road to which Moira had driven. I looked up. 'She's married to Brian Turner,' I said. It wasn't a question. I followed through with two. 'Is that what happened to the key to the Centre? Did she give it to him?'

Valerie was looking down.

I saw the soft folds of her neck and remembered how, once before, I'd felt like hurting her. 'Did she?'

She delivered up a mumbled: 'It wasn't like that.'

I didn't want to hurt her. Not any longer. I just felt resigned. 'She lost it,' I said.

A silent nod.

'Or Brian took it from her.' I was making the connections now. I added another. 'Was he responsible for the Janet Morris set-up?'

That startled her into looking up. 'What set-up?'

'Janet Morris was never raped,' I said. 'Whoever phoned was only pretending to be Janet.'

'No.' Her lank hair swung first one way and then another. 'It wasn't . . . it couldn't . . .' Her denial was so half hearted she couldn't even finish it. The implication of what I had told her was sinking in – if somebody from Brian Turner's police station had phoned the Crisis Centre with a lie about Janet Morris, that must mean that he . . . She said it out loud: 'He knows.' Her voice was dulled. 'About Moira's visits to the Centre.' Her eyes were locked in terror. 'Do you know what he'll do to her? Do you know what he's like?'

Yes, I nearly said, I know exactly what he's like. Because instead of doing something to Moira he did it first to Janet Morris and then to me. Brian Turner was a wife-batterer who didn't restrict his violence to the home. He was also a drug dealer and, very possibly, a murderer as well. But I didn't tell Valerie any of this. I asked instead: 'How did you expect him not to know about Moira's visits to the Centre?' I kept my voice gentle. 'After you met up with him?'

'With him?' She frowned.

My sympathy curdled into impatience. 'That day you left a note for Moira. The day I turned up at your flat. You were meeting him, weren't you?'

'No.' Her denial was vehement. 'Not Brian Turner. I'd never see him.'

'Somebody else from Parchment Road, then?'

I got a second 'No', less positive this time. Uncertainty didn't come easily to Valerie – she opened and closed her mouth a couple of times before she managed to spit the words out: 'He was from CIB2.'

Hearing that, I put my irritation on hold. After all, I had been caught in the exact same way. 'Name of David Newlands?' I asked.

'No.' She was on safe ground now. 'Not Newlands. This one was called Dowd. Chief Superintendent Gavin Dowd.'

There was a commissionaire sitting at a high desk. He seemed to look right through me. 'Can I help you?'

'Chief Superintendent Dowd,' I said.

He glanced down at the large-leaf book that was spread out in front of him. 'You have an appointment?'

'No.'

He looked up sharply.

'Tell him Kate Baeier is waiting for him,' I said. 'I think you'll find that he'll see me.' But only if he was who he had told Valerie he was, I nearly added.

It seemed that he was. After speaking softly into a phone, the commissionaire pushed the book round. 'Sign here.' He was very careful: only after he'd seen the curve of my signature completed did he hand me a pass. 'Someone will meet you at the eighth,' he said.

I took the lift up to the eighth floor. The doors opened. Someone – Gavin – was waiting. He moved towards me.

'Let's get this over with,' I said.

He pointed down the corridor. I started walking, feeling him close behind. Deliberately I wiped off memory of the other times when we'd been that close. He didn't need to tell me where to go – I saw his name on the door at the corridor's end. I stopped. He opened the door, I walked through.

He had always come to me before. I stood and registered this small part of his world that he had hidden from me. I saw a picture window facing out on to the Thames, a substantial desk, on which lay a set of files, a black executive's chair behind the desk, a more modest black leather seat in front of it, a photo of Charlie Parker, his cheeks ballooning out as he blew on his alto, and, opposite that, a bright Klee print.

I'd forgotten how fast Gavin could move. He was already behind his desk. 'Take a seat.'

I sat, seeing that there was an item in the room I hadn't registered. On the wall within Gavin's grasp was what I could only assume was some kind of blackboard. I couldn't be sure: it was covered by a curtain.

'Trusting to the last,' I said, tilting my head in its direction.

His eyes didn't waver from my face. 'I owe you an apology.'

'Oh.' I raised an eyebrow. 'Really?'

'I lied about where I worked. I couldn't tell you. Not after I met you first in Parchment Road police station. I was on an investigation, you see. I didn't think that what I told you, mattered. I didn't think I . . . I . . .'

'Would get me into bed?'

His frown said my words had been in bad taste. 'Would end up feeling so serious about you,' he said. 'I —'

I cut him off. 'Let's skip the sentiment, shall we?' I didn't wait for his consent. I went on: 'You visited Valerie Watson, didn't you?' I stared at him.

He stared back. Unmoving.

'You asked Valerie about Janet Morris. When Valerie told you what she knew, you suggested she stop pursuing Janet. Why did you do that?'

'I didn't think it was in either woman's best interest.' His voice was calm.

I levelled my voice. 'My, aren't you the chivalrous one?' I went on: 'You visited Janet Morris in hospital, didn't you?'

His head began to move.

'Don't bother denying it,' I said. 'I saw your car. What did you want from her?'

He snagged his bottom lip with his teeth and started working on it. I watched him, wondering how I could have ever found him attractive.

'Look.' He leant forward. Before he could tell me what I was supposed to look at, his phone rang. He picked it up and barked out an impatient 'Yes.' That's all, apparently, that was required of him. He listened briefly before putting the phone down. 'There's something I have to attend to,' he said. He stood up. 'I won't be long.' He left the room, making sure to leave the door wide open.

It didn't take me long to close it. And I could move as fast as him. I went behind his desk and raised the white cover. There was a blackboard underneath, on which were scrawled chalk hieroglyphics. Arrows pointed at mysterious initials. None of them rang any bells with me.

I dropped the curtain and turned my attention to the desk. I started rifling through the files. Again, none of the titles sprang out at me. I wondered whether he had had the foresight to lock all the Parchment Road papers away. Knowing Gavin, I thought that it was more than likely.

I put the files back in their places and pulled a hardbacked black book closer. It was some kind of work diary. I flicked through, seeing how Gavin was heavily into initials. I turned to that day. There was some committee pencilled in for the afternoon, but apart from that only one other entry. *The Huntsman*, it said, followed by one of the omnipresent sets of initials: *PCR*, and the time: *10.15*.

I thought I heard footsteps. I closed the book.

Chapter
forty-one

When he got back, I was sedately in place.

'Sorry about that.' Something seemed to have reinforced his ego. He powered over to his chair and, sitting, smiled at me.

'Had a break on the Ellis case?' I asked.

His smile was abruptly cut off. 'I can't talk about it. Not at this stage in the investigation.'

I looked at him.

He started justifying himself: 'My first sight of you was in Rodney Ellis's office. I didn't know how well you knew him. I had to assume . . .'

I wasn't interested. I pushed my chair out.

He leaned forwards, willing me to stay. 'I know you've been pulled into something you don't understand. It will be over soon. I promise you.'

I didn't think his promises were up to much. I stood.

'Don't go.'

I was already halfway to the door.

'Kate?'

I turned and shot a question his way: 'Are you going to trust me with what you have?'

His sigh was all the answer I needed. I turned away and put my hand out, aiming for the doorknob. And then I remembered. I twisted round. 'Does a Superintendent David Newlands work here?'

He answered that with a question of his own. 'Why?'

'Take it as journalistic curiosity,' I said. 'Does he work with you?'

'Yes.'

'How old is he?' I saw Gavin was hesitating. I poured scorn into my voice. 'Come on. That can't be a secret.'

'He's fifty-two.'

Much older than the man who had come to see me. 'Gone on a continental holiday, has he?'

Gavin frowned. 'He's in the Azores.'

Leaving an impostor to use his credentials, I thought. I wrenched the door open.

'Kate.' Gavin's voice was urgent. 'Don't do anything stupid. It will be all right if you would only . . .'

'Sure it will.' Especially I thought, now that I was out. I closed the door gently behind me.

I parked in a street outside the back entrance of the Parchment Road police station. I had come prepared with sandwiches and coffee and pieces of fruit. Which was just as well. I was there for six hours, watching police vans delivering suspects and police personnel changing shifts. All that time I put my thoughts on hold. I wasn't going to dwell on it, any of it, not until it was over.

At eight Gracie, the WPC whom I had seen crying on the night James Shaw had died, emerged. I watched her walking down the street. She looked about as weary as I felt.

I started up the engine and kerb-crawled behind her. She must have had a really bad day: she didn't even notice. She passed an alleyway. I put my foot down on the accelerator and, overtaking her, parked half on the pavement.

'What the . . .'

I pushed her into the alley, backed her up against the wall and held a knife against her neck. A plastic knife courtesy of the sandwich shop – although she didn't know that. With my other hand, I twisted her hand up behind her back.

'Now repeat after me,' I said. ' "If you're looking for Janet Morris, she said she'd be at Francio's . . ." '

She tried to pull away. I had been expecting that. I dug the knife into her earlobe. 'Want the *Reservoir Dogs* option?'

She shook her head frantically.

I ground the knife in. 'Say it!'

It came out haltingly. 'If you're looking for Janet . . .'

It was all I needed. 'It was you,' I said. 'You phoned the Crisis Centre pretending to be Janet. And you phoned me twice as well.'

She went limp. Another trick. I tugged at her hand, driving it almost as far as her shoulder blades. She winced.

'It was you, wasn't it?'

'Yes.'

'That's better.' For reward I hauled her arm even higher. 'Nobody raped Janet, did they?'

'You're hurting me.'

Which, frankly, was good to hear. I twisted some more. 'Did they?'

There were tears in her eyes. She shook her head.

'So why did you set her up?'

I no longer had the advantage of surprise. She looked defiantly at me.

'Somebody asked you to?' I said, shoving my face up close to her, to show how serious I was.

This time I got a nod.

'What had she done?' I tried an appeal, woman to woman. 'Refused somebody's favours?'

Gracie laughed. So much for woman to woman. 'Janet! You must be joking. She was the relief bicycle. A regular Martini.' She saw me frown. 'You know. Any time. Anywhere.'

I twisted the knife in further. 'What had she done?' Lucky it wasn't sharp or I would have drawn blood.

'She was a grass, telling all sorts of tales out of school,' Gracie muttered. 'So I was told.'

'Always believe what you're told, do you?'

She bit her lip.

'And do it as well? Like that night they killed James Shaw. I saw you there, you know, crying in the cell.'

'I didn't do anything.' Her eyes widened.

'Oh yeah?' I started improvising. 'I spoke to Melville Adams before he died. He had a tale to tell. You had a starring role in it: the kind your mother won't like to hear about.'

'Nobody will believe that jungle bunny.'

I pushed her head, banging it against the wall.

She laughed. 'Anyway, he's dead.'

I smiled. 'And I have him on tape, describing your part in James Shaw's murder.'

That got her. She burst out: 'It's not true.' Her eyes were watering. 'It was an accident. They were just a bit rough, that's all. I had nothing to do with it.'

'They?'

She started crying. 'I can't tell you. I can't. They'll kill me.'

I said it again: 'They?'

Her face told me that it didn't matter what I did, she wouldn't say.

282

'OK. Nod if I get it right. Is there someone in the station controlling all this?'

A beat, and then she nodded.

'Did Frances Ellis know about it?'

I got another nod.

'It's your chief super, isn't it?'

This time, she didn't move.

I was afraid the knife would break. I wrenched at her plait, pulling her head back. 'Isn't it?'

'Yes.' She squealed in pain.

'Who –'

I never got to finish the question. I heard an authoritative 'What's going on?' followed quickly by a rising 'Gracie?'

I turned my heard and saw an unfamiliar policeman walking towards us.

I spat words into Gracie's ear. 'Say anything and I'll tell them it was you spilled your guts about Brian Turner's little drug-recycling business.' I let go of her hand.

'Gracie?' He was almost upon us.

'It's OK,' I said. 'Just doing a consumer survey. Testing the strength of plastic knives.' I laid it in her hand. 'This one did quite well, don't you think?'

Chapter
forty-two

I'm sure there must be as many as a hundred Huntsman pubs in southern England. I know of only one. By eight-forty-five I had parked within a block of it. I got out and started walking. It was sited on a corner of one of the streets that lead off the New North Road. All around were prosperous-looking, low-rise council blocks, the kind that haven't yet fallen prey to urban blight.

I went in, just to check. The place was crowded with serious drinkers. A motley collection of animal heads were stuck in the walls, their glazed eyes focused on their fate. Probably came courtesy of the Essex Road taxidermist, I thought, looking at the clientele. They were mostly men, bellies so distended that the only thing they were in a position to hunt was small change for the next pint of beer. There wasn't a single familiar face.

I realized then that I hadn't had a drink since Gavin's reaction to my arrest had sent me on a binge. I played with the idea of breaking the drought. I looked at my watch: eighty-fifty. I had time before Gavin was due to meet the mysterious PCR.

I wasn't even tempted. I wanted to be sober. I turned and walked out.

I reparked my car, away from any lamppost but near

enough to the pub so I could see its door. I settled back to wait.

There was a fish-and-chip shop opposite the pub. Between the two, there was enough traffic to keep me interested. Strings of teenagers threw saturated fats at their arteries and old chip packets at the pavement, courting couples shared pieces of fish while their elders walked dejectedly into the pub past toddlers who sat in pushchairs bawling for more food and more attention. All human life: I was glad I could keep it at a distance.

By ten I started getting serious. I moved over into the back seat – a casual glance was less likely to find me there – and lowered myself on to the floor. That way, I could see the pub door as well as the rear-view mirror, which could tell me what was coming up behind.

He was prompt, was Gavin. At precisely ten-fifteen, his headlights flashed in the top mirror and then passed by. I saw his Saab in the side-view mirror. There was nowhere to park on my side of the road, so he crossed over and stopped close to the fish-and-chip shop. His lights went out. His door opened.

My eyes moved to the left, taking in the pub door. If I focused on it, I would see him entering and, perhaps, spot the person he was going to meet. I counted to ten, reckoning that this was enough time to get him across the road.

He didn't come into vision. I thought I was counting too fast. I slowed myself down and tried for another ten. Still no Gavin.

Maybe he was waiting in the car. I looked to the right. And did a double-take. The Saab was there, dark and silent, but it was empty. Gavin had gone. I couldn't believe it: I was only ten yards away and I'd lost him. My eyes swung left. I saw a man dragging a dog through the pub's brightly lit door. No Gavin.

Maybe there was something obstructing my view. I pushed myself up until I was sitting on the back seat. No. Nothing.

I heard the jangling of the chip-shop door. My gaze was drawn inadvertently to it. I saw him then. Gavin. Standing inside the door. He wasn't alone. He was talking to another man. The owner of the initials PCR.

Of course. I should have known. Lloyd Adams had, at his brother's funeral, told me this man's name. Police Constable Reynolds. Gary Reynolds. The man I knew as Action Man, the one who rode shotgun on Brian Turner's drug missions and who had been behind the desk the day James Shaw had died.

I was out of the car. I don't know why. I wasn't even conscious of getting out. I felt as if someone had kicked me in the stomach. I doubled over, retching. I nearly fell but, as the pavement came closer, I pulled myself together. I breathed out, long and hard. I knew that there was no point in my being there: there was no way I was going to confront them. I got into the front seat. The key was in its place. I turned it, listening to the engine sparking. Then, coolly, calmly and without thinking about what I was doing, I drove off.

I was inside my flat – locked in. I didn't feel safe. Something about shutting the stable door after the horse has bolted, I thought. Gavin had already violated my trust.

And Janet Morris's as well. I thought about what must have happened. She must have complained to CIB2 about the goings-on in Rodney Ellis's police station. Poor woman – she'd got Gavin. Who was himself involved and who had passed her complaints straight on to the Parchment Road mafia, which had then set her up as one of a hated breed of policewomen who falsely accuse their brother officers of rape.

Poor, gullible, stupid Janet. Just like me. When Newlands had told me James Shaw had died of a cerebral haemorrhage, I had felt secure because Gavin had said the same. Now I knew that this was the sign that they'd concocted their stories together.

The phone started ringing. I picked it up. I heard a man's voice. 'Miss Baeier. I must apologize for the lateness of the hour. My wife got the impression that this was an after-work number. The name's Jacks. Ian Jacks.'

'Mr Jacks. Thank you for calling.'

'You requested that I should?'

I tried to infuse efficiency into my voice. 'I am investigating the death of Steven Parker,' I said.

He interrupted, repeating the same words his wife had used but in his own rounded tones. 'At long last. I know there are those who find my persistence irritating, but when inefficiency stands in the way of police investigation I consider that worse than negligence.' He took a breath. I got the impression that asking him anything would slow up delivery of the story he was obviously dying to tell. I held my tongue. 'I have sent numerous letters to the authorities pointing out their negligence,' he said. 'I have received nothing substantial in reply. Of course it is now too late to see justice done, but, nevertheless, I am determined to put the record straight. I am considering asking my Member of Parliament to intervene.'

I thought that if it had taken him twenty-six years to think about contacting his MP, I'd be an old woman before he came to the point. I risked a question. 'What exactly is it that you saw?'

'A man, of course.'

A man? That was hardly helpful. 'Another witness, you mean?'

'For God's sake, woman,' he snorted. 'Haven't you bothered to read any of my letters?'

I went all formal. 'I'm sorry sir. I need it in your own words.'

That seemed to go down well. 'All right.' He was flattered. 'I'll attempt to be succinct. As I told the investigating officer, there was indeed a woman in the car. But she wasn't driving. There was a man with her. I couldn't have identified him – it all happened much too fast, you understand – but I know it was a man who ran that little boy down.'

'You're sure?' I don't know why I asked. I knew that he was sure. And that he was right. Ramona Martin had said the same thing.

His voice continued in the background telling me precisely how certain he was of what had happened. I listened with only half an ear. I was too busy thinking – about the man who had been with Frances. Her husband, Rodney Ellis. Who had got his chum Tom Harrison to cover up for him, to put in his report that, contrary to what all the witnesses had said, a woman had been driving the car.

'. . . which makes one think that all this talk of democracy is a sham,' I heard Ian Jacks saying. 'Don't you agree?'

I would have agreed to anything to get him off the phone. But it wasn't necessary. 'I'll bid you goodnight then, Miss Baeier,' he said. 'I've had a long day.'

I pulled myself together. 'Of course. Goodnight. And thanks for ringing.'

The moment I said those words, someone rang at my doorbell. I put the phone down. It was gone eleven – far too late for a casual visitor. I went over to the window.

I could see the stairs leading up to the front door but not the door itself – that was obscured by window ledges. Whoever was down there was the impatient type. I heard the doorbell ringing again. I looked up and down the street. And knew immediately, by the sight of his parked Saab, that it was Gavin at my door.

If I had checked, then so had he. He rang again. He knew I was there. I stood, silent, wondering what to do. I heard the chinking of keys.

He could have mine, I thought.

I grabbed my bag and moved fast away from the window. Of course he could have my keys. I'd been so trusting. He could have taken them any time he'd been here and made copies. I ran into the back, to the window that overlooked the garden. I wasn't going to stay in my flat. I couldn't. I pushed the window up and climbed on to the ledge. It seemed like a long way down.

I heard a door open.

I swung one arm out, grabbing for the drainpipe that ran the length of the house. When I thought I had a firm enough grip, I let the other hand join it. Then, without giving myself time to stop and change my mind, I jumped.

Chapter
forty-three

I slithered all the way down the drainpipe, grazing my skin. When I landed on the ground my right arm was burning. I didn't have time to look at it. I'd have to leave the first aid for later. I scrambled over the garden wall.

I was in the neighbouring garden. I ran across, climbing over its side wall, which landed me in another garden. I wasn't clear and wouldn't be for a while: a chain of back gardens stretched before me. I climbed the next wall, and the next, each time more slowly, until I reached the end of the row.

The last barrier was far higher than the ones that had preceded it. I stopped to catch my breath. That done, I ran at the wall, grabbing for the top. I clutched at a brick but not for long. My grip faltered; my fingers slid off. Now they also were hurting. I turned, walked a few paces back, and tried again. And again after that. By the time I finally succeeded in grasping the top, I didn't know whether I had the strength to haul myself over it. My breath was coming out as strangled gasps. I couldn't do it; I felt myself slipping.

I thought about Gavin and the clinking of his keys. Using reserves I didn't know I had, I hauled myself up, so hard that when I got to the top, momentum carried me over.

I landed on the pavement and sprawled forwards. I lay there struggling for breath. I didn't know which part of my body hurt the most. I did know that I felt defeated. I played with the idea of giving up, of lying there and accepting passively whatever it was that would happen next.

Gavin's image came again. I got up slowly. Some ancient reflex had me trying to brush myself down. Where my hand touched flesh, it came out wet. I stopped brushing.

For all I knew Gavin had posted guards. I couldn't fetch my car. I limped down the road, heading for the lights of the main Camden roads. On the corner I saw a heap of rags – a homeless person sleeping. I stood, looking down. He – she? I couldn't tell which – was covered by a long overcoat. I took a tenner out of my bag and, holding it in one hand, hooked up the coat.

'Oy.' Bony fingers shot out from the heap. I flashed the tenner. The fingers snatched, at the same time releasing the coat.

I put it on. It stunk of meths. I breathed more shallowly, trying to keep the fumes at bay, and then, stepping out into the light, I raised my hand.

I knew the coat had done the business when a taxi drew up. I opened the back door and got in, but I smelt too bad. The driver turned, his nose wrinkling, his mouth about to open.

'It's OK,' I said, my enunciation courtesy of Ian Jacks. 'I was cleaning my brushes after a spot of painting and the bloody turpentine spilled all over me.'

His look told me that the accent was a fail. I didn't move. I sat in his cab, waiting his reaction out. His expression changed not once but twice: in the end he decided that evicting the demented was more of a risk than an unpaid fare. He sighed and turned away. 'Where to?'

I told him, then I sank back into my seat.

I made the taxi-driver's week by adding a substantial tip to the fare he hadn't expected. As he drove off, I looked at Rodney Ellis's house. It was swathed in darkness. So were the others surrounding it. The whole street was quiet, serene like roads in Camden Town could never be.

I walked up the path. My footsteps resonated. I reached the door and hesitated, but it was too late, now, to go back. I pressed the doorbell. By the speed at which the light clicked on, I knew that he hadn't been asleep. I heard his footsteps and then, through the glass, I saw him coming closer.

When he opened the door, a spotlight blazed so bright that I was temporarily blinded. 'Miss Baeier,' I heard.

My eyes had adjusted. I could see Rodney Ellis standing in front of me. He was fully dressed in blue-grey suit, white shirt and matching blue tie that showed he had taken care to choose his clothes. Sometime in the last few days that is – the suit was crumpled, the tie askew, the shirt grubby.

The last thing I wanted to do was feel sorry for him. Besides, I bet I looked worse. I spoke: 'I've come about Steven Parker.'

I knew by his reaction that he'd spent his whole adult life anticipating those words. He dipped his head and left it down, waiting, mutely, for what came next.

'You ran him over,' I said.

He lifted his haggard face. I saw something which looked almost like astonishment flashing across it. 'I?'

'You were driving the car.'

He said a soft 'No', directing it inwards, as if the denial was aimed not at me but at himself.

'You killed Steven Parker,' I said.

He said something else then, so softly that I couldn't really hear it. It sounded like: 'I wish.'

I found myself trapped in repetition. 'You were driving the car.'

He looked at me. 'I was at work,' he said.

Of course he was. That's how he'd risen so high: he must always have been at work. The perfect policeman – with the wife who drank too much and who'd hung out with her husband's friends while he was gone. I didn't know what to say. I tried: 'I'm sorry.' I didn't know whether he knew why I was apologizing. It didn't seem to matter. He stepped back and closed the door on me.

I could see him, through the glass, standing in the hall. Like husband, like wife, I thought: both of them haunted by a mutual past. I turned and went the way I had come, down the path and out on to the street.

Nothing had changed. It was still dark and quiet out there. I began walking, aiming to steer myself out of the back streets, into a more central area where I might be able to find a taxi. 'I'll go to Carmen's,' I told myself.

When a car purred up beside me, I wasn't the slightest bit surprised. I stopped.

Sergeant Tom Harrison leaned over and opened the passenger door. 'Can I give you a lift?'

The street was deserted.

'Come on. You'll never get a taxi here.' He was smiling, kindly. 'You look as if you've been hurt,' he said. 'You'll never make it under your own steam.'

I knew I didn't stand a chance. Not there I didn't. I got in the car.

He shifted over to give me room. 'You live in Camden Town, don't you?'

I nodded.

'Wise woman. Always pays to stay centrally. I'll take you back.'

'I can always get a . . .'

'No.' He was driving at a law-abiding thirty. 'I wouldn't dream of it.' He turned left at the bottom of the road. 'I was visiting Rodney when you came. Poor man. He's taking her death hard.' He glanced at me. 'Not that I'm not. Frances and I, we were like this.' He held his left hand up and crossed his fingers.

I uncrossed my fingers and inched them nearer to the door handle.

'Now let's see,' he said meditatively. 'Which is the best route?'

By best, he must have meant the most deserted. He drove through the back streets of London, past law-abiding citizens all sleeping soundly in their beds. He was a good driver, he kept at an even pace, anticipating what came next. That way he didn't have the inconvenience of stopping at a single traffic light.

'I've got one errand to run,' he said. 'You don't mind, do you?'

I didn't think it mattered whether I minded. Or whether I spoke.

He turned to the right. I knew where we were now: in his patch, heading deeper into Hackney.

'The isolation of power made Rodney lonely,' he said. 'That's one of the reasons I never bothered with the exams. It's the camaraderie I like, the feeling of belonging.' He glanced at me and smiled.

I tried to return his smile, trying not to show how much my thoughts were focused on a zebra crossing ahead and on a couple of men walking towards it.

'There's nothing like the feeling of a well-oiled firm,' he said. 'Us against them, pitting our wits against their wrong-doing. We're not so different, you know. We walk the same mean streets. What separates the two groups is that our side has discipline, organization, guts.'

I concentrated on the men, willing them to move.

'We have to be better than them,' he said. 'Because if we aren't, they'll gut us.'

They moved, over the zebra crossing. For the first time, Tom Harrison was unprepared. He braked.

It was my chance. Perhaps my only one. I wrenched at the handle.

Which is precisely what he'd been waiting for me to do. There was a soft thunk – my lock and all the others with it, going down.

Tom Harrison was looking at the road ahead. 'Take central locking,' he said. 'Great timesaver, especially if you've got young kids. But tell me seriously – do you think anybody would have thought of inventing it, if it wasn't for the rise in crime?' His broad hands played on the steering wheel, turning the car.

We were in a narrow street. On either side prefabricated factories. Function, not form, was king here: the buildings were long and low, surrounded by mute pieces of machinery and piles of junk all fenced in by razor wire.

'It's just there,' Tom Harrison said, slowing down the car.

He brought it to a stop outside a high gate. He got out and fiddled with the gate's lock. I didn't move. There seemed no point.

He was back. 'I knew you would be sensible,' he said. 'Right from the beginning.' He killed his headlights and drove slowly into the yard.

Chapter
forty-four

He was holding my door open. 'Come with me.'

My joints were stiff. It took me a long time to get out.

By the time I managed, he had already moved away. He was leaning over the open boot. When he withdrew his hand, he was holding a long wooden bat. He winked jovially. 'I'm a sportsman at heart.'

I remembered the headlights of a car blinding me, the shadow of a man coming closer holding something long and straight. A man who had nothing to do with my father. A man who was standing in front of me now.

I cleared my throat. 'Did you set up that little charade on the South Bank to help Gavin win my trust?'

He frowned. 'Gavin? Who's Gavin?' He looked genuinely bemused. Not that it worried him for long. His expression cleared. The name had slotted into place, not as a major player but more a minor irritation. 'The action at the South Bank was a warning,' he said, 'to give you a chance to stop snooping, but you didn't, did you? Your type always thinks they're so clever.' He smiled. 'We were never worried about Dowd. We can run rings round him, especially now we've booked the woman he's shafting for dealing heroin and . . .' He left the sentence hanging without explaining what the 'and' implied. My imagination was already scaring

me enough: I was rather pleased he hadn't gone on.
'Come.' He took me by the arm, pushing me to the factory
entrance.

My senses were so acute, I smelt aftershave and the
starch on his shirt. His self-confidence was outstanding. I
knew that he must have been driving that day twenty-six
years ago. The question that had been nagging at me while
he brought me here, the question of how he'd had the nerve
to interview witnesses to the killing of Steven Parker, fell
away. This man had no nerves at all.

I put the thought aside. I needed to engage him. He was
inserting a key into a huge padlock. 'What's the point of
kidnapping me?' I asked. 'Did Gracie go running to Papa?'

Papa. A strange choice of words. It was I who had once
thought of Tom Harrison as a father-figure.

His teeth were so white they had to be false. 'Women
have got more stamina than men.' The lock fell. He kicked
the door open. 'Not Frances, of course. But then she never
got over betraying her husband in bed.' He stepped to one
side.

I tried another question. 'Why put Adams in the Crisis
Centre?'

He shrugged. 'That was Brian's little joke. He had an
obsession with that place – something to do with his wife.
You're lucky, you know. You don't want to meet Brian
when he's in the grip of an obsession. He's inspired, I can
tell you. Would have been drummed out the force a long
time ago if something didn't always pitch in and save him.
Take what he did to you – getting you over to the Centre,
making sure your fingerprints were there, and then handing
out your photograph to all and sundry, planning to persuade
somebody to identify you. Brian, I told him, it's not going
to work. But it did, didn't it? Turner's luck, we call it. He

297

found an honest citizen who genuinely recognized you and who even came up with a plot element all of his own – telling us that he saw you opening a note Valerie Watson had left for Brian's missus.' Tom Harrison directed an exaggerated wink my way. 'Naughty, invading privacy like that. It can get you into trouble, you know. Especially when Brian's sweet Moira realizes hubby has the keys and goes running to her friend Valerie screaming blue murder and what Brian will do to her, and Valerie, not knowing she was dumping you in the proverbial shite, agrees to cover up for Moira. Never trust a dyke, you know. That's what Brian would say. Not that you're his favourite person either. When he saw you at the club, he wanted to get you. I held him off.' He pointed ahead, mock chivalrous. 'After you.'

I took one, tentative step forward. It was pitch black. My foot hit something. Something metal. I heard it ringing out. I leaned down quickly and picked it up. It was small and round and fitted in my pocket.

Tom Harrison was by the wall. I heard a click, and the place was flooded with light, hundreds of watts burning. I looked around. The factory was empty save for a few hulks of discarded machinery on the floor, each surrounded by huge cardboard cartons. They'd been there a long time; parts of the cardboard had been eaten by mildew and by something else, their once perfect edges shredded into pieces.

Tom Harrison saw me looking at them. 'Rats,' he said. He pointed at the wall. 'If you wouldn't mind?'

I stood my ground.

He grabbed me by the arm and hustled me over, turning me round, shoving my hands up high, my legs away. Then he searched me, the hands of a professional patting my clothes. He clicked his tongue at the state of my arms and once again, when he found the metal object that I had just concealed.

'OK.' He kicked my feet.

I lost my balance, falling clumsily on to the floor. I thought vaguely that because it didn't hurt, I must be beyond pain.

'She's all yours,' I heard him saying.

I looked up. I was staring into the barrel of a gun. The hand that held it belonged to Lloyd Adams.

His hand was steady. Keeping it pointed at me, he leant forwards and yanked me up. Probably had a thing about shooting prone women, I thought.

'You killed my brother,' he said.

I shook my head. 'No.'

'You slag. Nobody does that. Not to me. Nobody kills my brother and gets away with it.'

I knew I shouldn't have but I couldn't help smiling.

A mistake. The gun touched my forehead. 'You think it's funny, do you?' It felt clammy. 'What did you think – that I wouldn't find out? Or that I wouldn't care? Because my brother had a habit, you think I would let somebody kill him and get away with it? He was still my brother. He was –'

Tom Harrison's voice cut through Lloyd's, 'Look, son. There's only one thing I have against you – you talk too much. You wanted her. I delivered her. Do me a favour, speed it up, will you?'

Lloyd's eyes were bloodshot. I wondered what he'd taken. He didn't look at Tom Harrison, he was fixated on me. 'You going to pay for what you did,' he said. He stepped back. The gun was pointing at my pelvis. It was his turn to smile. 'I'll enjoy this.'

I was still numbed by Lloyd's appearance. I fought with

299

myself to get my sluggish mind in gear. As he moved the gun up, slowly up, I launched into speech: 'She's quite a woman, your mother.'

Of all the things I could have said, he wasn't expecting that. His jaw dropped.

I tried not to hurry. 'I spoke with her at Melville's funeral. About giving people chances. I think what she was trying to say was that she regretted throwing Melville out. And would regret it her whole life.'

His hand had steadied. 'My mother's my business.'

'Sure she is. But how do you think she'll feel about what you're doing? Shooting me without giving me a chance?'

'You killed her son.'

'No.' I kept my gaze steady. 'I didn't kill him.' I made my eyes jump over Lloyd, indicating the place where Tom Harrison stood. 'He did.'

Tom Harrison laughed. Loud and confident.

'He and his friends killed James Shaw that night they had Melville banged up,' I said. 'Afterwards they got scared. I had crossed them twice: first by muscling in on their attempt to scare off one of their own colleagues, a policewoman by the name of Janet Morris, and then by wandering round the police station on the night of James Shaw's death. They weren't sure what I'd seen. They sent a man round who pretended to be part of CIB2 to check it out. They knew, by the way I talked to him, that I hadn't been there when James Shaw was offed. But there was somebody from the real CIB2 after them – somebody I knew. They saw an opportunity to get him through me. They planted heroin in my bread bin. Now, if my friend gets too close to the truth they can easily get rid of him by saying he was sleeping with a dealer. Which left your brother as the wild card. He must have been brought in about the time somebody was beating on James Shaw. They needed to know what he'd seen. So they used me again. They set me up to test Melville. They knew your brother well. They knew if I went to him, suggesting that he should contact a policeman about what happened that night, Melville wouldn't be straight about it. He wouldn't, would he? What he'd do is try and use the information to get more heroin.' Even though I was making it up as I went along, I knew that what I was saying made a terrible kind of sense. 'Which is just what Melville did,' I continued. 'He stopped trying to score from you and instead went straight to source. To Brian Turner. Tom Harrison's underling. Either he had seen something or else he pretended that he had. He told Brian that he wanted drugs for silence.'

Tom Harrison was unperturbed. 'Jesus. You got to admire her. She sure knows how to spin them.'

My gaze was reserved exclusively for Lloyd. 'They gave him drugs all right. And his silence as well.' Out of the corner of my eye, I could see Tom walking past Lloyd, walking closer.

'They set me up to catch Melville,' I said. 'To find out what he knew. Not knowing what I was doing, I sent him straight into their waiting arms. Whatever he told them was enough to make them want to get rid of him. They killed him and then they tried to fit me up for his murder, but I guess someone higher up wouldn't swallow it – the problem of a complete absence of motive on my part, I suppose. They can probably make the drug charge stick but they're not satisfied with that. They want to kill me too: and they want you to do it.'

Tom Harrison flooded his voice with easy contempt. 'Listen to her. The condemned woman talking shit. There's just one problem with her story. Melville didn't see anything. How could he? He was locked up tight. In his mind as well. Come on, Lloyd. You know how he was that night.'

A nerve was jumping in Lloyd's eye.

'We know as well.' Tom Harrison sounded so confident. 'So why would we bother going to all this trouble? It doesn't make sense. Go on. You've got your chance. She killed your brother. Get rid of her.'

Tom Harrison did something then. A policeman's trick. He turned away. Deliberately. Showing Lloyd his back. Showing him he wasn't scared.

I could see that it was working. I could see Lloyd's eyes refocusing on me. I could see the gun steadying. I had only one more guess to play.

'Harrison is lying,' I said. 'I think Melville did see something. Or at least he pretended he did. They set him up: I know they did. And I can prove it. I bet Melville mistrusted the police, I bet he would never go to them for a hit unless he was desperate. But he was desperate, wasn't he? He had no money and you had cut off his free supply. Why did you do that? Was it because someone told you to? Someone like Tom Harrison?

As soon as the words were out, I knew I'd got him. Not by Lloyd's response, but by the way Tom Harrison froze.

Something in me wanted to shout out, to stop what was going to happen. I couldn't.

It happened fast. The gun turned. I was watching Tom Harrison. I didn't see Lloyd shoot, but I heard the sound, a sharp report, and I saw the shot's effect. Tom Harrison fell over slowly and silently. On to the floor.

I had no time to worry about him. I looked back. I saw the gun coming my way. I saw it aimed at my chest.

302

I'd run out of words. 'What for?' was all I could think of saying.

Lloyd's face was impassive.

I said it again: 'What for?'

I had no idea what he was going to do. I wasn't even sure I cared.

His hand dropped so that the gun was pointing at the floor. He walked away.

He didn't go far. When he reached Tom Harrison he stopped. He kicked out, his foot sinking into Tom Harrison's stomach. I heard a groan.

Lloyd heard it to. He leant over and placed the gun on Tom Harrison's temple. I turned my head. I heard another, more muffled shot. I told myself not to look back.

I couldn't help myself. I turned to see that what had once been the inside of a human being's head – blood and what looked like oozing pus – was leaking out on to the sawdust floor. I heard myself retching. I saw Lloyd reaching into his inside pocket. He pulled something out, bent down and tucked it into what had once been Tom Harrison's coat. And then, finally, he walked away.

Chapter
forty-five

       I managed, by walking half the way and then hailing a taxi, to get back to my flat. The place was still bolted from the inside. Gavin had never had the keys.

I waited until dawn and then woke my neighbour. His shock at my climbing out of his window and up into mine put a temporary stop to his torrent of outrage.

I went inside, and closed the window and sat beside the radio. It was the lead item on the early morning news, told in those solemn tones that newsreaders reserve for major tragedies – a policeman shot dead in a deserted warehouse in Hackney. They said they couldn't release his name until they'd informed the next of kin. They also said they'd found the murder weapon lying close by. There were no fingerprints on it.

Since it was big news, they rolled the pundits out. There was plenty of talk of the cowards who'd shot a man in the back and some about the necessity of arming of the police. No mention was made of any drugs.

I hadn't slept all night. That didn't bother me. I unbolted the door and went out to my car.

Richmond was waking up. As an old Volvo dawdled down the street, a paper boy came trudging towards me.

I walked up to Rodney Ellis's door.

It was open. I went in. And called his name.

No answer.

I reckoned I knew where he was. I walked through the house and into the living room. The french doors were wide open. I went out into the garden.

I found him at its very end. He was crouched down by a bed, using a small trowel to make futile motions in the rich soil. I crouched down next to him.

He turned to look at me. He didn't speak.

I did. 'You know that Tom Harrison is dead?'

He nodded.

I spoke again. 'He was blackmailing you, running a firm within a firm. Dealing drugs. And other things I guess.'

I was wrong. What Rodney Ellis was doing did have focus. He was making a hole. A long, thin hole. Gently he took the earth from it and piled it by the side. His voice, when he spoke, was almost contemplative. 'Tom knew what Frances had done. He protected her. I waited for him to ask for payment. He never did. I stopped worrying about it – or at least that side of it.' He glanced up. 'Then, twenty-five years later, Tom fixed it so that he was posted under me. That's when it started. He thought he could do anything he wanted. I tried to stop him. I threatened to tell. But he knew I couldn't. It would have killed Frances.' Another trowelful joined the pile. 'I tried to ignore what was happening. When James Shaw died I told myself it was an accident – the Pl. M bore that out. But then Melville Adams died and my officers swore they found drugs on your premises. I knew you were no dealer. I knew then that I had to speak out. I told Frances. And she . . . and she . . .' The trowel smashed into the careful heap, scattering it in all directions.

He started rocking. Back and forth.

'Were she and Tom having an affair all those years ago?'

I thought he gave a nod. I couldn't be sure.

His voice confirmed it. 'Only until that day. After that, they stopped.' He looked at me. 'I didn't know what had happened, really I didn't, not until after the Parker case was closed. I didn't know what Tom had done for her.' He swallowed. 'For me.'

Not for Rodney, I thought, nor for Frances. For himself. I opened my mouth. I was going to tell him that he and Frances had been wrong, that she had never killed anybody. That she must have been too drunk to remember that it was Tom Harrison who'd been driving.

I looked at him. His eyes had the same glazed look as the dead animals on the Hunstman's wall. I closed my mouth. What I had been about to say would only add to the torture he was enduring.

I got up. His voice joined me. 'I'm finished,' he said. He picked up the trowel. 'Not that I care.'

Gavin came at lunchtime, accompanied by a uniformed policeman, who stayed in the room while Gavin told me formally that CIB2 believed I had been the victim of a corrupt police ring operating inside Rodney Ellis's station. He confirmed that James Shaw had died of a cerebral haemorrhage but said that several officers were being investigated for involvement in the death. He also said that Brian Turner was in custody and that the charges against me had been dropped. He gave me back my passport. Then he asked me if I knew anything about Tom Harrison's death.

'No.' I looked him in the eye.

'There were a set of fingerprints in Sergeant Harrison's

car,' he said. 'We haven't matched them yet. Do you think they might be yours?'

'It's possible,' I said. 'I've been in his car. Not last night. Some time ago.'

'Any witnesses to that?'

I didn't hesitate. 'Sure,' I said. 'A policeman. Sergeant Brian Turner.'

Gavin looked at me, holding the silence. I let him hold it. The policeman, standing in the background, coughed.

'And what if Sergeant Turner disclaims all knowledge of this?' Gavin asked.

I shrugged. 'Well, then you'll just have to decide which of us you believe.'

They left soon after that. I walked them down. After I had opened the door, Gavin told the uniform to wait for him in the car. When the man was safely out of earshot, Gavin turned to me. 'Why didn't you answer your door last night? I knew you were there. I came to warn you.'

'I saw you talking to Gary Reynolds,' I said.

His eyes closed, just a fraction, as he took that in. He knew what I meant – that I had suspected him of being part of the gang. I didn't tell him that only after I was taken to the warehouse did I realize how wrong I'd been.

'What was it?' I asked. 'An elaborate plea bargaining?'

He nodded. 'We knew much of what had been going on but to prove it, we needed an insider. We had tried before with Janet Morris but she got scared.'

'She didn't get scared,' I said. 'She got victimized. Somebody must have seen her talking to you.'

His face was sombre. 'Perhaps you're right, but the way they set about getting her – by reporting a false rape to your friend Valerie – was so obscure I thought they couldn't be entirely serious. That was my mistake – and a bad one.

I tried to help. I told Valerie to lay off agitating about Janet Morris. I thought that might take the heat off her.'

'You thought wrong,' I said. 'Janet ended up in hospital. Meanwhile I assume your drug-dealing friend Gary Reynolds will get off.'

Gavin shrugged. 'That. Or a reduced sentence. Depends how well he makes our case.'

'And Rodney Ellis? Are you going to punish him more?'

Gavin frowned. 'More?'

'His wife.'

'What happened to his wife isn't relevant.' Gavin's voice was hard. 'There was wrongdoing on a massive scale going on in the Parchment Road station. Rodney Ellis was the Chief Superintendent. If we can prove that he knew, and countenanced, what was going on, then as far as I'm concerned, he deserves everything he gets.'

Gavin's anger had got him going. He turned and started walking down the stairs.

'Gavin.'

He stopped.

'You didn't trust me.'

He looked back. 'And you? Did you trust me?'

I went back upstairs. I sat on the sofa and thought about what Gavin had said.

The phone rang. I got up to answer it, taking it so that I was looking out of the window. I heard my father's voice. I saw that Gavin's Saab had gone.

Erica Cadogan was fast. She'd already told my father that the charges had been dropped. I listened numbly to the outflow of his congratulations. When he had finished, he told me that the legal documents were ready for signature. I looked out on to a dull, overcast day and I told him what I would do.

Chapter
forty-six

My heels rang out against the granite cobble-stones. I kept on walking, breathing in the strong aroma of roasting fish. A horn blasted – somebody objecting to my walking in the middle of the narrow street. I stepped on to the pavement and let the car pass by. Above me a woman, dressed all in black, was hanging washing from her tiny wrought-iron balcony. The sun played intricate patterns on the cobblestones. I took off my jacket, enjoying the feel of Lisbon in spring.

The car had gone. I went to the end of the street, to my mother's *palacio*. Its dusty pink terracotta façade was barely visible through the tangle of untended fig trees. The huge iron gates were padlocked together. I went into the tyre shop next door and was given a set of keys.

The lock was rusty with misuse – it took me some time to set it free. The estate agents must have taken prospective buyers through a side entrance, I thought, as I walked to the ornate front door. I had a key for that as well.

Inside was dark and cool and musty. I went down the long hall and into what had once been our living room. The wooden shutters were drawn tight. When I pulled them open, sun streamed in. The place had been empty far too long. Ochre paint was peeling off the walls, exposing the aquamarine that had been my mother's previous choice.

I stood in the middle of the elegant room remembering my last glimpse of her. She'd been weaving through this room on her way to oblivion. Then I'd had no choice but to let her go; now I followed in her footsteps.

The place she had chosen for her final collapse adjoined the living room. A small but beautifully proportioned space, it had always been her special retreat. Here she had spent her days drinking as she sat staring out at the internal patio. The high windows had once brought the sight of the bougainvillaea she loved in to her; now all I could see was a jumble of dark green leaves, dusty from lack of care.

When I'd been growing up, this room had been forbidden territory, accessible only on those rare occasions when my mother had drunk enough to lift her out of her depression but not too much to sink her back into maudlin despair. Because it was off limits, it had taken on the aura of a magic place, one I ached to possess.

Now I saw it for what it was: a retreat, closed off from the outside world, safe from prying eyes.

I didn't want to be there. I left.

I walked through the rest of the building, expecting memory to well up. All I got was repacketed versions of incidents that I had mentally relived so many times before, they'd lost their edge.

Which was how I felt about the place. I walked down the hall and out of the front door, into the gardens. They were overgrown, exotic blooms swamped by leaves and thickening trunks, figs shrivelled hard on twisted branches. I tried the side entrance, but the top bolt was so rusted that I couldn't force it open. I went out the way I'd come, putting the lock back, depositing the key next door.

I pushed suspicion away; I wanted a rest from it. I

walked down the cobbled streets, through narrow stone arches to the stairs that led down into the centre of the city. I had almost eight hours before I was due to meet my father at his lawyer's office. I decided to spend the time lazily, at the bottom of the long run of cobbled steps, in a café drinking *bicas* and the occasional glass of grappa while I watched Lisbon's sophisticates stroll by.

I didn't go down the steps. I wheeled round suddenly and went the way I'd come. When I got to the *palacio* I veered right, continuing up the hill.

The cemetery's gates were open. I walked through them, and stopped. I had forgotten where they'd put my mother. But then it came back, that day when we had gone, my father and I, ten yards separating us, through the first two aisles and on to the third.

That's where I went. The closer I got to the place which was hers, the more slowly I moved. The marble plaques were four layers high. I wasted time by reading what have been carved on them -- the names, the dates, the inscriptions which ranged from the heart-rending to the banal. There were small vases attached to each site, many of them filled with fresh flowers.

Not my mother's. Her vase was empty. It looked like it had been empty for years. I stood, staring at her plaque, seeing her name, the day she was born, the day she died, and her husband's name – General Alfonso da Souza-Baeier – more prominent than anything else.

Her husband. My father who had come to Sam's graveside bearing flowers and yet who obviously never came here. My father who kept telling me that he had changed.

My mother's grave told me that my instincts had been right. My father didn't change.

*

I went to a bar. I didn't drink. I stood, the phone attached to my ear, watching a group of men tuck into grilled salted spare ribs and boiled potatoes succulent with olive oil. When the operator came on tap, I asked her for the number of London's Highgate cemetery and then I asked her to connect me.

It didn't take me long to find out what I wanted. Yes, the gate man at the cemetery said, someone had paid him to let them sit and watch. A small, swarthy man it was, who spoke little English. He would arrive as soon as the cemetery opened and he would sit all day, hugging a mobile phone, looking out of the window. After five days, my informant confessed, the man had made a brief phone call. That was that. He'd gone and not returned.

I put the phone down and paid for the call.

There was a flower-seller by the cemetery gates. I bought a bunch of spring flowers and left it by my mother's grave. Then I took a taxi to the offices of the local council Lisbon's *camara*.

I went up to the planning office, filled first one form and then the other, showed my passport and was shown in turn to the room in which were stored the documents which might tell me what was going on.

I looked methodically through the various planning permissions. The mystery of why there'd been rust on both the *palacio*'s outside gates was soon solved. The answer was simple: no one had been through them. No estate agent. No prospective buyer. No rich man who was going to restore the *palacio* to its former glory.

And the reason? Simple again. My father wasn't selling. He was keeping the place. But he was also changing it. He'd been so confident that he could fool me, that he had

312

already applied to the *camara* for a permit. To turn the *palacio* into a semi-public building – an up-market research institute-come-library which would bear his name.

I walked under the smooth stone arches and into the air-conditioned building. A receptionist told me how to reach a secretary. The secretary led me straight into a conference room.

My father and his lawyer were sitting around a polished wooden table. When I entered they both got up. My father pushed his chair away and came limping towards me. He held his arms out, readying himself for the embrace he thought was coming.

I kept my cheek averted as I walked round him. I went to sit as far away from him as I could, on the other side of his lawyer. I saw the two men exchange one glance. But they were professionals. They got down to business.

The lawyer opened a file. He read out to me the document I would be signing. It was a kind of glorified consent form, which released my father from the conditions of my mother's will, letting him do with the *palacio* as he pleased. When he reached the end, he glanced up at me.

'Strange wording,' I said. 'Wouldn't it have been simpler to just let me give him permission to sell?'

The lawyer was a smooth one. He answered in the kind of calm, rounded way that used a lot of words to say nothing. Then he told me that I should read the document myself.

I read it. It was, word for word, as he had said.

I gave it to him. He turned the pages, turning to the end where there was a space waiting for my signature. He put it down in front of me. He looked at me. I looked back. He handed me a fountain pen. It was a fancy one, inlaid with gold and an inscription from a grateful client. I turned it round, admiring it.

And then I laid it down.

For the first time since I had sat, I looked at my father. I saw him waiting expectantly. I said two words. 'A library.' That's all I needed to say. I saw him comprehending. And I saw something else – defeat – dull his eyes.

We both knew that my mother would have hated it – his name given to the building she had loved. If I was to take her part, I would refuse to sign. That was how it had always been: me defending my mother, the victim, from the father who only knew how to make victims squirm.

I nearly did that. It would have been so easy. I could have got up and walked out of there knowing that I had finally been the instrument of my mother's revenge; that I had thwarted the man she had grown to hate. I could have done that and disappeared, gone travelling, avoided him again. Now I knew how sick he was, I also knew I wouldn't have to hide for long.

I nearly did it. I nearly got up and left.

But something held me back. My mother was dead. The *palacio* was as well. My father had control of the place. If I refused to sign, he'd let it rot. My mother would have agreed to that – her will showed that she liked her revenge served cold.

But I wasn't her and I didn't have her stomach for revenge. I picked up the pen and signed.

I heard him releasing his breath. I got up. I got up and walked towards the door.

'Kate?'

I kept on going.

I heard him stumble. 'Kate?'

I turned. He was standing by the table, leaning heavily

on his stick. His face was so pale, the skin looked almost transparent. He said my name a third time: 'Kate.' He was breathing heavily. 'If I had known you would be so sensible about the property, I wouldn't have had to bend the truth.'

I looked at him. 'If you didn't bend the truth you wouldn't be you,' I said. And then I turned away.

This time, when he called my name, I didn't respond. I went out of the room, closing the door gently behind me. I would let his name live on, I would give him the memorial he so desperately desired. What I could never give him, however, was my good will.

I had meant to stay in Lisbon. I changed my mind. I took a taxi to the airport and booked myself on the first available flight to London.

It was getting dark by the time I arrived. I didn't go home. I reckoned Leicester Square was my best bet. I was right. I found a postcard shop which doubled as a souvenir stall. They had what I was looking for: a chocolate milkmaid, her tinsel-painted tresses – blonde of course – hanging halfway to her waist. I had it gift-wrapped and then I put it, along with a short note, in a taxi, and sent it round to Gavin.

And then, smiling, I made my way home.

☐ Sweet Death, Kind Death	Amanda Cross	£5.99
☐ Face Value	Lia Matera	£5.99
☐ Designer Crimes	Lia Matera	£9.99
☐ Catnap	Gillian Slovo	£5.99
☐ My Sweet Untraceable You	Sandra Scoppetone	£5.99
☐ Snow Storms in a Hot Climate	Sarah Dunant	£5.99

Virago now offers an exciting range of quality titles by both established and new authors. All of the books in this series are available from:

Little, Brown and Company (UK),
P.O. Box 11,
Falmouth,
Cornwall TR10 9EN.

Alternatively you may fax your order to the above address.
Fax No: 01326 317444
Telephone No: 01326 317200
E-mail: books@barni.avel.co.uk

Payments can be made as follows: cheque, postal order (payable to Little, Brown and Company) or by credit cards, Visa/Access. Do not send cash or currency. UK customers and B.F.P.O. please allow £1.00 for postage and packing for the first book, plus 50p for the second book, plus 30p for each additional book up to a maximum charge of £3.00 (7 books plus).

Overseas customers including Ireland, please allow £2.00 for the first book plus £1.00 for the second book, plus 50p for each additional book.

NAME (Block Letters) ....

....

ADDRESS ....

....

....

☐ I enclose my remittance for ....
☐ I wish to pay by Access/Visa Card

Number ☐☐☐☐☐☐☐☐☐☐☐☐☐☐☐☐☐

Card Expiry Date ☐☐☐☐